ETHIC

Ashley Antoinette

Ashley Antoinette Inc.
P.O. Box 181048
Utica, MI 48318

ISBN: 978-0-692-08855-5

Trade Paperback Printing April 2018
Printed in the United States of America

Distributed by Ashley Antoinette Inc.
Submit Wholesale Orders to:
owl.aac@gmail.com

RECOMMENDATION FROM THE AUTHOR

This book is a spin off from my novel, Moth to a Flame. If you have not read it, STOP. It is advised that you do so BEFORE beginning this book.

If you have read the Prada Plan series and Luxe series it will enhance your enjoyment of this book, but they are NOT required before beginning ETHIC.

Dedication

I dedicate this book to my fans, but especially to the ladies who have fallen in love with ETHIC. You guys love him so much that I was forced to write a book where he was the focus. I created this character in 2009 and I am so honored that he still resonates with so many women, years later. He is timeless and I hope you enjoy this ride as you continue to fall in love with ETHIC through my words.

-xoxo-

Ashley "Ash" Antoinette

Chapter 1

The sound of crickets serenaded the cemetery, as Ethic sat on the white blanket, his knees up, his arms wrapped around him, as he clasped his wrist with one hand, while digging his heels into the ground. He watched his two children read, as they leaned against *her* headstone.

"I am a little, black king. I can do any..." his son, Ezra, paused, as he looked up at Ethic. "Da- what's this word?" he asked, as he turned the book towards Ethic.

"Anything," Ethic confirmed. "Try the sentence again."

"I am a little, black king. I can do anything," his son read.

"Good job, Eazy," Bella coached, affectionately calling him by his nickname, as she looked up from her Harry Potter book.

"Keep reading," Ethic urged. "Your mom wants to hear you finish the entire thing."

It was their thing. It was how they stayed connected to the beautiful Raven Atkins. Although Raven wasn't Bella's mother, Bella was used to the routine. Her own mother had died when she was just a baby and Ethic had started the practice with her. On the first of every month, they went to the cemetery and visited both graves, taking a blanket, a basket of food, and books in tow. It was how they stayed close to one another and to those they had lost. It was always a hard day for Ethic, but it made it easier for his kids, so he did it faithfully, never missing this time with them. Ethic was a cursed man. Falling in love with two women and losing them both, tragically. It seemed that death followed him wherever he went. Ethic had been so guarded and secluded since Raven's passing. He had tried to find someone to fill the void. Only one woman had piqued his interest over the years and he had met her by chance. Disaya Morgan. She had been a great distraction from the pain, but she hadn't been fully available to love him. She had a situation of her own that she couldn't abandon, thus leaving him alone to mourn a ghost that no one could compare to.

The sun began to set, illuminating the cemetery in an orange hue, letting him know their day was coming to an end.

"Let's pack up," Ethic said, as he watched his children climb to their feet. "Put everything in the car. I'll be there soon," he told them. He watched them walk toward his Range Rover that set a few yards away, and then he knelt in front of Raven's headstone. "I miss the shit out of you, Rae. Every day, every moment. You're a hard act to follow, ma." He placed the bouquet of flowers he held directly in front of her headstone. Kissing his fingers, he placed them to her name. "Until next time, love. Rest up."

Ethic blinked away his emotion and swiped his hands over his face. When he stood, all traces of vulnerability were erased from his expression. He never exposed his melancholy to his children. He stuffed his hands in the pockets of his hoodie, as he headed back to his car. They drove through the city, a place he both loved and hated.

Flint, MI was home. Within the perimeter of the city, Ethic was the crowned king. It wasn't a title he boasted proudly. He didn't, particularly, like the reputation at all. Claims like that are what led to the downfall of a lot of men before him, so he let the hood whisper, without ever verifying anything. His younger years of mobbing through the city as Benjamin Atkins' lieutenant had earned him a reputation. No

2

one knew that he was, actually, Benjamin's connect. He made the streets freeze with the snow he brought to town, but that was a long time ago. He never liked the limelight that came with the game. He preferred to get money quietly, which is why he allowed people to think that Benny Atkins had been the man on top. Even now, when he was trying to walk a straight line and keep his hands clean, his exit from the game was never acknowledged. He had turned in his walking papers, but still, the game wouldn't leave him alone. His breed of hustler was rare, and the young ones admired him. Often, doing whatever it took just to be in Ethic's good graces. Ethic disguised the wealth he made in a distribution trucking company, several, automotive repair shops, and other real estate investments throughout the Midwest, but he hadn't been able to truly rid himself of the reputation he had rightfully earned. At 34 years old, his priorities had changed and the risks that came with the lifestyle were no longer worth it to him. As Ethic's strong hand gripped the expensive leather of his Range Rover, he studied the streets he used to rule. They had changed over the years. Businesses had tanked, causing the former gold mine to become a ghost town where there was no code of conduct. The rules had evolved, and the players had revolved to what was now an all-out war zone. Flint wasn't the same and he did 80 miles per hour to get his children out of the city limits and back to the suburbs where he could keep them safe. Flint was where the lawless reigned. He wanted his children to know nothing of that part of his life. Ethic peered into his backseat, as Bella read her book and Eazy transitioned to his hand-held video game. His children didn't have a care in the world. They were his reasons for flying straight and the smiles on their faces reminded him that they were the only constants that mattered. He tucked his turmoil away, as if it was an old piece of clothing that he could put in the back of his closet and forget about. He couldn't dwell in his feelings. That was what women did. Sulking about what he couldn't have wouldn't do anything but keep him stagnant. As he pulled into the driveway to his home, he noticed the C-Class Benz that was parked curbside. He sighed, as he threw his Range Rover in park. He almost didn't want to get out. He didn't have the energy to put up the charade with the beautiful woman, waiting faithfully for him in her car. She was always there, waiting, hoping that he would choose her; and although they had been on and off for years, he never settled down. She was never his pick. Dolce was just someone warm to lay next to – sometimes - on the cold, Michigan nights. As he processed the empty feeling that weighed on him, he couldn't help but feel a bit of guilt over the way he handled her. *Do I give her this feeling? Is her loneliness caused by me?* He thought. What torture the world would be if hurt was just one, big cycle. Were men and women going around loving the ones they could never have and neglecting the ones right in front of them? *Damn,* Ethic thought. His mind was complex. The smallest notion could leave him reeling, as he dissected the possibilities of its merit. Love was one of those puzzles that left him exhausted and frustrated. He just could not solve it.

"Hey, you," Dolce said, as he stepped out of his car. Ethic took his time replying. He took his time doing everything. The world seemed to wait with baited breath as it anticipated his next move. He paused because he knew it would be easy to deflect what he was going through onto her. Her unannounced visit had thrown him. Her unrequested presence annoyed him, but he had to ask himself if the slim, leggy woman with an inviting smile and wanting eyes would have irritated him if he hadn't just come back from visiting the gravesite of the love of his life.

"I wasn't expecting you," he said, his tone even, as he opened the back door of his car. Bella bounced out.

"Hey, Dolce!" she greeted, before running across the massive lawn to Ethic's home, heading for the front door.

Ethic reached down to grab Eazy, who was dead weight in his strong arms.

"I thought you would need a good meal and some good company?" Dolce said, as she held up the single, plastic, grocery bag she carried. Ethic wondered why he found it hard to take her seriously. She was a decent woman who offered something convenient. It may not be everything he required in a woman, but at least she was there. At least she put him above all else. When she bit into her bottom lip and added, "And I need some good…"

She let her words linger and it wasn't hard to fill in the blanks. Ethic sighed, as he remembered why she just didn't do it for him. She was too available, too easy; too much like a replica of every woman he crossed paths with these days. Her weave was long, her waist was unrealistically shaped, her ass too fat. *Her brain too empty,* he thought. He would rather appreciate the value in a dinged-up quarter than accept a shiny penny. Dolce was shining but her worth was insignificant.

He took the plastic bag from her hand, holding his heavy child with one, strong arm and the groceries in the other. Despite his lack of enthusiasm regarding her presence, he was still a gentleman. There were no thrills in causing her embarrassment. He nodded his head toward the house. "I'm a little tired, but dinner I can do," he said.

Just the mere thought of being in his space, under his roof, at his dinner table put a hope in her eyes that Ethic hated because he knew he would never give her the *more* she sought.

He walked into his home, eager to see the face of his oldest child, Morgan. She looked so much like Raven; he often found a sense of peace just from the mesmerizing beauty in her amber eyes. It was like Raven had left a piece of herself buried deep inside her little sister and she was growing up to look just like Raven. In the eyes of the law, and by the decree of the adoption papers, Ethic was Morgan's father, but he was truly her big brother. He could never, and had never tried to, take the place of Benjamin Atkins; but he would take care of Morgan with unconditional love, as long as air filled his lungs. She had made it a challenge every step of the way, however, and today was one of those days.

"Where's Morgan?" he asked Bella, who came racing down the stairs.

"She's not in her room." Bella shrugged.

"Where's Lily?" Ethic asked, referring to his nanny. The elderly, black woman had been a godsend to him, helping to take care of his children and keep his home intact, for years after Raven had died. He had allowed Morgan to skip their monthly cemetery visit, because he knew visiting would upset her. He hadn't expected her to be gone upon his return.

"She must have gone home for the night. She's not here either," Bella responded.

"Relax," Dolce said. "Morgan's 17. She'll be a grown woman soon. You can't keep the leash so tight. Lily doesn't need to keep an eye on Morgan. You have to start trusting her to make some decisions for herself. She will only try harder to pull away from you, if you don't. I'm sure she's fine. You put Eazy down. I'll start dinner." Dolce took the bag from Ethic's hand, but her words did little to soothe him.

He ascended the stairs to the castle he called home. The 7000 square feet of luxury were more for the children than for him. He had spared no expense in getting it built from the ground up. He had purchased it to give them a foundation and to remind him that all his ill deeds in the streets had been for something. He wanted Bella, Eazy, and Morgan to be protected behind these walls, but Morgan seemed adamant on playing outside the safety net he had provided. No matter how much he gave her or how far he moved them away from the hood, she always found her way back. It was like the streets called her. As he opened the door to her room, his jaw flexed in impatience as he smelled the remnants of marijuana in the air. He laid his son down on the soft duvet and then pulled his phone from his pocket.

Be home in half an hour, Mo. If you're not here, I'm putting word out to have you brought home. It will be much less embarrassing if you head home on your own.

Ethic pressed send and swiped his face in exasperation, as he blew out a sharp breath. He didn't want to be that guy. It disappointed him that he had to result to such strict tactics to get through to Morgan, but the only way to keep Morgan safe was to keep her removed. He had seen firsthand how the streets of Flint could swallow a girl whole. It had happened with Raven. He couldn't sit back and let the same happen to Morgan. If he had to be uncool in her eyes... so be it. He knew his ways were overprotective, but it was a byproduct of losing Raven. Or was it a result of losing his mother? Or was it a reaction to losing it period? Did he hold on too tightly out of fear of losing the women he cared for? Ethic didn't know, but at that moment, he didn't care. He lacked patience when it came to her safety, and there was no leniency when it came to that. He just wanted Morgan home; and if she didn't walk through the door in the next half hour, Ethic had no qualms about sending word to the block to retrieve her.

***

The smoke from the Kush-filled blunt danced in the air, as Morgan grooved to the vibrations of the speakers that sat behind her. The fact that she couldn't hear the music made her love to dance even more. Other girls danced to the beat, in a predictable way, trying too hard to be cute, swaying to the music more for attention than enjoyment. Morgan was completely different. The way her hips rode the beat was awkwardly beautiful but natural. Even though she didn't seek attention, it came to her effortlessly. She bopped to the beat of her own drum, using the heavy bass that vibrated her chest as her guide, while snapping her fingers between the rotations of the blunt that was being passed around. She closed her eyes, as the pulsations from the music traveled up her spine. She was in a vibe. She may not be able to hear the music, but she could feel it. She was standing in a circle full of pretty faces, but she was the only one that shined.

Her bohemian-chic box braids hung down her back and the tiny, diamond stud in her nose complimented her well. The red scarf she tied Tupac-style around her head put some grit behind her baby face. She tried to draw on her maturity with expensive cosmetics, accentuating her pouty lips with red lipstick. She was Benjamin Atkins' youngest daughter, and although her father had died years ago, his legacy lived on. Because of it, Morgan was royalty. She couldn't help but feel like she was princess by default. *None of this shit is for me. This is hers. This love is just residual from Raven. They don't even really know who I am.*

Morgan felt her best friend, Nish, tap her on the shoulder, as she held up a plastic soda bottle filled with purple liquid. Morgan focused on her lips. "You on this?" she asked.

Morgan had gotten used to reading lips. She could spy on an entire conversation from across the room - just by paying attention. The things that other people missed, Morgan usually picked up on. Her perception was keener because it had to be. She took the bottle and passed Nish the blunt, before lifting it to her lips. She didn't even get to taste the concoction before the bottle was taken from her grasp. She lowered her head, angrily, her eyes shooting daggers until they fell on his.

"Let's go, Shorty Doo Wop," he said. Messiah stood in front of her, face cross in irritation. His icy demeanor made his smooth, dark skin even more attractive. She loved the way his lips curved when he called her that...when he called every, pretty girl that. She had seen him refer to countless girls with that nickname. It seemed to be his nickname for the beautiful ones. She was just glad she made the cut.

It was moments like these Morgan wished she had the confidence to use her voice. She hadn't tried to speak since she was five years old. She still remembered the flush of embarrassment that filled her when her kindergarten classmates had laughed at the way her voice sounded. She hadn't spoken since that day. Hundreds of thousands of dollars had been poured into surgeries and therapy to help restore her hearing. First, her father, and then Ethic had poured money into different, innovative technology over the years. They had done all they could to help her, but the fact that she couldn't hear herself made her afraid to allow anyone else to hear her speak as well. She didn't want her words to come out jumbled or awkward. She didn't want her tone to sound weird or to highlight her handicap; so instead of saying something flirty to this god of a man in front of her, she rolled her eyes and smirked. She snatched the bottle back and he pointed a stern finger in her face. "Don't play with me," he said.

All I want to do is play with you, she thought. She handed over the bottle and threw up two fingers to her friends, as Messiah led the way out the party. She knew Ethic had sent him. He had a way of tracking her down that made her feel like she wore a leash. Morgan just wanted to live her own life. She didn't care if she fucked it up, as long as she had the freedom to make her own choices. She desperately wanted to fly free.

"You gon' make a nigga have to body something out here," Messiah said. "Got your stomach and shit all out. Why the fuck your shorts so small, man? You ain't got to carry it like that. That face is enough to get you all that attention you're begging for."

So, he does think I'm pretty, she thought. Morgan didn't miss the insult that accompanied the compliment, but she would accept anything if it was coming from him. *If he was passing out baby daddy passes and food stamp cards, I'd be first in line.* That thought made her laugh aloud.

"Now I'm funny, huh? Got me up in here, pulling you out of clubs and shit. How'd you get in anyway, with your young-ass," Messiah said, a small smirk playing at the side of his lips. He was too stubborn to reveal a full smile, but the way his mouth tugged upward at one corner was the sexiest thing Morgan had ever seen.

She shrugged, knowing he didn't know sign language, so there was no need for her to try to respond.

"Get in," he said. Messiah was up and coming. After his partner had been murdered in cold blood, Messiah had stepped into a position of power, taking over a cocaine operation that ran half the city. Not only was he moving weight, but he wasn't afraid to lift anything of value that came into town. He often sought guidance from Ethic. She would catch him at Ethic's body shop, sitting for hours, as they read The Wall

Street Journal and Ethic taught Messiah about stocks and bonds. She had seen him around town with different women, but none of them seemed to stick around long. She was just waiting to turn 18, so that she could shoot her shot. *He could have his pick of any woman in the city. He's not checking for me,* she thought. "Pretty girl," he said, as he snapped his fingers to jolt her out of her reverie. "Quit daydreaming and get in. I got to shoot you all the way out to Grand Blanc, before I go handle this business," he said.

She nodded, as he opened the door for her and she stumbled into the car. She knew if she walked into Ethic's house drunk and high, he would overreact and she sighed at the thought of the argument that was to come. *He thinks he's my father,* Morgan thought. When Messiah slid into the driver's seat, she turned toward him.

"Can you at least give me a few hours to sober up?" she signed.

She could see the confusion on his face, but he was too polite to ask her what she was trying to say. She grabbed his phone from the cup holder of the Range Rover and called herself so that his number would pop up on her screen. She denied the call and then opened a text message.

If I walk in the house like this, Ethic will kill me. Can we go somewhere for like an hour, so I can sober up?

He read the text and sighed, before swiping a hand over his full beard. "Yeah, alright," he said, as he put the car in drive and maneuvered his way through the crowded parking lot. Morgan rolled down her window. She didn't mind all the gawking women, looking at her in shock, as she rode shotgun next to Messiah. All his groupies were present, and she knew leaving the club with him would cause nothing but speculation.

"I'm not a catch, shorty. You brag about the good boys. I'm the type you keep a secret," he said, honestly. *If only you knew,* Morgan thought, as she bit her bottom lip. She felt privileged just to have her hips spreading in those buttery leather seats.

They rode through the city and Morgan wondered if Messiah was as comfortable in the silence as she was. Silence was all that existed for her, but she hoped it wasn't awkward for him.

They pulled up to Stepping Stone Falls, and a knot formed in her stomach. She hadn't been to the nature reserve since her father had been killed. She used to love to see the water cascade down the waterfalls, as she sat on her father's shoulders. *It was our thing,* she thought, sadly, as she closed her eyes. *I used to be able to see his face. I can barely remember his smile anymore.* She had gone somber; and now, she just wanted to go home.

The interior lights came on and she watched Messiah exit the car. He dipped his head down and said, "I'll be right back. Stay in the car." She looked in the side mirror and noticed another car pulling up behind them.

Her eyes were glued to that mirror, as she watched Messiah greet another man. She knew the deal and tore her eyes from the scene because his business was his business. She respected his privacy. When he got back in the car, he tossed a black, duffel bag in her lap.

"Count up for me?" he asked.

She nodded and unzipped the bag to see that it was full of different denominations of bills inside. She focused in, as she organized and counted the money.

"Fifty bands," she signed. He was lost, and she smiled, picking up her phone to text the message to him.

He looked at his phone and then mimicked her hand movements. "This is how you say 50,000?" he asked.

She nodded.

"How did you lose your hearing?" He asked. "You ain't got to answer, but I always wondered."

He always wondered? Does that mean he thinks about me? She thought.

I was born deaf. My sister was born perfect and I was born like this. I used to hate it. Now, I'm kind of grateful that I can drown out the noise. The world is filled with too much bullshit.

He read the text and nodded. "Real shit. Sometimes, I wish I could block out the world too. That's what Ethic is trying to do. Keep the bad shit from you. Why you out here chasing trouble?"

"You're trouble?" she signed.

He mimicked her body language. Moving his hands in the same way. "Trouble," she mouthed.

"Yeah, I'm trouble," he confirmed. She was addicted to the way his full lips moved when he spoke. She felt her body react, as a pulse started in her panties and traveled through her body, making her shudder.

"I don't think so," she signed.

He shook his head, as he gave a rare smile, understanding that one. He quickly corrected himself and the smile disappeared. She had already witnessed it, though, committing it to memory, instantly.

Morgan pointed out the window toward the falls and then popped open the door, before he could protest. She stood in front of his car, headlights shining around her, as she bent her finger, beckoning him to come to her. The fact that he didn't come right away made her want him more. He wasn't a puppet to anyone. He didn't follow orders. He gave them, and he made her wait, as he contemplated whether he wanted to join her or not. She held her hands up in a pleading motion and pouted. He didn't budge, so she removed her shirt and dropped it on the ground, as she stepped out of the light and into the darkness that covered the rest of the reserve. Morgan shed a piece of clothing, with every few steps she took, leaving a trail for him to find her when he finally decided to join her. She stepped into the water, gasping at how cold it was this time of year. She eased into the water, her nipples hardening under the fabric of her bra as she shivered. It was exhilarating, the bite of the cold water against her skin. It made her feel alive. The reflection of the moon shone over the water and Morgan got lost in the beauty of the night. When she turned back to shore, she was waist deep. She saw Messiah standing on the beach, holding her clothes in his hands. His arms were outstretched in perplexity.

She was glad she couldn't hear, because if she could, she knew he would be calling for her to come back. He would be trying to talk some sense into her and she just wanted to blow free like the wish weeds she used to pull when she was a kid.

She turned her back to him and stared at the moon, transfixed, until she felt the ripples of the water change patterns, letting her know someone else had gotten in.

"You're crazy as shit," Messiah said. She saw his lips moving but there was too much space between them, and his skin mixed with the dark night made it impossible for her to tell what was spoken. She moved closer to him and he tensed. His shoulder-length dreads were pulled back off his face as he stared down at her.

"It's time I take you home." She shook her head.

She reached up to touch his face, but he caught her wrist. Her heart raced, just from the fact that he was touching her.

She took his hand and placed it on her chest. Her weighted breaths caused her chest to heave. She wanted him to feel her heart beat. He looked at her, drawn into her uniqueness, into her freeness. She was like a fire, silent in her destruction and uncontainable. Messiah was walking a fine line. Ethic was a man he respected, and he didn't want conflict, yet still, he couldn't pull away. She reached out and put her hand on his tattoo-covered chest. He was like a mural of ink and she secretly wondered what each one meant. He kept his cool and his face was unmoved, but he couldn't hide the beat she felt through his strong chest. She closed the little space that remained between them and hopped up around his waist. Her legs circled his back and her arms went behind his neck, as he held her up with one arm around her back.

"We got to go," he whispered. His strong body was tense, cautious. He pulled her hand, as he began to step toward the shore. She pulled back. Almost instantly, his strong arm was around her waist, pulling her into him. She shook her head, declining his request to leave. He closed his eyes and rested his forehead against hers, before pulling away abruptly. Just like that, their connection was broken. She sighed, as she followed him toward dry land. He bent down to put on his clothes, and then turned away to give her some privacy, as she stepped into her own.

He had to get out of her proximity before something happened that he would regret. Morgan was a beautiful girl, but she was young, jail bait; and at 17, she wasn't ready for what he offered at 25. He was in the streets heavy, with no intentions of slowing down. Messing with Morgan would be a direct violation of Ethic. He was lucky to have Ethic's council at all. Messiah didn't want to burn that bridge, not over pussy, no matter how pretty it was. Men wanted to conquer Morgan simply because of who she was, and he didn't want that. He didn't want to prey on her for her namesake. It just could not happen between them. He wasn't into young girls. His conscience and who he was as a man would not allow it.

Morgan walked past him, filled with embarrassment and feeling foolish that he had turned her down. She climbed inside the car and turned towards the window, as he entered as well. This time, the silence was loud as they avoided conversation the entire way.

Morgan couldn't get out the car fast enough. As soon as Messiah pulled into the driveway, Morgan bolted from the car, slamming the door so hard that Messiah cringed.

He climbed out the car and followed her into the house. By the time he caught up to her, Ethic had her frozen in sight.

Morgan was in tears and Messiah's stomach twisted, knowing that she was crying because of his rejection.

"Are you hurt?" Ethic asked.

She shook her head.

"Are you high?" Ethic grilled.

Normally when Ethic asked a question, he already knew the answer, so Morgan knew better than to lie. Under his intense stare, Morgan shrank. She didn't want to lie to him, so she opted for silence, looking off to the side as her eyes watered. It was in these moments when Ethic reminded her so much of her father that she felt the saddest. He shouldn't have to discipline her. She should have parents for that; but her father had been gunned down by the police, years ago, on a Sunday morning. On the day that belonged to the Lord, the devil had come and snatched the foundation of her family away. She remembered it, like it was yesterday, and it still hurt. Now, Ethic was left playing the paternal role. Although she loved him, it wasn't the same.

Morgan could see the disappointment in Ethic's eyes, and for a moment, it felt like she was sitting in front of the late, great Benjamin Atkins himself. Ethic was cut from the same cloth as her late father.

"Go upstairs, Morgan. Sleep it off. We'll talk about everything in the morning," Ethic said. Morgan nodded and then retreated up the stairs.

Messiah wanted her to look back at him, just so he could look in her eyes one more time, but she didn't.

"I appreciate you going to get her, homie," Ethic said, as he pulled out a knot of hundred-dollar bills.

"Come on now, put that up. We don't count favors. Anytime, OG; it's nothing," Messiah said. He slapped hands and embraced Ethic, before breaking out. He didn't want to leave things as they were, but it really wasn't his place to fix Morgan. She had been broken way before Messiah came along, so he would let sleeping dogs lie.

Chapter 2

"**S**he's just trying to spread her wings a little bit. She will be okay."

The sound of Dolce voicing her opinion on things that didn't involve her irritated him. She came up behind him, wrapping her arms around him, as if she was his peace of mind. She wasn't that for him. That wasn't her place in his life; and the more she tried to force it, the more it turned him off. He removed her hands and turned to her.

"It's getting late," Ethic said.

"I could stay," Dolce offered.

"Not tonight, alright? I'll get up with you," Ethic said, as he stared down at her. Obligation made him lift her chin and kiss her cheek. He could, practically, see her deflate from his refusal. He wasn't trying to hurt her feelings. That wasn't his intention; but giving her more than casual sex wasn't an option, and tonight he wasn't even beat for that.

He was a man conflicted, scarred, burned by emotion he couldn't seem to get a grip on. To a man that was used to being in control, his current state made him feel weak. *I've got to get my mind right,* he thought. Dolce's eyes were pleading with him, her body language begging him to take out his angst within the heaven between her legs. Women were equipped with superpowers in that way. Within their opening lied bliss, and Dolce was offering it to Ethic, without uttering a word. He had never missed a sign from a woman and Dolce was giving

18

him the green light to fuck his problems away. A lesser man would have taken her up on the offer, but Ethic just wanted to breathe.

He walked over to the door and held it open as she walked out. She turned, sharply, huffing in angst, as she pointed a warning finger in his face. "One day, you're going to look up and I'm going to be gone."

"I know," he replied, simply. He closed the door. The weight of the world was too heavy for one man to carry. He thought about the things he had done, the lives he had taken, the poison he had pumped into the veins of his community, and he couldn't help but think this loneliness was his karma. Ethic believed that God made man and woman in pairs. The reward for a good life lived was to meet that soul that was intended to be your mate. The consequence for a life squandered was what he was living through now. To find an amazing woman, not once, not even twice, but three times, and to lose them all was nothing short of punishment. Ethic had struck out and now he had to navigate through parenting a teenage girl, and his own, two children - alone.

He wanted to go upstairs and talk to Morgan about her behavior. Perhaps, punish her for being reckless, but he didn't know how. She reminded him so much of Raven that it hurt to watch her grow. It angered him that she was slipping down the same, slippery slope that had destroyed her sister. His head wasn't right at the moment. *I'll address it tomorrow,* he thought. *When I cool down.*

He peeped in on his sleeping young ones and stood outside Morgan's room. He grabbed the handle on her door, but halted, knowing that space was needed tonight - for them both. *She can be mad all she wants, as long as she's home and she's safe,* he thought. He had won the small battle. He would handle the war in the morning.

Ethic descended the steps to his home until he reached the lowest level of his three-story home. It was where he went when he needed to remove himself. When he wanted to unplug from being a father, a gangster, a mentor…when he just wanted to be human; when he wanted to be the man that he would have been had the streets not made him a beast, he went down there. It was his sanctuary, and no one else was allowed to disturb the energy in that space. He pulled off his shirt, his temple of a body looking like nothing less than a work of art. Each tattoo on his dark skin symbolized significance in his life and told a story of a boy whom had navigated his way to manhood alone. He was life's exhibit of survival; the epitome of what this world did to black boys, turning them into men too soon, and then getting upset when these men, whom didn't know themselves, lacked maturity. Grown men, who were still boys inside, broke things because they, themselves, were broken. Rules, hearts... men like Ethic were just prone to breaking shit; but they had no idea how to repair themselves when the shoe was on the other foot.

He pulled out the gym mat and stepped out of his pants, before reaching into a drawer and removing a pair of Nike, athletic tights. The fabric fit his muscular legs like a second pair of skin. He remained shirtless, and then removed his socks, before stepping up to the mat. Meditation was the thing that stopped him from pulling triggers. It had taken him years to figure out that his gun was only to be used when every other alternative had been exhausted. He would lay a nigga to rest, should the need occur. He was made up 100 percent G; and at times, gunplay was necessary, but only self-control could help him make the decision. Yoga and meditation taught him to always have complete autonomy over his mind. Love had fucked that all up; because no matter how hard he tried, he couldn't stop the pain he felt. Love had made him susceptible to weakness and he had to get a handle on that shit.

He reached over his head, making a temple with his fingers, as he looked toward the ceiling. Every muscle on his exposed chest flexed, as he began his routine. His strong core held him up, as he moved fluidly through difficult poses as he cleared his mind and pushed his body to the limit. Sweat glistened on his dark skin, as he controlled his breathing. His stamina was endless, and he went through his hour-long ritual with ease, ending on the floor, with his eyes closed and legs crossed, breathing deeply. His blood pumped wildly, reminding him that he was alive. The pain told him he was alive, and that this feeling he had was a part of living, a part of being privileged to be six feet above ground. As he stood and grabbed a towel to wipe away his sweat, he told himself if he couldn't shake the feeling, he would learn from it and make sure that he never felt it again. As he cut out the lights and ascended the stairs, he shut off his heart. Ethic flipped the switch that allowed him to love, allowed him to hurt... allowed him to live. He went back into his shell, promising himself that he wouldn't expose himself again.

***

Sitting at the window seat, staring out over the sprawling, green lawn, Morgan felt like Rapunzel, trapped in a tower and dying to be free. Nobody understood her. How could they? No one knew what it was like to walk through a world without fully experiencing it. They had no idea how loud things got inside her head. Morgan hated that she wanted to be accepted by the same people she despised. She hated them for the superficiality; hated them for being so normal, and for not appreciating the blessing that came with being able. Able to

21

hear, able to just exist without people feeling awkward around them. Morgan always felt like she was under a microscope. Curious eyes gawked in surprise, wondering how she could be so beautiful yet be so flawed. People always stared, so Morgan put on a show, acting out, frustrated with people and their judgments. Nobody understood her, not even Ethic; and although he tried his best to make her feel loved, she simply felt like she didn't belong. She wasn't his daughter. Her family was gone, and she didn't quite fit in anyone else's life. Nobody accepted her like her family had. When they were alive, she barely even realized she was different than anyone around her. They made her feel secure. But as soon as they went in the grave, all her insecurities surfaced.

She picked up the phone and looked at Messiah's number. She stored it in her contacts, before tossing the phone to the bed. She wished she could call him. If she had a voice, she would. She desperately wanted to belong to someone, not out of obligation the way Ethic had inherited her, but out of need... the way a man wanted a woman to be only his. She wanted someone, anyone, to choose her, and to love her. Flaws and all. Until she found it, she would drown the loneliness in liquor and weed to distract herself from the things she couldn't have.

***

The rays of the sun broke through the curtains, disrupting Morgan's restless sleep. It blazed through her closed lids, illuminating her mind, and forcing her to open her eyes. She dreaded the discussion that was to come. The parenting. She never really took to the idea of anyone disciplining her, because that was the job of the people who made her. Ethic had not, therefore, his concern seemed manufactured. *He's just going through the motions. Nobody gives a fuck about a kid that doesn't belong to them,* she thought. She was just waiting for her 18th birthday to come around. She had already graduated high school. She would break out and never look back, even if she had to leave with just the clothes on her back. Morgan was itching to live life by her own rules.

She climbed out of bed and sauntered downstairs. Smeared mascara and remnants of last night's *Ruby Woo* still stained her face.

"Mo' Money!" Bella signed, calling Morgan by the nickname that she had since they were kids. Morgan smiled. She had a special place in her heart for Bella. She took a seat at the dining room table and took a fork to Bella's plate.

"Is this my shirt, Bella?" Morgan signed. Ethic had made sure everyone living under their roof had learned sign language, so that they could communicate with one another.

"The fact that a 12-year-old can fit it means you shouldn't have it on," Ethic interrupted. He didn't sign because he knew Morgan was zeroed in on him, anticipating his parental wrath.

"Ha, ha," Morgan signed. "So, what's my punishment for last night?"

Ethic's face was serious. He was always so stern, as if he was in a constant state of deep contemplation. She was prepared for him to lock her in her room forever; but to her surprise, he said, "Let's wash it, a'ight? I haven't been as focused on you or them like I should, so I'm partly to blame. I need you to move smarter, though. I don't want you in the city. You hear me? I need you to understand who you are."

He made it sound like she was a porcelain doll that would break if handled too much. She wasn't looking for a fight, however, so she simply nodded. *I'm lucky he didn't take my car,* she thought. *Oh shit, my car,* she remembered, realizing she had left it in the parking lot of the club. She didn't want to bring it up. She didn't need to give Ethic any more incentive to reprimand her.

"Your birthday's coming up," Ethic said.

"You're not canceling my party?" Morgan signed.

"Of course not," Ethic replied. "Your father threw you a party every year. I still remember when I met you and Raven at your sixth birthday celebration. You were the prettiest girl in the room. Benjamin was proud of you. He was proud of Raven. He introduced the two of you, as if he had his own, personal angels. I wouldn't break that tradition. I know what it means to you and what it meant to him."

Morgan nodded and blinked away tears, as she noticed the lights flicker in the house. Every inch of Ethic's home had been tailored to fit Morgan's handicap, including the doorbell. A twinge of guilt rushed over her, as she realized how much Ethic truly had done for her over the years. He may not have been her father, but he was the closest thing she had to one. His love for her was forgiving, just like her father's had been for her sister, Raven. "Thank you," she signed. "I'll get the door."

She pulled open the door in haste and was shocked when Messiah stood in front of her. His dreads were pulled half up off his face and the back hung shoulder length.

Was that a smile? She thought, as she noticed a change in his disposition. It was so slight that she questioned if she had imagined it. His style was always so effortless. Morgan hated the guys from around the way who flaunted everything they had all at once. There was nothing gaudy about Messiah. His effortless cool drew her in. He knew he was paid. He didn't have to prove it, so he kept his style simple, with jeans, a V-neck and a leather vest. The Rolex on his wrist was all the accessory he needed; no chains, no earrings, just Messiah and the condescending smirk that he seemed to reserve for her.

She didn't know if he found her amusing or if he found her intriguing.

He held up the key to her car.

"Ethic here?" he asked.

She moved to the side, as he eased by her, brushing by her, arrogantly. He had no idea what he did to her. Her youth made what she felt for him so intense. When she was around him, the air felt too thick to breathe. His cologne, *Creed,* she thought, hugged her as he passed, and she had to grab the doorframe. He made her knees weak, without even trying, without even noticing. *He's so fucking arrogant,* she thought.

"What's up, big homie?" Messiah greeted. "My people took me to pick up the car and I drove it here. I didn't want to bring nobody out to your spot. I know how you are when it comes to shit like that. You think you can run me back to the crib?"

"Morgan can drop you," Ethic said.

Messiah turned to Morgan. "Drop me at the crib?" he asked.

Morgan nodded, before leading the way outside. She almost forgot that she had just rolled out of bed. She climbed into the passenger side of the car and cringed, as she glanced at her reflection in the visor mirror. As Messiah walked around to the driver's side, she hurriedly licked her fingers to try to slick down the edges of her hair, and then wiped her eyes with the sleeve of her shirt, to remove the day-old cosmetics that now resembled clown makeup. She was sure her breath smelled like corn chips - at least it tasted like it - and she sighed in frustration. *He had to pull up on me looking this good and smelling this good. Meanwhile, I'm sitting here looking crazy,* she thought, mortified. When he lowered into the seat, she snapped the sun visor shut. Young girls worried about the most trivial things and Morgan was no different. She was damn near holding her breath to make sure he didn't smell her funk.

Morgan wondered what he was thinking behind his brooding stare. He didn't speak, so neither did she; even though she desperately wanted to rehash the events that had happened the night before. He had paid her more attention than she had ever seen him pay anyone. He had opened up to her. She had felt it. *Or am I tripping? He's sitting here like I don't even exist.* It didn't help that he couldn't sign, and she couldn't speak. It was like the sun had come up and exposed all the reasons why she could never have him. She, desperately, wanted to go back to the dark, where it was safe to let her inhibitions go. In the dark, it had felt possible that Messiah would want a girl like her.

The silence was killing her, but she refused to beg him for his attention. She didn't want to seem pressed, so she settled into her seat and watched block after block pass them by. With every mile they drove, she felt the opportunity to be in his space dwindling. When they pulled up to a modest, two-story home on the Northside, she noticed a girl waiting patiently for him as she leaned against his car. Morgan turned up her nose, as jealousy seared her. The girl's beauty was typical: fat ass, slim waist, long weave...so on trend. There was nothing original about her. *Old Build-A-Bear-ass bitch,* Morgan thought, as she rolled her eyes, making no attempt to fix her face. Morgan knew she was hating. The girl was exactly the type that she would have expected Messiah to be attracted to. He probably had a collection of women that he alternated each day of the week. Morgan wanted to be the one he called on Sunday. His family. The one who dragged him to church to balance his sins and then fucked him on the same table they ate Sunday dinner on. A man gave his Sunday to the woman he loved. *That's why this thirst bucket is here on a*

Wednesday. Ol' hump-day-ass bitch, Morgan thought. She chuckled at that. *With my hating-ass. Damn, why couldn't God give me an ass like that?*

Messiah put the car in park and then climbed out. Morgan followed suit, as the bobble-head girl with the weave bounced over to the car.

"Hey, babe," she cooed. Morgan almost gagged, she was so sick. She knew the girl was putting on, staking claim, as she wrapped her arms around Messiah's neck and planted a deep kiss on his lips. He pulled back, slightly, not one for public affection. He rubbed his lips with his thumb, before licking his lips.

He turned to Morgan. "Umm… Morgan, this is Shayna. Shayna, this is Morgan."

Morgan waved, and the girl returned with a dry, "Hey."

"Thanks for the drop off," Messiah said.

"Thank you for getting my car," she signed.

"Car?" Messiah asked, as he mimicked her signs.

She nodded, with a meek smile. She noticed she always had his full attention when she signed. She appreciated the effort he put into understanding her.

"Aww…She's deaf, right? That's Benny Atkins' daughter. I used to know her sister. Well, not know her, but I used to see her around. Everybody used to want to be like Raven Atkins back in the day," the girl said, reminiscing.

Morgan was over this girl. She had just confirmed her groupie status. She was a hanger-on and Morgan had no interest in entertaining the conversation further.

Morgan frowned and lifted her hand, as she looked at Messiah as if to say, "Who is this bitch?"

His smirk returned. "Give me a minute. I'll meet you inside," Messiah said, as he passed the girl his keys.

When she disappeared inside, he turned to Morgan. "I'll see you around," he said. "No more hole-in-the-wall clubs, shorty. That ain't for you."

She nodded, as she headed back to her car. She was livid that she was the one he was seeing off, meanwhile, a lesser woman was waiting for him inside his home. Knowing that Messiah was off limits to her, she got into her car, without looking back before pulling away.

***

Morgan Atkins was a princess. Throne, crown, the whole nine yards. Her 18th birthday celebration proved exactly how much love her family had around town. Ethic had spared no expense, renting out a mansion on the outskirts of town. He had given her a real-life castle for the day. Morgan did nothing ordinary. Her event was like a local Met Gala, with formal attire required and all. Waiters walked around with hors d'oeuvres and champagne for the guests who were of age. A full spread was available in the kitchen; lobster and crab, specially prepared by a five-star chef, had been flown in from Maine. The all-white ball room theme was something out of a fairy tale, and Morgan looked like royalty. Her Escada gown was ripped straight off a runway; short and sexy, a sheer overlay dragged behind her when she walked. Her braids, along with the gold beads with henna tattoos, gave her a unique style that only she could pull off. Her winged eyeliner gave her a Cleopatra, Nefertiti, or some other black queen vibe. She was their equal because Morgan was just an effortlessly, gorgeous human being. Morgan was one of the pretty people, just as her sister had been, just as their mother had been. She came from a long line of inherited *beauty*.

"This is crazy," Nish said, as she posed for the cameramen that kept the bulbs flashing as Morgan's guests walked the red carpet and took pictures in front of a step and repeat. Morgan and Nish posed for over an hour, before moving inside where a huge crowd was congregated in the great room. Morgan looked around in amazement. Ethic hugged the corner of the room, clad in a simple, black, Tom Ford suit with Dolce, gleefully, on his arm. Anyone who was anyone and lived on the Northside was present - from Morgan's age to Ethic's. It was a turnout of epic proportions. The city's biggest D.J. kept the atmosphere jovial. Morgan was delighted. Ethic had pulled off a celebration for her, every year, to honor the tradition that her father had started; but this year, he had outdone himself. She felt slightly guilty for giving him a hard time. Morgan knew that her growing pains caused him great concern, but she just wanted to live life fully, without the childish rules Ethic smothered her with. She smiled, as guests greeted her, but when he walked through the door her face fell in disappointment. She had been, silently, searching the crowd, discreetly looking for him, hoping to drift through a waft of his cologne, but she hadn't seen him. Now that her eyes were on him, she wished he would just leave.

He brought that tacky, beauty-supply-store-weave-buying-ass bitch to my party, she thought. She felt like a brat, as she balled her fists at her sides. Morgan could have thrown a tantrum on the spot, but instead, she took a deep breath to qualm the sick feeling that was invading her stomach as they approached.

"There go your boy," Nish signed. "His girlfriend is cute. Cheap dress, but she's straight." Morgan and Nish went back to elementary school. While other girls used secret codes like Pig Latin, Nish and Morgan talked shit using sign language. They were their own, little club and had remained close throughout the years. Morgan had taught Nish how to sign over the years. At that moment, she wished she hadn't taught her at all. Morgan was jealous enough, without Nish rubbing it in.

Morgan rolled her eyes and turned to face Messiah, as he came strolling in. She took him in. The navy suit he wore was so dark it almost looked black, and it was tailored to perfection, with Red Bottom-studded loafers to accent it. The Versace shirt he wore underneath was trendy, and he wore extravagant jewelry; six, diamond chains, and four, diamond rings on his left hand. He wore his dreads French braided in two to the back and a gold, Presidential on his wrist. He was intoxicating, and his cologne made matters even worse. Messiah was a young man, getting money, and he always looked the part of a young boss. His normal, understated style was put away for the occasion. He didn't care if he looked like new money. It all spent the same. He carried a small box that had been beautifully wrapped and handed it to Morgan.

"Happy birthday, beautiful," he greeted.

Morgan took the gift and gave him a short smile. *At least he showed up. He could have skipped it altogether,* she thought.

"Thank you," she signed.

Ethic walked up and greeted Messiah. "Your young gunners outside?" Ethic asked, getting straight to business. Just because there was a reason to celebrate didn't mean he would drop his guard. Ethic would never put himself in a position to be caught slipping. He had to make sure the party was safe and that every guest who walked through the doors was weapon free. Every guest, except himself and Messiah, that is.

"Yeah, my niggas on it. We're good," Messiah concurred. He slapped hands with Ethic, who then eased back into his corner, allowing the flow of the party to resume.

"I'ma see you before I leave out of here, a'ight? I hope you like the gift," Messiah said.

Morgan nodded, as she watched him walk away with another girl on his arm.

She didn't feel much like partying after that, but she put on a smile, as the night thrived, and everyone had a good time. Morgan couldn't quite fix her mood, not with Messiah sitting across the room with his date in his lap. They were whispering, and the girl smiled, as if Messiah was telling her the best joke in the world.

Nigga ain't even funny. Goofy bitch just being extra, Morgan thought. She hated that Messiah had reduced her to a hater. Truth was, Shayna was gorgeous, and Morgan knew it. She had that grown woman feel that made Morgan feel as if she were simply a little girl with a school-age crush. She dug into her purse and retrieved her cell phone, as she stormed away from the crowd. She was sick, literally. She felt like she would throw up. Messiah was too close to her to be so distant, and she hated the fact that someone else was making him look good.

Morgan retreated to the restroom and she locked the door as she exhaled. She clicked on Messiah's number, her fingers stabbing the screen of her phone as she sent him a text.

Morgan:

Why are you ignoring me?

Messiah:

I'm not ignoring you, shorty. I see you, clearly.

Morgan:

You act like the night at the lake didn't happen. Like you didn't feel it.

Messiah:

It's not the time or place for this conversation. Where are you? Just come out and enjoy your party. People are looking for you.

Morgan:
How am I supposed to enjoy anything with that bitch smiling all in your face? I hate that she's here with you. I hate her, period.

Messiah:
Hate is a strong word, shorty. lol. You should save it for more appropriate things…like broccoli.
Morgan smiled at that and shook her head.
Morgan:
I felt something that night, Messiah. Something real.

Messiah:
Just drop it. We both know the rules. You're young and I know what you think you feel but…

Morgan clasped the phone, as she waited for Messiah to finish his text. He was brushing her off, dismissing their chemistry, as if she was too childish to distinguish real from fake. Morgan's pride was injured.
Messiah:
I can't, Mo. Off principle. It ain't right. I'm out. I hope you enjoy the rest of your day. Didn't mean to ruin the vibe.

Morgan rushed out of the restroom. She wanted to stop him from leaving, knowing that she didn't really want him to go; but by the time she emerged from her hiding spot, he was already out the door.

Ethic watched Morgan from afar, amazed at how quickly the years had passed. When he had first gotten custody of her, she was just a little girl. He had tried his hardest to replace the family she had lost; and although it was a cheap substitute, he hoped Morgan knew that he loved her like she was his very own. She had blossomed into a beautiful, young woman and he knew that he tended to hold on too tightly, but it was out of fear. He knew that all that glittered wasn't gold. He didn't want her to learn that lesson the hard way. So, he was overprotective; not just with Morgan, but with Bella and Eazy as well. They were his world and he would do anything to keep them out of harm's way.

"You've done her father a real service, Ethic," Dolce whispered in his ear. "Not many men would have stepped up to take care of her the way you have. You should be proud."

"I just worry. I see a lot of her sister in her. She wants to move too fast and I'm trying to get her to pump the breaks," Ethic admitted.

"She's not her sister," Dolce reminded him. "And if you would let go of the past, maybe you could move forward and appreciate a good woman that's right in front of you." Dolce's voice was laced in resentment. He had wounded her. She had been in the picture before he had ever loved Raven, and he had cast her aside to love other women, over the years. Hurting her was never his intention. He was always honest about where they stood; but somehow, she always ended up expecting more. She walked away, and he could tell by the way she threw her hips, with a mission, from side to side, that she was filled with attitude and anger. Ethic sighed.

I've got to stop fucking with her. She can't handle friends with benefits. She says she can, but her actions always speak the opposite, he thought. Ethic knew she was waiting around, hoping to get a ring by default, or even a promotion to an official title of girlfriend, but he just couldn't give that to her. That type of commitment required a connection that they just didn't share. Ethic knew it was wrong to string her along, but she was always so available to him. Even when he told her that he wasn't looking to make things serious, she still stayed. She still cooked, and sucked, and fucked, and catered to him, as if she was doing it to earn a prize. Their sexual chemistry was amazing; but in every other aspect between a man and woman, they were flat. Ethic didn't know if his standards were just too high, or if Dolce was falling short, but he couldn't give her more. He wondered if he was causing her the type of pain that plagued him. It seemed to be a cycle. People loved the ones that couldn't love them back. The ways of the world were just fucked up that way.

Ethic watched, as the servers brought out the magnificent cake Morgan had chosen. Her taste was over the top, but he never told her no. He granted her every wish because he knew her father would have. The crowd began to sing, and Morgan blushed as she covered her face, bashfully. The party was a success, but he couldn't wait to give her the gift he had purchased. He had watched Morgan overcompensate, her entire life, for not being able to hear. She had even deferred college, refusing to take a scholarship to Michigan State because she didn't think she could keep up. He believed that she partied and filled her life with distractions to try and be as regular as those around her. She was striving for ordinary when he knew she was bred to be extraordinary. Ethic just wanted to give her every opportunity he could. He had researched the experimental treatment that would restore her hearing for years, and now that she was old enough, he would give her the choice of whether she wanted it or not.

He let her enjoy her evening, sitting back in the cut, watching the door, cautiously, and never losing sight of

Morgan. Around midnight, the crowd began to disperse, and she walked over to him with nothing but joy in her eyes. Her happiness made him happy.

"Thank you so much, Ethic," she said, throwing her arms around him and giving him a huge bear hug.

"You're welcome," he replied.

"I'm going to hang for a bit. I'll be home before it's too late. Is that cool?" Morgan signed. She was 18, and technically grown, so Ethic knew she was only asking out of respect. This was the point in her life where she would begin to make her own decisions. He couldn't stop her from going out.

"It's not too late already, huh?" he signed back.

She side-eyed him and pursed her lips, as he rubbed the back of his neck while shaking his head. "I'm not ready for you to be grown, man. This is crazy," he said. "I wanted to give you another present, but we can do all that when you get home. Go have fun with your friend. Be safe. Move smart." He reminded.

She beamed a smile and rushed out with Nish.

"You got the bag in the car?" Morgan signed.

"Of course," Nish replied. "I'll drive while you change, and then we can swap. Hurry up, I'm not trying to get there too late. The line will be out the door."

Morgan smirked, knowing that she had never stood in a line a day of her life, and tonight wouldn't be any different. She had enjoyed her party. It was tradition and she didn't have the heart to tell Ethic that she had no interest in one this year, but she was ready for a real turn up. On a Saturday night, there was only one place to be.

Chapter 3

Messiah sat in V.I.P at *Afterhours*. The nightclub was filled to capacity, but his eyes were glued on one woman - Morgan. She was putting on a show. His temple throbbed, as she swung her long braids and her hips rolled to the beat. Gone was the couture, model look she had donned earlier. She was a vixen - one that knew she had every man in the club ogling her. There was a party going on all around him. Shayna and her friends mingled with his people, popping bottles of champagne, but Messiah's mood had been spoiled. The sight of Morgan half-dressed, garnering the attention of every dude in the building, had him ready to dead something without thinking twice. He told himself it was out of loyalty to Ethic. She wasn't supposed to be out there, shaking her ass. He was just being a good soldier. Right? Or was it something more? Did the disdain spark from the image of her, showing off something that he wanted her to keep a secret? Her beauty was hard to miss, even without her accentuating it. She tried so hard, with tons of makeup and false lashes, but Messiah noticed it most when he saw her out of her element. Like, when he popped up at their crib to return her car. Nights like this one, she was too obvious, too loose, and he clenched his jaw in irritation, as he saw her bend, slightly, in front of one of his adversaries, while working her derrière with expertise. *Clown nigga on the dance floor, freaking off. He lucky I don't rob his bitch-ass,* Messiah thought.

"You're acting real funny tonight," Shayna said, as she sat beside him and extended the blunt she was smoking to him. He pushed her hand away.

"Fuck out of here," he dismissed.

Her eyes followed his to the dance floor and she popped her lips. "That retarded-ass bitch is the reason you're over here sour-faced?" she shot.

"Fuck you just say?" he asked, as his face screwed in disgust. He never lost his cool, but she saw the blaze in his eyes. He gripped her by the elbow and grabbed an open bottle of Ace from the ice bucket. He poured it all over her, as he pulled her roughly through the section, before tossing her outside of the velvet ropes. "Throw her ass out," he told his two goons, who secured his section, making sure only those he invited entered his space. He had caused a scene and Shayna was laughed out the club, as she shouted, "Fuck you, Messiah!"

"You good, G?"

Messiah looked at his best friend, Isa.

"I'm solid. Bitch just in here talking reckless. Pour up," Messiah said.

"In all the years I've known you, nigga, you're never down to drink around a crowd. What happened to all that holistic shit that nigga, Ethic, be putting in your head? Sober body, sober mind and shit," Isa said.

Messiah reached for another bottle of champagne and titled it toward his mouth. "It's needed tonight, trust. The way I feel, I might blow a nigga head off."

"She's just having fun, bruh. She's playing with these niggas in here. She knows she got it. These thirsty mu'fuckas in here are puppets on her string," Isa said. He had never known Messiah to invest his energy into any woman, let alone one as young as Morgan, but the jealousy that danced in Messiah's eyes were a dead giveaway to things he wouldn't dare say.

Messiah wanted to deny what Isa was insinuating, but he wasn't the type to spread falsehoods, so he opted to take another gulp of the liquor instead.

The mood lighting in the club made the way Morgan was moving her body even more sensual, and Messiah's chest was tight, as her dancing partner's hands roamed her. His section wasn't short of groupies, there were always women hanging around, willing to do whatever to be chosen for the night. Messiah usually didn't fall for the trap, but he needed leverage; or at the very least, someone to take his mind off Morgan. She was the forbidden fruit. Not only was she young, she was Ethic's pride and joy. Getting involved with her would be teetering on disrespect and Messiah knew how Ethic handled impertinence. Messiah feared no one, but he wasn't looking to offend a living legend either. He valued the guidance Ethic so graciously offered. He turned his back to the dance floor, opting to appreciate the random beauty that was vying hard for his attention.

***

Morgan was the life of the party. The ecstasy in her system made her feel like she was flying. She was loose, wild, and the free feeling she had chased most of her life was finally hers. She appreciated it, even if it was only temporary. Her hurt feelings were replaced with confidence and a sensuality that she had never felt before. Why trip over the interest of one man when she had the eyes of many? As Morgan danced offbeat, she felt him watching. She wanted him to see how many men wanted her... how she could have her pick of them. *How dare he bring someone else to my party and act like I'm invisible... like I'm a kid? I'm a grown woman and he won't notice it until someone else has me,* she thought. A sheer sheen of sweat covered her body, causing the thin fabric of her short dress to cling to her. Her taut nipples were visible through the dress. She was on fire and she liked it. From the feeling of the guy behind her, she could tell he did too; and from the look on Messiah's face, she had accomplished her mission.

"Damn, you just out here fucking shit up, huh?" Nish yelled over the loud music. The song ended, and Nish handed Morgan another drink. "Last call."

Morgan took the glass and tossed the shot back, frowning, as she felt the shot of liquor burn her throat all the way down.

"You and your homegirl want to grab food afterward?" The guy hugged her from behind, whispering the words into the crevice of her neck, not knowing that Morgan couldn't hear him. She eased out of his grip to walk away, but he pulled her back. She turned to see his lips. "You leaving with me?" he asked.

He wanted the trophy. She could see it in his eyes. He wanted to be the one to take Benjamin Atkins' daughter home. She knew what that felt like...to want to win the prize. She had competed for her father's affection when her sister, Raven, was alive. When she was little, she competed for affection with Ethic because, biologically, she wasn't his and he couldn't possibly love her as much as he did his own children - no matter how much he assured her otherwise. Right? Tonight, she competed against every other woman in the club that wanted the upcoming king of the city...Messiah. She competed for him and, still, he acted as though she didn't exist. She glanced in Messiah's direction, noticing that he was headed for the door with a girl flanking, stumbling, not too far behind. Her envy made her agree. He was leaving with someone, so she would too. She was the master at tit for tat.

She nodded, as the guy grabbed her hand and led her out the club.

The parking lot was the after party and the real reason why people showed up to the hole-in-the-wall at all. Inside the club, it was too dark to truly size up the opposition. Under the shining street lights was where the real from the fake was discerned. Diamonds and rims, foreigns and Chevys, it was all on full display, as partiers hung out on the hoods of cars, still pouring, still sipping, still enjoying the high of the night. This was Flint, this was the life; a Saturday night on the strip of Clio Road, and she was headed to the car of a big fish - Lucas. He wasn't as major as Messiah, but he was getting money and was a respectable catch. While she was jealous of the girl on Messiah's arm, there were plenty of women envying her, as she climbed into the passenger side of Lucas' black Cadillac Escalade.

Messiah got on his Kawasaki Ninja. The Yves St. Laurent motorcycle jacket he wore made him look like he was a model, instead of an actual rider. He handed the girl he was with a helmet, as he pushed his own down over his head. Isa mounted the bike next to Messiah's, as the rest of their crew prepared to ride behind them. They weren't a gang, but it was rare that you caught Messiah without his shooters.

"You not gon' put a stop to that?" Isa asked, as he nodded towards the Escalade.

"She choosing. Ain't my business," Messiah said, arrogantly, as he revved his engine, loudly, while the random girl wrapped her arms around his waist. He sped out of the parking lot, starting a chain reaction, as Isa and the rest of their team whipped out behind him.

The fun ended for Morgan when she saw Messiah leave. Suddenly, her interest in leaving with Lucas waned. Messiah had brought her down; and suddenly, she felt the urge to go home and cry face down in a pillow. He was always around, always moving and shaking in the same places she liked to frequent. It was torture being around what she knew she couldn't have. Now that he was no longer paying attention, she wished she had gone home instead. She turned to the backseat where Nish was cozied up with one of Lucas' friends.

Morgan was too young to know the power of the feeling that was filling her gut. It was instinct, telling her to get out the car, but she was already fighting so many misconceptions. She was just trying to be down. She knew if she messed up the flow of the night, they would think she was lame or childish. They pulled out of the parking lot, and despite her nagging gut ringing in alarm, she went anyway. This pressure she felt in her chest that made it hard to breathe, hard to swallow…it told her she was different from everyone around her and she just wanted to be the same. So, she stayed silent, as Lucas placed a hand on her thigh, inching his fingers up toward the place between her legs as they drove. She tensed, and he slipped her a pill.

"You need to relax," he said.

She knew it was ecstasy. She wasn't a stranger to the euphoric feeling it provided; and if she was going to go through with this, she would need help. She knew Lucas' expectation of her and it was too late to say no. She took the pill, grabbing the bottle of vodka that was being passed around the car to rinse it down with. It only took minutes to take effect, and she felt the indecision leaving her, as they pulled into a motel.

"I thought we were getting food?" she signed, as she turned to face Nish.

"Relax, we can order something," Nish signed back.

"Y'all talking shit about us right in our face, huh?" Lucas asked, with a smile.

"Nah, just a little girl talk," Nish answered. "Relax; these niggas are a big deal, bitch," she signed. Morgan and Nish weren't impressed by the same things. Nish was chasing material things that could be bought and sold, which in turn meant she was up for sale, willing to rent her body out to the highest bidder. Morgan was chasing a feeling. A feeling of unconditional love, acceptance, appreciation for her uniqueness. She knew before she stepped across the threshold of the seedy motel room that Lucas couldn't give her that, but she wasn't looking to spoil everyone's fun.

Morgan got out the truck and followed everyone inside. The stale scent of tobacco filled the dated room.

Morgan poured herself another shot, taking it to the head; the burn giving her confidence, as Lucas pulled her down onto his lap.

"You're sexy as fuck," he growled, as he leaned back on the bed, his elbows supporting him.

She tried to pull back, but he pulled her down with him. Her dress riding up, exposing her thong, as Nish pulled out her phone.

He was attractive, but he wasn't Messiah, and she wasn't feeling how hard he was going.

"Chill," she signed. "Slow down."

"What she say?" he asked, as he looked at Nish.

"She said she wants you to fuck her," Nish said, belligerently, as she stuck out her tongue and turned the camera toward herself, so she could show out for her viewers on social media. "I'm live right now and my baby, Mo, about to get that cherry popped," she bragged.

The guy she was with leaned into her video. "What about your cherry?" he asked. They were visibly high, as he stuck his tongue down Nish's throat.

"You got to pay to play over here," Nish responded.

"You ain't said nothing," the guy responded, as he flashed a money roll for the camera.

"This nigga about to hit that retarded pussy," the guy said. "That shit look fat from the back, though." He took Nish's phone and turned it back to Morgan, as Nish laughed at the joke.

Morgan pulled away. "Stop, it's not happening tonight." She signed, as she climbed off him, pulling down the thin fabric that barely covered her behind. She turned to Nish and noticed her laughing.

"This nigga too thirsty," Morgan signed. "You ready to go?" Morgan frowned, as she pushed Nish's phone out of her face. "Nish!"

"Relax, baby," Lucas said, as she sat up and pulled her back onto the bed. "You scared of the dick?"

Morgan pushed him, hard this time, and headed for the door. She snatched it open but the weight of his body behind her forced it closed.

It was times like these when her voice was needed. When she had to be able to say stop or no. Nish's look of amusement told her that they weren't taking her seriously. She just wanted to leave. She wanted to get out of this room and away from this man. She grimaced, as he pressed his erection into her. She felt dirty, as her face pressed against the wood door. She struggled against him, but he was too heavy and too burly. She wasn't getting loose until he let her. She could feel his lips on the back of her neck; they were moving, but she couldn't make out what he was saying.

I don't want this, she thought, as tears of disbelief clouded her vision. His tongue felt like a snake on her skin and his calloused hands pulled her thong to the side. Her body went limp when he broke into her. This was a burglary. He was taking her, and she couldn't help but think she was partly to blame. She felt him break her hymen, and tears came to her eyes, as she struggled against the weight of him. She had started this, with the seduction in the club, the dancing, all to make Messiah jealous. She had ignited a fire she could not put out; faked interest when there was none, and she had ignored that feeling, that alarm that had told her to get out of his fucking truck. Her mind screamed, *no!*

She had never done this before and there was no delicate approach. This was an attack. He rammed inside of her, and when she closed her eyes, she felt tears wet her cheeks. He was ripping her in half, proving a point that he was defiling Benny Atkins' daughter.

Please, stop. Please, just let it be over, she thought. The fact that he wasn't wearing a condom made her skin crawl. There was nothing she could do but take it; and when he was done, she crumpled onto the floor.

"Morgan?" Nish called, her laughter waning when she finally realized that Morgan was crying.

Lucas waved her off. "She'll be a'ight. Come here. You up next. Bruh, go get in that. Shit is amazing," Lucas bragged. Nish cut off the camera and looked back at Morgan. She was, visibly, shaking. The decision to be uncool and check on her friend was overridden by her desire to be down. Nish wasn't like Morgan. She didn't come from a family that was well known. She had to suck and fuck her way to the top, just like every, other, little ghetto girl in the city. That was her mentality. Sad as it may be, good sex was all she was known for, and she was okay with that. If she put it on Lucas and his homeboy the right way, she knew they would throw her a few dollars. And if they bragged on how good she was, every baller in the city would come sniffing for a taste. It wasn't hooking, it was just the game. Morgan had never had to play it. That's why she was devastated. *What did she think would happen? You don't come to the motel at two in the morning, unless you're trying to fuck,* Nish thought.

"I told you, she's good. Now, come here," Lucas said, roughly pulling Nish onto his hardness as he licked his lips. He was rolling on the E pills he had taken. It had him ravenous and Nish was desperately trying to be chosen.

"You got something stronger than weed? I'm rolling but my high coming down," she said. "I get nasty when I feel good," Nish teased.

"You get nasty, huh?" Lucas questioned, intrigued. "Walk with me to the car. I got a little something."

Morgan reached for Nish, as they passed her, but Nish shook her off. Nish knelt in front of Morgan. "Relax. My turn. Have a drink. Have some fun, for once," Nish said. "I'll be back. Homie will entertain you."

Morgan struggled to her feet. Her legs felt like they would give out at any moment. Devastation and anger flooded her. She could see the lust in this random guy's eyes, as he approached her.

Was this rape? Was she giving off vibes that this was okay? She didn't want this. This wasn't how her night was supposed to turn out.

Morgan didn't know what she had done to invite this violation. Was dancing in a club and barely-there clothing the signs that had given these men the green light to have their way with her? If that were the case, she wouldn't dare do it again. The attention, the spotlight, feeling sexy, chasing maturity, none of it was worth the humiliation she felt now. Suddenly, she just wanted to go home. She wanted to be the girl complaining from her locked room. She yearned for Ethic's overprotectiveness. If she had listened to him, she would have never been in this situation.

A million regrets ran through her mind, as she was swarmed with confusion. Her head was spinning. She was nauseous and the fear that she would have to endure another body inside her made the contents of her stomach come flying out.

"Damn, bitch, you throwing up on my shoes and shit," the guy said. He pushed her hard to the floor, disgusted, as he stepped around her vomit. She scrambled for the door, as she pulled down on her dress, wishing it had a little more fabric to cover her ass. She had never felt more exposed than she did now. The wetness between her legs disgusted her. Remnants of Lucas was leaking out of her, and it wasn't until that moment she realized he hadn't even used a condom.

"Where you going? Huh?" he asked, as he pulled her by her hair, so roughly that she felt him ripping the braids from her scalp. She grimaced, as he flung her on the bed. "Turn around," he growled, as he flipped her roughly. Morgan tried to crawl to the other side of the bed, but the guy caught an ankle and pulled her toward him, spreading her legs wide, as he put his weight on her back, pinning her.

She had never been so scared. The room spun, as she clawed at the dirty sheets beneath her. She needed to brace herself. She felt him hanging between her legs. She went crazy, flopping her body, wildly, to try to stop him from entering her. The guy put a forearm to the back of her neck and stuffed her face into the mattress. Her lungs screamed for air. The more she fought, the harder he pushed. She couldn't breathe. She tried to sip the air, whatever relief she could find, but he had her head pressed so firmly that she knew he had no problem killing her.

"Stop fighting, bitch." He grew frustrated by her lack of cooperation and was too caught up in his assault to realize she couldn't hear his command. He punched her in the back of the head and Morgan saw flashes of white, as her head rang from the blow. She stopped moving, stopped resisting; because if she didn't, she knew she wouldn't make it out of the room. His weight eased, slightly, and she was able to gulp in air. She screamed in agony, as he rammed himself into her. It was different than what Lucas had done. This man was taking her anally and without any lubrication. She howled. The pain was so great that she couldn't stand it, but she had no choice but to endure it.

She was grateful when she felt him pull out and empty his seeds on her back.

"Retarded bitch," he stated, as he hawked up a glob of spit and marred her body with more of his fluids, before buckling his pants and fleeing from the room.

She rushed into the bathroom and closed the door, locking it behind her. She had lost control and she covered her mouth to stifle her cries, as she sobbed uncontrollably. She was too afraid to step out into the room. She, desperately, hoped Nish came back for her. *How could she just watch?* Morgan thought. She didn't know if they were coming back for more, but she would barricade herself in the bathroom until housekeeping came in the morning.

*＊＊

"Yo, bruh, you might want to look at this," Isa said, as he slid his iPhone across the table. Messiah took his arm from around the young lady he was entertaining, and frowned, as he picked it up.

47

When his eyes landed on the video on the screen, fire coursed through his veins.

"This live?" he asked, his jaw clenching in anger.

"Yeah, man," Isa said. "That little bitch, Nish, streaming that shit on IG."

Messiah's heart settled in his stomach, as he watched Morgan fight against Lucas in the video. It was obvious that she wasn't a willing participant. Even if she was, Messiah would have reacted the same. He heard Nish and another voice making insulting jokes, as they witnessed Morgan struggle, but did nothing to help.

Social media revealed all, and he took note of the location before he stood to his feet.

"I'm right behind you," Isa said, already aware that they were about to get into some gunplay.

"I got it," Messiah shouted over his shoulder. He pushed open the door to the diner with so much force that he cracked it. He hopped on his bike, feeling nothing but pure rage before speeding off.

He was across town in less than 10 minutes. Messiah didn't know how he had gotten so emotionally invested in Morgan, but he hadn't been able to take his mind off her since the night at the falls. Most girls oversold themselves. They made promises and talked too much, but Morgan just existed. He felt everything she thought she couldn't convey, just by the way she looked at him. It was like she pleaded with him to hear her and he did. He just couldn't reciprocate. It wouldn't be right. The two of them didn't make sense; but to see someone hurt her and put it out for the world to see, had him in the mood for murder. Messiah was best avoided when he was in this state of mind. Men had lost their lives for less. He wanted to be angry at Morgan, for putting herself in such a precarious position, but all he could think about was getting to her. What she had endured was punishment enough. The embarrassment, the violation. He knew she would have to walk around their small city with even more judgement than she had on her before. Walking in her shoes couldn't be easy... he knew it. He walked into the office.

"Lucas Hill's room. I need the key and I need the number," Messiah said, as he placed a small knot of hundred-dollar bills wrapped in a rubber band on the countertop.

Flint was a city where everybody knew everybody. He and Lucas had been longtime rivals for years. Messiah was always one step ahead of Lucas, and it had resulted in jealousy that had compounded like interest on a loan. *I should have snatched her out the club when I saw her dancing on this nigga,* Messiah thought, feeling as though he was part to blame in the way the night had turned out.

The old, white woman at the desk pulled on her Newport, expertly balancing the long ash that had burned out on the end. She blew the smoke toward the ceiling, as she slid the money into her pocket. She didn't say a word, as she slid him a key card and held up seven fingers.

Messiah rushed out, heading toward the door. He drew his pistol, and then slid the key into the door. The room was empty. The only sign that anyone had even been there at all was the crumpled sheets and empty liquor bottles that were left behind.

"Fuck," he whispered. He pulled out his phone and shot a text to Morgan.

Where are you?

The buzzing sound drew his attention toward the purse that was tossed on the floor.

Soft whimpers could be heard through the bathroom door and he rushed to open it.

"Morgan, open the door, it's Messiah," he said. Authority and worry laced his tone. It took him a second to register that she couldn't hear him. He stepped back, in frustration, and lifted a wheat-colored Timberland boot as he kicked the door, springing it open. The look of terror on her tear-stained face, as she looked up at him, tore through him. When she realized who he was, she rushed into his arms, crying hysterically. Messiah bit into the side of his jaw as his teeth clenched and he held onto her tightly. Every tear she shed was like tiny rocks dinging his chest, trying to break through the wall, trying to expose how much he cared. He held her, firmly, as he let his body sink to the dirty floor. The murderous thoughts that ran through his mind caused his chest to heave up and down, as he rocked her back and forth.

"Shh, it's okay," he whispered. "I got you."

He told himself that he was there because Morgan was like a sister, like family, but what he was feeling was more than that. It was territorial, as if Lucas should have known better than to lay hands on someone he coveted so dearly.

They sat there like that for over an hour, until she had cried it all out. She stood to her feet, wiping her nose with the back of her hand. He stood as well. He stared at her, his concern apparent.

"Let me take you home," he said.

"I can't go home," she signed.

He got the gist of it. Her disheveled appearance. Her puffy eyes. It would be a dead giveaway that something had gone horribly wrong.

"I'll take you somewhere," he said. She nodded and gathered her purse, before he grabbed her hand and led her outside.

Morgan rested her face on his back, as she climbed on the back of his bike. He could still feel her shaking, as she wrapped her arms around his waist.

He shook his head, as he kicked off the stand and revved the engine before taking off into the night.

Morgan closed her eyes, as the cool wind chilled her, and she hugged him even tighter. He was an instant remedy for her affliction. She secretly wondered if she had caused all this just to get this type of attention from Messiah. Her tears were silent, unforced. They just kept coming, sliding down her face, wetting the back of his leather jacket, causing her skin to stick to it slightly. Everything flew by them in a blur. The speed and the water in her eyes made this feel like a bad dream. She just wanted to start the day over and erase the stupid decisions she had made that had led to such a disastrous night. Morgan placed her hands under his jacket, so that her skin was touching his. Her hands laid flat on his chest. The beat of his heart was so intense that she breathed to its rhythm and it soothed her. She hugged him tighter. God, why couldn't this man be hers? Why couldn't he see past his relationship with Ethic, past her age, past her hearing, past this night? He would never admit it, but she was sure her differences scared him. She wanted to be mad at him for that, but she had dealt with it her entire life. People judging her, thinking she was stupid, or lacking because she couldn't hear. It was frustrating; especially so with Messiah, because she had never wanted something so badly. He steered the bike with one hand, as he placed a hand over hers, reassuringly. He intertwined his fingers with hers, making a joint fist over his heart and Morgan sucked in a baited breath. Such a simple gesture made her turn to mush inside. *He cares. He can't do stuff like that and not care,* she thought. Just as quickly as he did it, he took his hand away, refocusing on the powerful machine they rode.

Messiah was selfish with his love in that way, only giving her crumbs that made her want to taste it all. He was holding back, and trying to bait him into jealousy had ended dangerously for her. On the back of his bike she felt safe, she felt owned, as if she was an object to possess. As if she was his most prized, and wished it could stay that way.

When they pulled into the driveway of a large home, she frowned. This wasn't the house he had taken her to before. It was beautiful. A large, family home, with a manicured lawn, made completely of brick.

He cut the engine and they climbed off, removing their helmets. She motioned toward the house, with an inquisitive look.

"This is my crib. Nobody knows about this place. I don't bring anybody here. Ever. That's the only way I get to sleep with both eyes closed," he said.

Morgan smiled, slightly, because he trusted her.

"You can stay here for the night and get yourself together. Text Ethic and let him know you're staying with one of your homegirl's tonight," Messiah said.

She did as she was told, as she followed Messiah inside.

The house was beautiful. Modern and new. It barely looked lived-in at all.

"There's a guest bedroom upstairs. There are fresh towels in the bathroom," he said. "I'll be back."

He turned to leave, but Morgan grabbed his hand, turning him back toward her.

She shook her head. "Stay," she mouthed the words, as she signed. "Please, stay."

Morgan could see the blaze in his eyes. She knew where he was headed. She was aware of his reputation; and though she was flattered that he would react on her behalf, she just wanted him there with her.

Messiah exhaled, as if it pained him to oblige her. He was the type of nigga who scratched an itch immediately. If he let it linger, it would drive him crazy. He had never learned to tether his aggression. His temper was so hot that once it was ignited, nothing would stop him from exploding. He had a vengeful spirit. Disrespect begot disrespect. He lived by a code that was so G it was hard for others to keep up; and when they slipped, he punished them. He had been waiting for an excuse to lay Lucas down for years, anyway. This beef had been cooking for a long time. Morgan was just the needle that broke the hustler's back.

He was as cold-blooded as they came; but for some reason, the sight of Morgan in front of him, trembling, as large droplets of emotion clung to her long eyelashes, moved him.

"Don't worry, I'm not going anywhere," he said. "Come on."

He led her to the bathroom where he turned on the shower. "Everything you need is under the sink," he offered.

He pointed, and she nodded. When she turned, he noticed blood on the back of her dress. It was like gasoline to his fury.

He dug his phone out of his jacket pocket.

Meet me in an hour and a half. You know where.

He sent the text to Isa, but he was sure his man was already anticipating the play. There was no way Messiah wasn't going to see Lucas tonight. He would make sure Morgan was straight, but as soon as she closed her eyes, he had every intention of committing murder tonight.

He gave her privacy and left the room, going into his master bedroom to retrieve something she could sleep in. He didn't entertain women in his home. He didn't trust anyone enough to reveal where he closed his eyes. *A bitch will get you murked even quicker than these lame-ass niggas, nowadays,* he thought. He rifled through his clothes, knowing that there was nothing feminine to find. *A t-shirt and hoop shorts will have to do.*

He went back to the bathroom, but halted, as the sound of muffled cries infiltrated the hallway. He felt intrusive, as if he was bearing witness to a moment that wasn't meant for him to see. Messiah didn't know what to do with emotions. It had never been his job to cater to the feelings of another person. He had never wanted the responsibility; because in his mind, he knew he would be no good at it. Defending her honor, he could do, but restoring it felt like a challenge that was meant for a father. She had none. Ethic tried to play the role, but Messiah knew Morgan resisted it every step of the way. He balled his hand, using the knuckle of one finger to rap softly on the door. Again, out of habit, because she couldn't hear him. That was the problem. He didn't know how to be with her. It was so easy to forget that she was deaf. He pushed the door open, slightly, and peeked his head in, coyly, not wanting to pry. He hoped she was decent. He only wanted to help; and if he was honest, he desperately wanted her to stop crying, because hearing her was chipping away at something inside his chest. He hurt with her, as if they shared a connection where one felt the other's torment. It was odd - at least to a man who extended his time and effort at a minimum. This feeling was new.

Her cries stopped, suddenly, as their eyes met, as if she had been caught being hurt... exposed... being human. She sat on the side of the toilet, the bloody dress still on her.

He stepped inside and leaned against the door. He wished he had a mother or sister who could help him deal with this girl. Morgan, with her vulnerability and her beauty, was knocking at the door inside him that he kept locked. She was asking him to love her, without saying anything at all, and Messiah didn't want to; but surely, this ache he had on the left side of his chest, behind all the brawn and muscle, was love.

He crossed the room and got on his knees in front of her, as he began to remove her clothes. He started with her jewelry. The diamonds on her neck and wrists were brilliant, just another accessory that exasperated the girls around the city that were, simply, not on Morgan's level. She was another breed, a dying class, a vintage version of a model of hustlers' wives that no longer existed. She just didn't know it. She was Justine Atkins' daughter; her beauty was inherited. If only Morgan knew her worth. Her last name was the reason why Messiah hesitated. Her history was the reason why he respected her. Kendrick had described it best: "There was loyalty and royalty inside her DNA." Messiah was undressing a queen, and because of this, he did it respectfully, hoping that she would be able to get herself together enough to finish the job before her beautiful body was exposed. She sat there, however, soft tears falling, head bowed, disgracefully, as she wrung her fingers nervously.

Messiah started with her dress, next, rolling it up her smooth skin and pulling it gently over her head, as she raised her arms. Her panties were gone, and she wore no bra. Messiah reached around her, running warm water into the spa-sized bath and she turned to submerge inside the tub.

He washed her, gently, slowly, his strong hands rubbing the knots of tension out of her shoulders, as he cleaned her from head to toe. It felt like a privilege; as if he was washing the dirt off the toes of a queen, because she was truly too special to walk through the grudge of the earth. Morgan was like a goddess and he was simply mortal. She wasn't supposed to be susceptible to the tangible ails of the streets. She was above them. If she realized that, she wouldn't pursue it, but he knew she was just trying to find a place where she belonged. She was displaced, the only one left standing with her family name, and she was searching for something. She was attracted by the allure of the game. He had to stop her from self-destructing, even if only for tonight.

He tried to wash away her tears, his wet finger wiping them, but they were only replaced with new ones. He turned her chin to him and she looked at him, her bottom lip quivering.

"I'm sorry. Nobody's going to disrespect you again. I promise. That's my word," he said. "Come on, we're done." He let out the water and held open a towel, as she stepped out of the tub. Her body glistened. It was the work of art he had always suspected existed beneath her clothes. He felt like not even he should have had the privilege to see it. It only angered him more about the events that had landed her at his house tonight. She tied the towel, securely, around her body and followed him into the master bedroom. He dressed her and then sat beside her on the edge of his bed. There were so many things he wanted to say to her, but they had an entire language between them.

"You're going to have to teach me some signs. There are things I can't say because I don't know how. Things I can't understand. I want to be able to. It's important," he said, as she stared at him.

Morgan nodded, her heart aching for this moment, but realizing it was ruined by everything that had occurred. "I can teach you," she signed.

He pulled his phone out his jacket pocket and handed it to her, opening the notes. She typed in the words instead.

He nodded, not liking the bruised feeling that existed inside his chest. It was like he had been hit and the tenderness that an injury left behind was inside him, consuming him. It was like she held the key. The key that unlocked the cage surrounding his heart. She was digging, past all the muscle, past his ribs, past all the walls he had formed over the years, determined to touch him on the inside. He didn't like the feeling. Unfamiliar with the way infatuation left a man weak, he only knew that Morgan being around him was a potential problem. He had his choice with the women in the city and no one made him feel as touchable as this young girl. Morgan affected him, despite his efforts to keep her in the off-limits zone. He stood to his feet.

"I have to go," he said. There was no more delaying the inevitable and concern flickered in Morgan's eyes.

"I have to," he repeated, before she could protest. She knew there was no stopping it. Her recklessness had set a chain of events in motion that no one would be able to prevent. "I'll be back. Try and rest," he said. She watched him walk away, his stride filled with rage and determination. She was flattered. Wars had been sparked over less, but Morgan didn't want Messiah shedding blood on her behalf. She had already lost too much. She couldn't stand the idea of losing him before she even got the chance to know him - fully… to love him, to have him as her own.

Unsure of what to do, but knowing that nothing was not an option, she rushed to her phone. Ethic was the only person who could stop Messiah from doing something stupid. Morgan knew that she would be exposing her lies by asking Ethic for help, but she would have to put herself aside to make sure Messiah was okay.

Chapter 4

E thic hated when the streets baited him. Losing control and allowing the game to lure him back was a weakness. As he drove through the city, pushing the horses under the hood of his foreign car to the max, he knew that the devil inside him had been awakened. There were just certain people in his life that were off limits. Morgan was one of them. The fact that someone had hurt her had him in a blind fury and he couldn't get to his destination fast enough. He appreciated Messiah's effort, but Ethic would put in this work himself. He battled between his humanity and his ruthlessness, daily, trying his hardest to keep himself from reigning over the city with an iron fist. He had learned the art of humility, had developed an appreciation for the simple life, but he had never lost touch with the streets. He had been raised in them, rooted in them, and a man always knew how to tap into the roots of his soul. Ethic was a gangster, and not in the corny way that men claimed to be. He was effortlessly deadly, callously calculating, and unforgivingly deceptive. He played the good guy well because he desperately wanted to be a man of character, a man that his children could be proud of, and a man that a woman could love. But when he had too, he tapped into the darkest parts of him. Only when he must. Often, when he was pushed. Always, for the ones he loved. He was the king of the city; and because he had been on a soul-searching journey, his discreetness had been mistaken for weakness. He was about to light the entire fucking city up. Lucas had trespassed, and the thought of the young hustler violating Morgan, was enough to make him move without apology. It was enough to make him call Lily in for overtime to watch Bella and Eazy, while he handled the disrespect.

Lucas was a young hustler around the city. He was 25 and raking in a lot of cash on the city's Southside. He was flashy, loud, a real-life character, who was used to having his way. Where Messiah ran the North End of the city, Lucas was his adversary across town. Bad blood existed between them, often over turf, often over women. The two men just differed on principle alone; but Ethic had kept Messiah on a leash, each time Lucas tried to bait Messiah into beef. "War is bad for business," Ethic had said. Now, he wished that he had given Messiah the green light to eliminate the threat. Now, Lucas had crossed a line. There had to be consequences to that. Ethic hadn't felt this type of anger in years. The last time he had allowed himself to act with this much rage, it had ended tragically. His dear love, Raven, had lost her life. He had tried to control his ire, by leaving the streets behind, but the worst parts of him were bubbling, threatening to surface. This was personal. Morgan was family to him, and knowing that she didn't possess the words to say no during Lucas' assault, had his temperature rising, simultaneously, with his speedometer.

He already knew where to find Lucas. The dumb hustler was so flamboyant that he wanted the entire hood to see him shine. He lived off Circle Drive, one of the old neighborhoods in Flint that reflected a time when the city was booming from the automotive industry. Lucas wasn't smart enough to stay low, while he got rich. He was dumb enough to let niggas know where he rested his head. Now that Ethic was ready to behead him, he knew, exactly, where to go. That was the problem with young niggas these days. They didn't respect the rules. They moved incorrectly. Ethic pulled up on the darkened block and immediately knew that Messiah had arrived before him. Every street light had been broken out to avoid any neighbors witnessing the melee that the night would bring. Ethic's headlights illuminated through the back of an older model Chevy Tahoe. He knew it was stolen, and he knew Messiah and his goon lay in wait inside. He cut his lights and picked up his cell. Messiah answered on the first ring.

"Morgan called me. Send your people home and come hop in the passenger seat," Ethic said.

Messiah didn't protest, and Ethic waited, patiently, as Messiah put the order down. Moments later, the old truck started, and Messiah climbed out before it pulled away. Ethic's temple throbbed, as Messiah got in.

"You're moving flawed," Ethic said. "I respect the fact that you're moving at all, considering this isn't your beef."

Messiah was more invested than Ethic could even imagine. He had no idea the murderous thoughts that were racing through Messiah's mind.

"What I tell you? Murder is something you do alone and only when..."

"Completely necessary," Messiah interrupted, finishing his sentence.

"No offense, OG, but it's necessary. You didn't see her," Messiah said, his tone flat and serious. "And Isa is my man. I trust him."

"You don't know who you can trust. You can't trust anybody when it comes to murder. The same nigga that help you put a body in the grave will be the same nigga pointing the finger at you in a court of law. Go home and make sure Morgan's good," Ethic said.

Ethic knew Messiah had plenty of bodies on him. The tattooed tear on the outer corner of his eye was a misprint.

Ethic was sure he had sent more than one to their maker. He knew the burden that death put on a man's soul, however, and Ethic wouldn't allow Messiah to dive deeper in a pool of sin. Not on his behalf.

"No offense, big homie, but this ain't about you," Messiah said. Messiah had never feared anyone, not even Ethic; but he would be remised if he didn't admit that it took every ounce of courage in him to admit that he was acting on Morgan's behalf. A man only went that far for a woman he had stake in.

The flicker of recognition shone in Ethic's eyes. Now wasn't the time to address Messiah's vague admission.

"A man takes care of his woman. If this is about a woman, then a man would be at her side. If it's about you, then we can walk in there and handle it together and burn something. The type of man that I would want my daughter with, and trust me, Morgan is like a daughter to me…that man would walk away and make sure she's good. A real man never puts himself in a position to leave his woman. Murder is 25 years to life. Is this some street shit between you and him? Or some kind of show of love for a woman? Because, if it's for love, you got it backwards. Love keeps you at her side, healing wounds. This shit here… is all motivated by hate. This shit here… removes you from a woman's life faster than the blink of an eye. One minute, you're here defending her honor, catching a body. The next, you're trapped behind steel bars, watching her search for even half of you in the next nigga in line," Ethic said. His tone was scolding, and Messiah could hear the anger in his voice. He weighed the words on his soul. He, desperately, wanted to be the one to end Lucas, but he knew that Ethic was judging him in this moment. How Messiah moved would determine if Ethic would approve or disapprove of his feelings for Morgan. It would reveal whether Messiah was the type of man a father would allow to date his princess, despite blood relation.

Messiah blew out a sharp breath, and without saying another word, he pulled open the door, flipped the hood to his sweat shirt up and headed in the opposite direction of Lucas' house.

Ethic nodded, slightly proud that Messiah had the self-control to walk away, but more than a little irritated that the young gunner had his sights on Morgan. It was a conversation for a different day, but one that would be had.

Ethic eyed the house. The glow from a television shone through the broken blinds in the front window. It was the only light coming from inside. He reached toward his touch screen and pressed a special sequence of buttons, causing the screen to lift and reveal the hidden compartment behind it. He pulled out the pair of leather gloves that lay inside and placed them over his hands. The ski mask was next, and he rolled it around his head, so that when the time was right, he could pull it down over his face with ease. He then retrieved the dirty pistol that rested inside. Without serial numbers, it was untraceable. He screwed on the silencer and then parked at the corner, before exiting and walking casually up the block. It was a quiet neighborhood, but he was still cautious, holding his head low. Ethic had an entire city of young wolves, including Messiah, that could have handled this for him, but he tried his hardest not to glorify what must be done. There was no glory in murder. There was no honor in it. It blackened his soul and came back to haunt his life so drastically that the only woman who loved him was a bitch named Karma. He didn't want Messiah to do as he had done. He wanted Messiah and the other young men he saw every day, the ones who saluted him, the ones who respected him, and the ones who saw him as a street legend, to do the opposite of what he had done. He wanted them to tap into their royal blood and excel, to take over the city with their minds, instead of diluting their worth by playing up to the stereotypes that had been placed on them. Black boys were more than hustlers, ball players, and rappers. He had fallen into that brainwashed trap; and sure, it had made him rich, but at the same time, it had made him poor. His morality and mentality had been for sale, just like his ancestors that had been shackled before him. The only difference was…Ethic had put the mental chains on himself. He was grateful he had avoided the physical ones - the bars, the steel, the confinement that this game ultimately led to. Nah, Ethic wouldn't contribute to the cycle by having broken boys follow his path in the streets. He would put in his own work and pray for Messiah and the young niggas behind him to find a better way. At least, they wouldn't get lost under his command.

Ethic went up the driveway and rounded the backyard. He pulled the ski mask down, concealing his identity, and then tried the back door. To his surprise, it was unlocked, and he used his shoulder to push it open, slowly, while gripping the gun in his hand tightly.

Stupid, he thought, as he shook his head at Lucas' carelessness. *He getting all this money and can't take the time to lock the door?* That was the problem with these 'new niggas;' they moved too quickly…to sloppily. They were too quick to do everything… snitch… kill… steal. This mistake would prove costly. Ethic followed the glow through the kitchen and into the living room where Lucas lay on his side, a thick blanket covering his body, and his back facing Ethic. It was almost too easy. Ethic pulled the trigger, firing a full clip into Lucas. The whispers of the silencer barely audible, as blood started to spread through the holes in the blanket.

Ethic walked over to Lucas and reached down to turn him on his back, to deliver a final head shot, for good measure. He reached for Lucas' shoulder and flipped him on his back, but pulled back in horror when he saw the little girl tucked in the grooves beneath Lucas. She was struggling for air to breathe, as Ethic saw the two bullets that had penetrated her chest. Lucas had been sleeping, with a little girl in his arms. She had been hidden by the cover, when Ethic had fired.

"No!" he whispered. "No, no, no!" He pushed Lucas out of the way, unaffected by his dead body as it hit the floor, but the little girl lying there, bleeding out, splintered him. He knew he should be making his exit, but he couldn't leave her there, dying, senselessly. Children were supposed to be off limits. *I didn't see her,* he thought. He scooped the little girl in his arms, but as he looked in her face, all he saw was Bella. At any moment, his past could come around full circle and affect any of his children. It was a sad truth, and the last thing he wanted was for this child to pay for Lucas' debt. Lucas' death wasn't worth the collateral damage that had been done. Nothing was worth the life of someone so young.

She's a baby, he thought, his heart shattering at the sight of what he had just done. That was the one thing about triggers, they couldn't be "un-pulled."

"Fuck!" He shouted.

His phone was in the car. He turned left and then right, searching for a house phone.

The little girl choked, as blood flooded her mouth. The fear in her eyes caused turmoil to erupt inside him. Ethic wasn't built for this… not anymore. Life had matured him. His children had shown him a side of himself that he never knew he had. He was no longer the ruthless man who could walk away, unaffected, after something like this. This would stain his conscience until the day he died. Ethic placed her on the couch, as he frantically dug through Lucas' pockets to find a cell phone. He had no remorse for the body on the floor, but this little girl, losing her life by the second, was torment to his soul.

He finally found it and dialed 911, not caring that he was sacrificing himself to save this child. He kept envisioning his children in the crossfires of war, bleeding out, because of some mistake he had made, and it burned his eyes with emotion.

This was it. This was the deed that would put him under the jail; and as the little girl died in front of him, he thought, *I deserve it*. This was the part of the game he didn't like. Innocent people got hurt. They were casualties of circumstance, and Ethic was to blame for this young life lost.

The sound of someone entering behind him caused him to turn, gun pointed, and he aimed at an old woman who held nothing but fear in her eyes.

Ethic froze, and so did she, as they both waited for the other to make a move. They stared at one another, the seconds seeming like hours, as they sized one another up. The old Ethic would have popped her, laying her down right where she stood, but enough blood had been shed. The night was already tragic enough. He didn't need the life of an old woman on his soul.

"You get out of here," the old woman spoke, finally, mustering all her courage, as she held up a black purse as if it could provide some sort of defense.

"What did you do?" she screamed, as she ran to the little girl on the ground, her fear taking a back seat to her concern. Ethic backpedaled out of the house, jumping the fence in the backyard to make it to the next block. Snatching off the ski mask, he walked, briskly, back around to his truck and pulled away into the night.

Chapter 5

The pit that filled Morgan's stomach was so vast that she felt like it would suck her inside out. Like a black hole, she felt something pulling at her. She was sick, as she sat on the stairway that led to the second floor, and watched the foyer, counting every second since Messiah had gone. *Please, let him be okay,* she thought. She was full of remorse, and wound so tightly, that when she saw the lock turn on the front door, she jumped out of her skin. She was on her feet, running to the door; and as he came through it, she wrapped her arms around him, hugging him as she cried. He could barely keep his balance, as she clung to him, like a second skin, cupping his face in her hands and kissing his lips, repeatedly. Messiah wanted to push her away. He knew that he should resist her, but the smell of her, the desperation emanating off her, it all magnetized him to her.

Fuck it, he thought.

His lips parted, as he kissed her, hungrily, stumbling backwards, pinning her to the wall as she caressed his face and his tongue took over her mouth. This kiss was soul-stirring; partly because Messiah never put his mouth on any woman. He didn't kiss. He didn't want to connect to anyone so personally. He didn't even lay a woman on her back when they sexed. Women were faceless to him; especially, the type that chased him. They all wanted one thing: money, and he wanted one thing: pussy. It was a transaction, and kisses weren't accepted…until now.

"This ain't right," he whispered, as he clenched his eyes shut and rested his forehead against hers. She was so young, so inexperienced. She was an Atkins girl. Everything rushing through his mind told him he was out of bounds, but that weak feeling, that ache in his chest, told him he was still going to play.

She ignored him, as she thought, *nothing has ever been this right.*

Messiah rubbed his goatee, as he took a step back. He was in deep contemplation, stuck somewhere between love for a girl and loyalty to Ethic.

"We can't do this until I talk to Ethic," Messiah said. "I want to do this, but I won't disrespect him. I can't. It's going against all the rules."

She nodded, and he pulled her close, kissing the tip of her nose, as he pulled on her long braids, causing her to crane her neck backward as his rough hands gripped her fragile neck. He kissed her, again, on the neck and she lowered her gaze to look him in his eyes. This was the feeling that she was supposed to feel when she invited a man to explore her. She was positive now that Lucas had raped her. He had taken liberties over her body that she hadn't granted. This chemistry, this message, this silent permission that she was giving to Messiah was unmistakable. Lucas had taken her virginity, and it saddened her, because now she couldn't give it to Messiah.

"Go upstairs and rest. You've been through enough today. Your head is all over the place. What feels right might not be right. If it's meant for us to fuck with each other, then it'll be. In the morning, I'll take you home," Messiah said. His lips were so beautiful to watch, and she was, briefly, grateful that she couldn't hear; because if she didn't have to look at them, she wondered if she would notice them at all. They were full and dark, as if he had smoked 100 blunts. She wondered how many women he had given the honor of tasting his lips, and a twinge of irrational jealousy ran through her. The way he bit his bottom lip, and then licked them, made her swoon as she sighed deeply, while acknowledging his words. She walked away, looking back at him, coyly, before disappearing up the stairs.

Messiah was going against everything he stood for. Money over women. He had never thought twice about a female. They were good company at night, but none of the many he had sampled had ever brought him back for seconds. He hadn't even touched Morgan and already he was ready to body niggas over her. That type of affection was scary. It was crazy and dangerous. It was irrational; but still, he felt it. It was forbidden but he knew he was still going to pursue her. He pulled out his phone and sent a text to Ethic. If he was going to do this, he had to face his mentor, man to man. It was only right. He only hoped Morgan was worth it.

***

Darkness encompassed Ethic, as he stepped into his home. The beep from his alarm system sounded, lightly, causing a sleeping Dolce to stir on the couch.

"It's late, is everything okay? You called me over here and then you rushed out without explanation." She stood and walked over to him, his silhouette illuminated slightly by the light that filtered inside from the porch. She touched him, but pulled back when she felt something wet.

"What is this?" she asked, as she pulled her hands back and reached for the light switch. The gloom he wore on his face and the blood on his jacket were evidence of his wrongdoings. "Are you bleeding?"

"It's not mine," he admitted. "Where are my kids?" he asked, suddenly feeling a sense of urgency to make sure they were okay.

"They're upstairs, sleeping. They are fine," Dolce reassured, as she frowned. "What happened?"

"No questions," he answered, his voice dark. Sadness lived in his eyes. Regret. Anger. Paranoia. It all reflected in his gaze, as he looked at her. He had blood on his hands; and although he had killed before, he had never carried the guilt of a child's murder. He pulled off his clothes, unable to keep them on his body any longer. The stained hoodie felt like it was hot to the touch, as if it was the one act that had given the devil ownership of his soul. He stalked up the stairs.

"Ethic!" Dolce called to his back, as she picked up the clothes and followed him.

He peeled out of his jeans and stepped right into the shower, turning the handle all the way too hot to scold the guilt away. He placed both hands on the wall in front of him and lowered his head, as he watched the water swirl around the drain at his feet. He was spiraling. His life was like a tunnel, and the only light he saw at the end was the flames that waited to burn him for the mistakes he had made. His chest felt as if it had caved in, and he remembered the last time death had put this crippling feeling on him. It was the day he lost his mother. He was seven years old when she had been murdered, and he had felt the same thing then, that he felt this day. Devastation. Utter loss. He felt Dolce's hands wrap around his body and he cringed. She just wanted to be near him. He just wanted to cast her away, but he turned around, water rinsing over him, falling into his eyes and on his face as he breathed deeply, his frustrations mounting.

"Fuck do you want from me?" he asked her.

He saw confusion in her eyes and shock fill her face. *She don't even know,* he thought. He often pondered about the motives of women. They had always been superficial creatures. Before he had been trapped in a burning car, years ago, ladies had wanted him for his looks. Afterward, some sought him for his money. Others wanted to be that special one that he claimed. They wanted the power and the glory that came with being his. Dolce had been in the ring, fighting for the spot for a long time; but deep down, he knew she was just more of the same. She wanted the title, nothing more; and if Ethic ever fell off, he knew she would flee. Her attraction was superficial, and suddenly, he wanted to punish her for it. He flipped her around and pulled at her hips, so that she was standing on her tip-toes, and there was a slight arch in her back.

"Take it out on me," she whispered, in a throaty gasp, as he entered her.

She was there. She wanted to be fucked, so Ethic was going to pour his aggression, his anger, into her. He was strong, wide, and hard, as he dug into her - all raw passion, no finesse. He wasn't gentle. In fact, he was more than she could handle, his back shots causing her to bite down on her bottom lip. She took it, because she knew he needed it, and it felt so miserably good. The mix of pain and pleasure that caused her to cry out when he hit the deepest parts of her was like nothing she had ever felt.

She tried to run.

"Take it," he whispered. His voice was almost pleading with her, begging her to take the remorse off his hands, as if he could transfer his fault to her through this act. It was non-transferable. The pain was his to bear. Only he was liable for what had occurred tonight, and he couldn't fuck his burdens away. He withdrew from her, growling in masculinity, as he spilled his seeds, mixing it in the stream of water and washing his beautiful, black babies down the drain to Dolce's dismay. She had been trying to get Ethic to slip for years, knowing that he was the type of man that would never walk away from a woman who gave him children. Her attempts at entrapment were to no avail. He was always cautious, even when his mind was somewhere else.

He washed his body and stepped out of the shower, wrapping a towel around his waist.

"You know you can talk to me, right? About whatever happened, about whatever is hurting you," Dolce said, as she turned off the water.

"Talking about real shit has never been our thing. Why can't you just leave us where we are, instead of trying to force us to a place where it's uncomfortable," Ethic said, in frustration. He walked into the room and she was right on his heels.

"Uncomfortable for whom?" Dolce challenged. "For you? Because this..." She pointed between them. "...this shit here is what makes me uncomfortable. I've been available to you for years. Even after you brought that bitch, Raven, up in here. Who picked you up when you were drowning, after she died? Then, you go off to New York to take care of some new bitch, leaving me here, just dropping what we have..."

"I don't owe you any explanations. We're friends who fuck at times," Ethic replied. He knew it was a bit harsh. Normally, he would spare her feelings, but she was picking on the wrong night.

"And that's it? After all this time? That's all I am? A friend to you?" Dolce said.

He didn't answer her, as he slid into a pair of grey, jogging pants, allowing them to hang low on his waist, exposing the deep, V cuts that lead to his girth. Even after sex, he hung noticeably in the sweatpants. The print of thickness pronounced and distracting, as Dolce yelled at him. He had checked out of the conversation. He didn't argue. The yelling and screaming, he wasn't beat for it.

"I never made you no promises, ma," he said.

Dolce scoffed. "You selfish, arrogant motherfucka," she said, as she snatched up her clothes and put them on, quickly. "Next time you think to call me to come watch your kids, or cook a meal, or to suck your dick, don't!"

He watched her storm out and sat down at the foot of his king-sized bed. He had so many things to deal with that remedying Dolce's hurt feelings was simply not a priority.

Chapter 6

Alani sat on her hands and knees, scrubbing, gripping the bristle brush so hard that her knuckles hurt, as she tried to clean the blood stains out of her wooden floor. Her blood-shot eyes burned, as she swiped at her tears with the back of her wrist. She had been crying for days. Her brother and her beautiful daughter were dead. She felt like she was drowning, trying to inhale air in a pool of water, and the slow suffocation was torture.

"Alani, let me help you, baby. You need to sleep."

The voice behind her belonged to her aunt, Nannie. Normally, the soft alto filled with wisdom and strength was soothing to her; but today, it was like nails on a chalkboard. She was irritated, taking her anger out on everyone around her, as she mourned the loss of Lucas and her dear Kenzie.

"Sleep won't come, Nannie," she whispered. "So, I might as well be doing something." She scrubbed harder and harder, using so much elbow grease that she was breaking a sweat. "This blood just won't come out!" she shouted. She bowed her head and sobbed, as she cried, "Why is this happening? God, my baby is gone. I told Lucas that all his bullshit was going to catch up to him. He was out here selling dope and throwing every dollar he made in the faces of every broke nigga in town. He was living foul, and it was only a matter of time before something went wrong. But that was his chance to take... it was his life. How did his karma come back on me? On Kenzie?" she wailed, confusion and grief caused her to double over. Her emotions were causing her physical pain. She could barely inhale, it hurt so badly. Alani just wanted to die because it would be much easier than being the only one left behind, mourning.

"It's only by the grace of God that I didn't get shot that night," Nannie said, as she sat down on the floor in front of Alani and grabbed the brush from Alani's hands. She began to scrub at the stained wood. "I know it hurts, baby, but I'm going to love on you, through the hurt. I'm right here with you. I've been with you since the day you were born; and as long as I live and breathe, you will always be okay. These are dark days, Alani, but there is always a light ahead. Keep your faith in God," Nannie said.

"What kind of God allows a three-year-old girl to be murdered while she sleeps? Huh? That's no God I trust. You may worship that type of God, but I won't. I can't," Alani said, as she stood and stormed out the house, snatching her purse up on the way out. She paused, midway, as she descended the steps. Her aunt was the only person she had left. She had never raised her voice at her. Guilt caused her to backtrack her steps, as she went back inside.

"I'm sorry, Nannie," Alani said, as she watched her aunt pick up the bucket and the brush from the floor.

"I know. It's not all on you though, Alani. I loved them too. I feel it too. Ain't no point in us feeling it alone. We need one another to get through this. I just want to be here for you, baby," Nannie said.

Alani nodded, as she teared up. She hated the way her emotions came in waves. It was up then down. One minute, she was mentally coaching herself to find strength, and the next, she felt like the world had ended. She would never be able to make it through the planning of two funeral services.

"Have you seen the life insurance policy?" she asked.

Nannie looked at her, sympathetically. "It's in your hand," she replied.

Alani looked down, as if someone else gripped the folder. "I'm losing it," she whispered.

"Don't be so hard on yourself. You want me to come with you to the funeral parlor?"

Alani shook her head. "No, I have to do this myself," Alani said, shaking her head. Seeing her daughter's body under the white sheet at the morgue had been the hardest thing she had ever done. It was an image she would never forget. She was a mother burying her child. Nothing about that was right and she didn't need anyone witnessing her breakdowns. She was trying her hardest to keep her composure, to only fall to her knees behind the safety of closed doors, and to stifle her wails at night, face in pillow. She just couldn't let anyone see the type of grief she was going through, because it was teetering on the edge of crazy.

She rushed out and jumped into her raggedy Pontiac G6. The car was so old they didn't even make the model anymore. The reason she had even left her daughter in Lucas' care was so that she could pick up overtime hours to be able to save up for the down payment on a pretty, little Jeep she had been dreaming about. It all seemed so selfish now, so pointless. She was worried about people in her city judging her, laughing at her for driving a bucket car, and had lost time with her little girl, chasing material things. She had left Kenzie with Lucas plenty of times before, always so she could work, but she now questioned if she was working to take care of her daughter or if the motive had truly been superficial. She had never thought it would result in such a tragedy. "I'm to blame for all this," she thought. "I should have moved Lucas out of Flint way before the streets got ahold of him; and I should have never left Kenzie with him. What was I thinking?"

Alani had tried hard to never judge her brother, but not once had she taken a dime of his ill-gotten money. She had watched him slink lower and lower into the bowels of the city's underworld. *I should have done more to stop it. Look what has happened because I sat around and did nothing at all,* she thought.

Her thoughts haunted her all the way to the funeral home. Even the sky seemed to be crying, as she stepped out into the rain, holding a copy of Essence magazine over her head to stop her fresh wrap from turning into a full-blown afro. By the time she made it inside, she was soaked. Her hair started to fight her fresh press, reverting to her natural curls, slightly. She huffed, as she took the hair tie she wore around her wrist and used it to pull her hair into a high ponytail. She caught a glimpse of herself in the mirror in the reception area. Her puffy eyes and red nose were evidence of the sleepless nights she had endured. She wore her melancholy all over her. Even her skin had lost its vibrant glow. Alani couldn't even imagine ever feeling true happiness again. Not as a childless mother. How was she supposed to forget about the little girl that had grown in her womb? Surely, she couldn't be expected to act as if she didn't know what it felt like to have two heart beats at the same time. Alani felt like she had been given entrance into an exclusive club, only to, suddenly, be kicked out. Her motherhood had been stripped, violently, from her. Her legs weakened slightly, as she suddenly had the urge to run back out into the rain.

"Ma'am? Are you Ms. Hill?"

Alani turned to find that the voice belonged to a black woman with sympathetic eyes. Alani could tell that it was a look that she supplied out of habit. The woman was in the business of burying people, of preparing the final goodbyes of the dead. She had rehearsed that compassionate stare long and hard. Alani could see the contrived kindness was nothing more than a job requirement. It was as common as a uniform or an

ID badge. Alani wanted to slap the false sadness from the woman's face. She was so angry these days, angrier than she had ever been. She needed someone to blame. Without someone to take this hurt out on, it was eating her alive from the inside out.

"I'm here to begin arrangements for my daughter and brother," she whispered. "They were brought here last night."

"Of course, we've been expecting you. Did you bring the insurance information?" the woman asked.

Alani went into her bag and handed it over. "It's not a lot. I have $10,000 on each of them…" she began to explain.

"Don't worry. That's plenty. We will work within your budget," the woman explained. "Come into our showroom. I'll introduce you to James. He will be your coordinator. I will go contact your insurance company, while he gets you started with arrangements."

Alani nodded, as she was led through a double door where a man was waiting for her. She stepped over the threshold into what seemed like a world of flowers and caskets.

"Alani, this is the owner, James Masters. I'm going to handle the paperwork. He will take care of you. You're in good hands," the woman said.

"That you are," he said. Alani took in his expensive suit, fake smile, and his greasy hair. His brown skin matched hers, but it was a shade richer, which let her know he wasn't from where she was from. He was the type of person who built his business in the hood, but wouldn't dare live there. He was getting rich based on the deaths, often murders, of black people and Alani wasn't naïve to the fact. "Let's sit," he offered, as he grabbed a book from atop of one of the fancy caskets and took a seat beside her. They flipped through the options and Alani felt instant intimidation from the prices. It seemed that even the simplest details were $1000 and up. She went through the book, not even eyeing the makes of the caskets or the type of flowers, but noticing the prices. Her heart was full of angst. She never knew that it was so expensive to put a loved one to rest. *I can't afford any of this. Even with the insurance,* she thought, dismayed. She wanted to do her brother and daughter justice and tears pooled in her eyes.

"You want the best for your daughter. This rose gold, pink, aluminum casket is a great option. It will never decay. It will withstand the elements well. I have mothers come in here and all they are thinking about is getting change from that insurance policy, but I know a good mother when I see one. This is perfect for your angel," James said.

She looked at him, her lip trembling. He was selling her hard; his voice full of awe, as if he was peddling her a brand-new car instead of a box that would go in the ground filled with her most precious possession in the world. She was overly emotional. Her hands shook, as she turned the pages, desperately hoping that the next page would reveal something…anything that was within her range. It was costing her more to bury her daughter than it had to birth her. Death was more expensive than life; and this man was too eager, too pushy. He held no remorse, no timidity about broaching the sensitive subject. This man had no shame about measuring her love for her kid based on what she chose out of this high-ass book. Alani felt like a failure.

The woman from before, the wearer of the fake smile, knocked on the door, softly, before peeking her head inside the room.

"Ms. Hill, can I speak with you for a moment?" she said.

Alani was grateful to be tapped out the ring. She stood to her feet, finally having an excuse to run from the room. As she stepped into the hall, the woman's expression caused Alani to frown.

"Your insurance company says the policy has lapsed. You do not have a current life insurance policy. Is there another policy, perhaps, at home?" the woman asked.

"What do you mean? I pay this policy every month," Alani whispered, her face heating with embarrassment.

"I'm only delivering the information as it was told to me," the woman replied. She handed Alani the documents back. "You can call them to find out more. Can you take a loan from the bank or a family member, in the meantime, to cover the burial expenses?"

Alani snatched the papers out of the woman's hands. "There's no one. It's just me. It's always on me," she mumbled those last words, as she gathered her shame. "I need to call about the policy. I'll be back."

The rain welcomed her back. This time, she was grateful for it. It mixed with her tears, helping to hide her torment, as she rushed back to her car. She pulled out her phone, but as she went to dial the number on the rain-stained papers, she heard the automated voice echo in her ear. "Please contact AT&T about your account."

Alani tossed the phone at the dash board, as frustration mounted, and she gripped her steering wheel in ire. Nothing could ever be easy. Every day was always one, big struggle. She was always behind, always robbing Peter to pay Paul, always playing catch up. She had managed over the years. She had always been able to make the pieces to the puzzle fit. Sure, things were paid late, but they were always paid. This time, she didn't know if she would be able to pull it off. Her mind wasn't even in the right state for her to think of how to make the impossible possible. Right now, she just wanted to have a hall pass, not to cheat, but to cry. It seemed black women were never given that luxury of emotional release. Her mind was submerged in grief and that blocked all logical thought. All she knew was that she didn't have the money she needed, and the fact that her daughter and brother were lying on a cold slab, waiting for her to come to the rescue, was damaging to her soul. She had always been their nurturer, their problem solver, and now she felt useless. She found her car key and went to turn over the ignition. The sound of it revving and then stalling caused her to laugh.

"Of course," she said, in disbelief. Her car wasn't starting. "When it rains, it fucking pours."

She exited the car. Her embarrassment kept her from going back inside, so she trekked through the rain across the street to the diner on the corner. She wasn't reminded that she hadn't eaten until the smell of bacon caused her stomach to growl, as she stepped inside. She sat at the bar and motioned to the waitress, serving the early morning patrons.

"Is there a phone I can use? My car is stalled across the street. I need to call a tow," she said.

"You got to buy something first," the waitress replied.

"That's fine," Alani said. She looked up at the sign. *$3.99 breakfast special.*

She needed every, little dollar at this point. The four dollars she was about to spend on one breakfast could buy her a whole pack of bacon that she could eat on all week, but her stomach urged her to feed it. *Four dollars ain't gon' make a difference,* she thought. "I'll take the special and a *phone,*" she said, her testy tone causing the woman to roll her eyes. She handed over the old-school phone, stretching the curly cord to the max, so that Alani could use it.

Bitch is going to spit in my food, Alani thought, as she took the receiver, wishing that she had been a bit nicer with her tone. A good breakfast would stop her stomach from touching her back and ease the sick feeling that had lived within her since finding out about the deaths of her loved ones. Or so she hoped.

She hooked up to Wi-Fi and searched for the closest company. The waitress sat down her food, as she ordered the tow.

Alani eyed the food, suspiciously, opting out of eating, as she placed exactly four dollars on the countertop before heading back out into the rain.

***

Ethic's hands were covered in motor oil, as he installed the carburetor into an old-school Buick Regal. He had to focus on something, on anything, to stop himself from thinking about the little girl's life he had taken. Albeit it had been a mistake, those types of slip-ups were ones that didn't go without fault. Someone had to shoulder the blame for the loss of life. The world was filled with enough evil. He had taken one of the good ones and now his soul was unbalanced. His spirit was disturbed and nothing but busy work could keep him from losing it.

One of his many investments over the years had been a distribution trucking company and a string of automotive shops around the state of Michigan. It was rare that the boss came in to get his hands dirty, but today, he needed to do something, anything, to keep his thoughts from haunting him. Rebuilding the beautiful, American-made machine was like putting a puzzle together. It took all his concentration and he often blocked out everything around him until the entire picture was complete. He had salvaged the car from the junk yard, years ago, and he was putting it together piece by piece.

"We got one coming in?" he heard one of his workers shout out, and he lifted his head, as he noticed a tow truck pull in front of his berth. His gut wrenched when he saw her step out of the passenger seat of the tow truck. He, instantly, recognized her. Her hair was a curly mess on top of her head, as she ducked under the handbag she held above her head. Her eyes were swollen and red. Still, he noticed the beauty in her, as she rushed inside the lobby to shelter from the rain. Her skin was smooth, resembling coffee that had been diluted with milk, and her slim build was complimented with wide hips and bowed legs. Even in her obvious distress, she carried an effortless beauty.

What is she doing here? He thought, as alarm filled him, and he held his breath, her presence ordering him to cease all movement. Her story had headlined the news.

Mother loses daughter, sister loses brother to gun violence, marks the city's 50th murder.

Even if he had missed the story that the media played on a loop, her face matched a face he had seen before. It was an older replica of the little girl that he had stripped from the earth. He stared at the woman walking into his establishment and knew the universe was playing a cruel trick on him. If he had thought he had found respite from his guilt, this face, this woman, was there to destroy all possibility of that. Even if he hadn't been the hidden figure behind the trigger, he would have noticed her. He had learned to ignore the sound of the bell above the door, but she captivated his attention. She was just one of those people, hard to miss, as was the pain in her blood-shot eyes. Sorrow filled him because he was, unknowingly, disrespecting her space. She was standing mere feet away from the murderer of her child, of her brother, and guilt riddled him like bullets. He was surprised the emotional shots he took didn't cause him to bleed out right there in the body shop. He hurt with her…for her, as if she was his beloved to mourn beside. Ethic had never been so silently remorseful. He was used to righting his wrongs, to remedying things he had broken. A real man knew when to apologize and acknowledged his wrong. He felt like a little-ass boy standing there, allowing her to remain in the dark about his actions. There was no way to repair this. There was nothing he could do or say that would lessen her agony. He couldn't speak an apology because to do so would incriminate him. As he blinked, the momentary darkness reminded him of Bella, of Eazy, and of Morgan. Each of their faces flashed behind his lids, with every blink. They depended on him. To confess his sins would force him to leave his children behind. He just couldn't do it and he felt like the lowest of the low…a coward…a murderer. No admission of guilt would come from his mouth, which meant no apology between them could exist.

The air thickened around him and Ethic wiped his hands on the towel beside him and bypassed her, as he walked into the back office. It was time for him to break out. With her there, the distraction he sought was no more. There wasn't one big enough, anyway, to stop him from seeing blood on his hands. He went to the sink and washed his hands, but as the black grime rinsed down the drain, all he could see was red.

"Yo, boss, we got a problem out here."

Ethic looked up, as Redneck Larry peeked his head into the office.

"You can't handle it?" Ethic asked.

"She asked for the owner," Larry said.

Ethic's throat constricted, as he reached for the paper towel to dry his hands. Did she know? Did she have super natural abilities to detect his guilt? Was her motherhood like an internal compass that helped her find her daughter's offender? Ethic was a man whom had faced many things, but this petite woman made him feel like he was a peasant who was preparing to meet the evil queen. How mighty would her wrath be? Logic told him that he had been careful. That there was no way she could identify him, but remorse was a hungry beast and his conscience was feeding it.

"Boss?"

Ethic snapped from his thoughts and stepped out of the office. For some reason, he felt disrespectful, greeting her with grease smeared on his forearms, and the coveralls only half casing him. His strong chest only covered by the dirty wife-beater he wore. He looked like a blue-collar worker who made honest money, but as he shook her hand, the softness of his well-manicured hands told a different story. The hair rose on the back of his neck at their brief connection because he knew his was the last hand she would want to grasp. The ball in his throat made him swallow deeply, moving his Adam's apple, as he wiped the top of his head, smoothing out his waves. Ethic was nervous. He had crossed many gangsters in his lifetime, none of which had ever made him sweat. This woman made him uneasy, with nothing more than her presence. He felt transparent standing before her.

"What can I do for you?" he asked.

"Listen, I wanted to talk to you about giving me a discount on the price of my car being repaired. I, literally, am having the worst week of my life. I'm not trying to give you no sob stories, but my shit is fucked up. My daughter died, my brother died, I'm missing work to plan the funerals, the insurance people on some bullshit, and my car broke down outside the funeral home. I can't afford to fix this car, but I can work it off. Sweep up around here or something. Scrub toilets. Anything. I just really need God to send me an angel right now, because if one more thing goes wrong, I'm going to lose it. What do you say?" She had to laugh at how ridiculous it sounded, but it was all truth, no exaggeration needed. Her life was in shambles. She was in shambles, and as she stood pleading with Ethic, she laughed. She gripped her stomach in laughter, as tears came to her eyes. "I'm sorry," she said, in between laughing fits. "This is just so ridiculous. How can life get this bad? I mean, I've been praying and praying, and I just find it funny that I'm praying to the same God that allowed this to happen in the first place. Shit's hilarious." Her laughter faded, as she planted her face in her hands. She turned away from him, in embarrassment. "You know what? Never mind," she whispered. She faced him now, taking a deep breath and squaring her defeated shoulders, as she cleared her throat. "This isn't your problem and I've never begged for anything in my life. I'll come up with the money. Can you just have it done as soon as possible?" she asked.

He watched her, as she stood in front of him. Her eyes were sad, but challenge lived behind her stare, as if she were determined to survive. Her hand was cocked on one hip and her face twisted in anger and frustration. Glistens of tears danced in her eyes and she was trying so hard to be strong that her bottom lip quivered. Her vulnerability and sadness were the most exquisite thing Ethic had ever seen. Her femininity was a work of art. She was beauty, a shattered kind, that was broken and all over the place, but beautiful all the same. He would have obliged her, even if he wasn't the one responsible for the havoc in her life.

"Fix her car," Ethic said, as he turned to exit.

"What's the discount?" Redneck Larry asked.

"It's on the house," Ethic replied. He reached the door and looked back, just in time to see her eyes widen in shock and her shoulders slag, slightly, as if he had physically removed a weight from them. Her burden was visible and palpable. He could feel it. The energy she carried left no room for anything but woe, and he understood, but she was infectious. Seeing his actions affect this woman disturbed Ethic.

"I swear on my life I will pay you back. I just need a little time. Thank you," she said, as she took a step toward him, hands pressed together as if he had answered one of her many prayers. He backed up from her, abruptly pushing the door open with force, as he crossed the parking lot to his car. He had to get away from her, out of her reach, out of her sight. He started his car and pulled away from his business, in haste. He could see her step out of the building to watch him leave, but he wanted nothing but distance between them. She was a reminder of his greatest sin and he knew that the irony of her walking into his shop, on the rare day that he was present, was nothing but God reminding him that he had lost his way.

Chapter 7

The emotions that dwelled within the chambers of an 18-year-old girl's heart were so intense. They were like a cosmic force in the universe, spinning, and burning, and building to an immensity so brilliant that its inevitability of explosion couldn't be avoided. Morgan sat on her bed, her body sinking into the plush mattress so deeply that it muffled her cries. The gloom of the rainy day matched her somber mood, creating the perfect soundtrack to her melancholy, as beads of water slid down the window pane. She felt everything...every emotion...they hit her all at once, simultaneously torturing her weary, young heart. Her need for *him* attacked her. He hadn't called. He hadn't responded to her texts. She had been torturing herself for days, checking her phone every few minutes, only to feel the sting of letdown when his name was never present on her screen. Messiah was MIA and she felt like she was being detoxed off a drug so strong that without it she would die. He had only given her a taste of his attention. A morsel of his affection, and already, she was willing to do anything for more.

Young love was potent, like crack to a dope fiend, like relaxer to new growth, like good dick to a nympho, like chocolate during a menstrual; when you needed it, you needed it. She saw the light in her room flicker on, then off, and she turned to see Ethic standing in the doorway. She sighed. She had wondered when he would speak to her. It had been days and he hadn't uttered one word. His silence was almost worse than any punishment he could come up with. It took a lot to make Ethic mad, but he was brooding. His demeanor filled the house with anxiety, as she waited. She was tired of the daddy role. When she was younger, she needed him. She wanted his guidance. She respected his role as patriarch in her life. It was old and stale at 18, however. She wanted the leash removed. She had been walking around on eggshells because his disappointment was like carrying around a heavy weight that only he could relieve her of. If he truly was her father, she would want his approval; but Morgan just wanted him to leave her alone and give her space to become whomever it was she was meant to be, whether it was fucked up or not.

"What do you want?" she signed.

Ethic folded his arms over his broad, strong, chest. "I don't know what to do with you, at this point, Morgan," he signed back.

"I never asked you to do anything. You chose to take me in. You're not my father." Her hands were moving so fast that he knew she was upset.

"But I'm your family. Family is about more than blood, and I want to keep you safe. Messiah ain't safe. Choosing to go to the motel with a nigga you didn't know wasn't safe. Someone, intentionally, hurt you and there was a price to pay for that. Messiah won't hurt you like that, but he lives a lifestyle that he can't protect you from. If something happens to you because of him, at the hands of him, or anyone who has a problem with him…" Ethic paused, because he could feel his temper returning. "He's not an exception, is all I'm saying. When you hurt, others get hurt; and this time, someone innocent was affected behind bad decisions you made, Morgan," Ethic signed, as his thoughts went to the little girl lying cold in a casket.

Speculation had already spread around the city about the murders. Morgan didn't know, exactly, what had occurred, but she knew that Ethic was behind both Lucas' murder and the little girl whose face had been on nightly news on repeat. Morgan was young, however, and she didn't quite value life in the same way Ethic did. *That little girl's death is on Lucas. His karma got her killed,* she thought.

"What about my hurt? What about what was taken from me?" Morgan signed. "He had me pinned against a wall, he was inside me, and I couldn't even say no. No one hears me, no one sees me. I'm just Benjamin Atkins' pretty, deaf, dumb, daughter! Messiah sees me!"

"Messiah is no good for you," Ethic replied, with sympathy. He pulled a pamphlet out of his back pocket. "My position isn't changing about him. I know you feel different and you act out because you want to bop around here like your little friends. Everybody sees you, Morgan. We hear you. I hear you. I believe that there is a queen in there and you're trying to dumb yourself down to be like everybody else. You not being able to hear allows you to look at the world through a different lens. I respect your perspective, Morgan, but I know that everything is harder for you. I know there is a part of you that I can never understand." He handed her the paperwork in his hands. "I think you're fine the way you are, but if you want to hear, there is a surgery that can help. I've been considering it for years and I have the money put up. You are chasing behind Messiah, but I want you chasing your dreams, baby girl. You can go to college, you can do more than flaunt around this town. Flint isn't the kingdom it used to be when your daddy was running things. It's the wild, wild West and I don't want you caught in the crossfire. Just think about it and let me know what you decide."

Morgan looked down at the paperwork, and when she raised her eyes again, Ethic was gone. For years, she had wished for this. She had never thought it could be possible;

but as she sat on her bed and flipped through the pamphlet, tears came to her eyes.

Messiah would have called by now if I was normal. I scare him. I scare everybody, she thought.

She had always been the girl who got stares.

"It's because people never saw a girl so pretty," her mother used to tell her.

Morgan knew better. The stares were caused by misunderstanding. They were from discomfort. She was the pretty girl who talked with her hands, who had no voice. She was tired of being that person. She knew, before she ever read one word of the information, that she would go through with the procedure.

She hoped the world sounded as beautiful as she imagined it did in her head; but most of all, she hoped Messiah's voice was as deep and strong as she suspected. She wanted to hear him say he wanted her; and even if he didn't, she had to hear his denial of her to believe it.

***

Messiah sat in one of his many cars. He was a collector of sorts. Old schools, foreigns, bikes; he had a thing for speed. It made his adrenaline race; and as he sat inside the big body BMW, rolling up, his music knocked so loud from the speakers that he couldn't hear his cronies' wisecracking around him. He wasn't much in the mood for flexing, but he couldn't go into hiding. He had to be on the scene, following his normal routine, to combat the whispers that he had been the hitter behind Lucas' murder. Niggas went into hiding after they got their hands dirty. Messiah was right there, out in the open, because he bore no guilt and wanted no implications, but his mind was a million miles away. Tupac was the soundtrack to his life as *Hail Mary* rang out in the night air.

The bass was so heavy that it rattled his chest, as he nodded his head ever so slightly to the beat. The car wash was packed, and the night sky sparkled with stars, as the city's finest pulled into the establishment for the simple purpose of being seen. Women walked by his car, with no destination, just to give him a glimpse of their assets. They wanted to be chosen and Messiah knew he had his pick of the litter, but tonight, his mood was off. Thoughts of Morgan infiltrated his mind. To his own dismay, she had found her way into a place where no man or woman had ever been able to before - his heart. Not even his mother or father occupied space there; but somehow, Morgan had broken the lock. He didn't like the distraction. When he should have been thinking about his next move, he was zeroed in on a woman - a young one at that. The tender feeling in his chest had him feeling like a sucker. He had seen how loving a woman had brought down the best hustlers over the years. His best friend, Noah, had gotten gunned down for thinking with his heart. Messiah refused to let the same happen to him. Love made men sloppy and unfocused. It was a weakness and Messiah prided himself on having none. He lived a life of limited attachments because he always wanted to be able to walk away from everything at the drop of a dime. *I'm already spending too much time on this,* he thought.

Messiah saw the thick crowd of people turn to look, as a Range Rover entered the parking lot. Messiah knew who it was, before the window ever rolled down. Only a few men had made it to foreign status in the city, and only one could cause such a frenzy when he pulled up. Ethic's street resume was extensive, but he moved like a ghost, rarely coming into the city limits and choosing to enjoy his wealth silently, as he masked as a successful businessman. Retirement hadn't subtracted from his legend, however, and as he pulled onto the scene it was like a celebrity had arrived. Ethic pulled, directly, in front of Messiah's car, blocking him in. He rolled down the window, revealing his stern face. Messiah turned down the music.

"Let me rap with you for a minute," Ethic's baritone announced, as Messiah stuck his head out.

Messiah knew it was an inevitable conversation. He knew Morgan was like a daughter to Ethic. He also knew that he didn't make the cut as acceptable to fit into Morgan's life.

"Yo, I'll be right back," he said to his squad, as he exited and walked around to the passenger side of Ethic's whip. He climbed inside, and Ethic pulled away. Messiah wasn't fearful of anyone, but Ethic's presence was heavy, as silence filled the small space between them.

"Do I even need to say it?" Ethic asked. The authority behind his question was clear.

"Nah, I got it," Messiah replied. "There is a line. She's on the other side of it. I ain't a bad nigga…"

"You're not good enough for her," Ethic replied, with a stern tone that told Messiah that he was truly talking to a man about his daughter. There was nothing contrived or forced about Ethic's love for Morgan. Blood couldn't make them any closer.

"That's all facts, OG," Messiah responded. "She's a special girl." Messiah looked out the window, as they spun the block. "I have nothing but respect. You've taught me a lot. You've probably kept me alive over the years. You've given me game, when you could have left me to learn it the hard way. I'll keep my distance."

"It's appreciated," Ethic answered. He popped the locks and Messiah realized they were back at the car wash. That was all the time Ethic had to spare for today. Messiah exited and watched as Ethic pulled away. Ethic had the pipeline to the city sewn up. His trucking business was a legitimate establishment, but when something needed to come in or out, whether it be drugs, money, or both, Ethic ensured safe transport up and down I-75. The auto garage and repair aspect were simply a way for him to employ some of his old partners around the city, and give them a legal means to an end. The real money was in what was coming and going on the semis. If Ethic wanted to, he could ice Messiah out and shutdown all his blocks by simply restricting his access to product. Messiah didn't want those problems. It was best to let that go. He walked back to his car to find it swarmed with a pack of pretty women as his homeboys entertained. Messiah wasn't in the mood for bullshit, but he knew there was no point in turning down new pussy. He and Morgan were done, before it could even begin. It was something he would just have to get over. He knew that Morgan was young and naïve, no matter how mature she claimed to be. She would be a distraction, and he would be directly going against his big homie, if he continued to pursue her. He pulled out his phone to text her and then paused. *It ain't worth it,* he thought.

"Hey, Messiah."

The melody of her voice was laced with thirst and he glanced up from his screen.

"What up? You need something?" he asked, slightly irritated. Nish stood before him, looking like a winner amongst the crowd. She was a beautiful girl, and he could tell from the look in her eyes, she knew it. He had seen her around, mostly with Morgan. She was young, freshly legal, so she hadn't been worn out around the hood. He knew it was only a matter of time before a young hustler staked claim to her.

"Just you," she answered.

"Just me, huh?" he answered, as he shook his head. *Bitches are dirty as hell,* he thought.

"Where yo' homegirl?" he asked, checking her temperature to see if her loyalty to Morgan would stand up.

"Who?" she asked, playing dumb. He smirked, because young girls were bad at playing dumb, and he knew the girl before him wasn't playing at all.

"Morgan," Messiah played along.

"Oh, I don't know. I don't mess with her like that. We really more like associates. She's a friend of a friend. Why we talking about her, though? I'm trying to talk about us," she pressed hard.

Messiah laughed at that. Another quality of young girls was their frankness. They hadn't perfected the art of flirtation yet. "There's an us?"

"There could be," she answered, with a smile.

Messiah had no interest in Nish, but he knew that if he took up with Morgan's friend, Morgan would lose all interest in him. Messiah knew it wasn't the best way to handle things, but he needed an out. He was afraid of the way he felt when in Morgan's presence. He knew, even with Ethic's condemnation, it would only be a matter of time before he went after what he wanted. The feeling she gave him was addictive and he was craving her. He had to make Morgan hate him, because if she wanted him, the attraction would be mutual, and he would risk it all to make her his girl. He had to kill the possibility and Nish was the perfect scapegoat.

"I don't know about all that. I ain't really looking for none of that. I'm more of a casual type of nigga," he answered. "All fun, no strings," he said.

He could see the disappointment in her face. She was looking for strings. She wanted a come-up, but she would rather take what he was offering than nothing at all.

Messiah hopped in his truck. "You coming?" he asked.

Nish jumped on the opportunity, without hesitation, climbing into his passenger seat.

Messiah rolled down his window to address his crew. "Yo, I'm up. Y'all good?" he asked.

"Yeah, we straight," one of his homeboys replied.

Messiah rolled away, with Nish riding shotgun, and guilt pressing hard on his conscience.

Chapter 8

"Nannie, this pie doesn't make up for the $500 worth of free labor this man is doing for me," Alani said, as she impatiently waited for her great aunt to wrap up the homemade sweet potato pie.

"It's not about making up for anything. It just shows appreciation," Nannie replied, as she placed the pie in Alani's hands.

Alani tried hard not to roll her eyes and pressed her lips together, stopping herself from getting too smart with the old woman who had raised her.

I don't have time for this. I need to be at work in an hour and a half, she thought.

"Relax. You can't work $20,000 worth of hours in a week," Nannie said. She had always been intuitive. Reading Alani's thoughts was nothing new. "I don't know why you're trying to work right now, anyway. Your heart is broken, baby. Your daughter, your brother...they aren't even in the ground yet."

"And they won't ever be, if I don't come up with some money... fast," Alani said. "I've got to go, Nannie," she said. "I need to catch the bus to pick up my car before they close, and then get to work so I can clock in on time. I'll see you tonight."

"Give him that pie! You always feed a fine man," Nannie yelled, as Alani headed for the door.

Alani turned around, frowning. "I never said anything about the way he looks. You're a trip, old lady," Alani said, smiling for the first time in days.

"Yeah, all that sugar you put in your voice about how he was so nice and so understanding told me he was fine," Nannie shot back.

Alani snatched up her purse. "And I got your old lady, little girl!"

***

Ethic pinched the bridge of his nose, in frustration. He wasn't used to his time being infringed upon. In the streets, he moved at his own pace, even when he was a young hustler, working blocks, he held some authority about himself. He was a one-man show, and he got money without anyone expecting anything from him - besides good product. Going legit meant that he had over 50 employees calling on him, depending on him, what seemed like every second of the day. It seemed like the boss was always needed, and he was slightly irritated that his day was being disrupted. He hit a U-turn in the middle of the street.

"Daddy, where are we going?" Bella asked.

"I have to make a quick stop," Ethic said.

He saw her face fall and he quickly eased her disappointment. "I promise, and you know I don't break my promises," he said, with a wink. She smiled and infected him, as his lips spread in happiness too. His children were the only people who got to see his vulnerability. They were of him, composed of the same blood, his legacy and the keys to his heart. He considered Morgan a part of that sentiment, which is why he expected so much of her. He pulled up to the shop.

"Aww, man, we have to come here? It's going to take all day," Eazy whined.

"Big man, stop whining. What I tell you about all that whining? It'll only take a few minutes. Climb out," Ethic said, as he opened the back door to his Range.

He could see that the woman was giving Redneck Larry a run for his money, before he even stepped inside. Her mouth was moving a mile a minute, and a thick vein of discontent had appeared down the middle of her forehead, showing her frustration.

When he opened the door, Redneck Larry said, "You've got to take it up with him." The white man turned to Ethic and blew out an exasperated breath. "The car isn't ready. There's a ton of more work that needs to be done, but we're closed, and I've got to get home to the wife."

"I've got it from here," Ethic said, as Larry gathered his belongings and rushed out the shop.

"I need my car," Alani started in, bringing the static directly to Ethic. He found it amusing that she was demanding a rush on a car that was being fixed for free. He knew better than to point it out, however. Ethic wanted no parts of this mad, black woman. The fire in her eyes told him that she would sear him alive, if he did anything other than see things her way.

He turned to look at the notes on the clip board.

"It would be wiser to invest in a new car. The fellas have fixed the alternator, your starter, and exhaust pipes, but there is a crack in your engine block and the transmission is slipping. It'll take about five days or so to get all that repaired," Ethic informed. "Even still, you're only putting a Band-Aid on it. This car won't last you another year."

"Well, I need every day of that year because I can't afford a new car. It was supposed to be done today. I was supposed to be at work 30 minutes ago. Is it drivable?" she asked.

"If you want to breakdown a couple miles down the road," Ethic informed.

She sighed the kind of sigh that only a black woman could muster. In the weighted breath, Ethic heard all her worries dissipate into the air. He hated that every black woman he knew carried too much on them. They were like magical beings that were expected to play 10, different roles every day, often switching them at the drop of a dime, without ever missing a beat. He often wondered how they did it. How they pulled it off... The single motherhood of it all, the nighttime student of it all, the homemaker of it all, the lover, the friend, the chef, the nurse, the maid of it all. He knew she was a part of that magical, melanin club, because all black women shared that same sigh. He hoped his girls never had to learn it. She ruffled her shoulder-length hair and he watched it fall back into place. Each, thick layer trained to fall at the nape of her neck, because he suspected she was also a part of the 'wear a head scarf to bed' club that black women had invented. She was a sister, through and through, and Ethic drank her in. She was falling apart; and although he could see the devastation quietly creeping into her stance, sagging her shoulders and causing her chin to quiver, he still marveled at her. She was a mess, her life was a mess - because of him - but she was like a walking piece of mystique, as he wondered how she was holding it all together.

"Where do you work?" Ethic asked.

"What?" she responded, thrown off by the intrusiveness of his question.

"You need a ride, right?"

He felt obligated to fix something in her life. The car he owed her, the ride he owed her. It was the least he could do.

"At a hospice center in Auburn Hills," she answered. "It's too far. I can't expect you to drive me 30 miles; and even if you do, I don't have a way home, so..."

"Let's go," he said. "I'll make sure you have a way home, don't worry about it."

She frowned, in confusion.

"Come on, guys, back in the car. We're going to drop my friend off here and then we'll get ice cream before we go to the movies. That cool?" Ethic asked.

"Yeah!" Eazy shouted, as he ran out the door. Ethic looked at Bella. "Yeah, I guess," she moaned, not thrilled with the idea.

"No, you got your kids with you. It's really not necessary," she said.

Ethic held open the door for her. "Get in the car," he said, nodding towards his truck.

"I don't even know your name," she said. "I come up in here, bitching and complaining, after you agree to fix my car for free, and you still gon' help me?"

"It's nothing. I'm Ethic," he introduced, offering her his hand. "This is Ezra, but we call him Eazy; and that little girl with the screw face is Bella."

"Alani," she answered, as she extended a dainty hand of her own. She handed him the pie box she had been holding.

"What's this?" Ethic asked, as he took it from her hands.

"A thank you gift for fixing the car," she said. "A pie. Do you like pie?"

"I'm afraid to say no. The way you come in her barking on my employees, I don't want to be on the receiving end of that mouth," Ethic said, smirking.

"I deserve that," she said, with a small laugh. "It's just been a rough week. I'm sorry for bringing drama to your place of business. I really do appreciate you working with me, regarding my car. Thank you, Ethic." Her tone of voice was so sincere, as if no one had ever done anything for her a day in her life. In fact, no one had. Alani had worked hard, getting a job at a local restaurant, working under the table at just 12 years old. Nothing had been given to her. Not even a pair of panties was handed to her. She had earned everything on her own. She didn't have much, but what little she had attained, had been bought off the sweat of her own back. This simple gesture wasn't so simple to Alani because Ethic was giving her what many people neglected to see value in...time. He took time out of his schedule to get her to work, when he owed her nothing at all. Or so she thought.

She climbed into the passenger seat and admired the butter-colored leather inside. *My ass even sinks into these seats differently,* she thought, as she made herself comfortable.

The sounds of Kendrick Lamar kicked through the speakers, not too loud as to draw attention, but loud enough to vibrate the seat she sat in. As Kendrick spit verses about being alright, Alani wished she could believe him. Her life was out of focus and she was stumbling through it with tear-blurred vision. She knew she had been demanding, ungrateful, and downright rude, regarding her car.

"And I know you said it's on the house, but I will pay you back every penny. I'm good for it," she said.

He didn't respond. He acknowledged her words with a nod. Or was he nodding his head to the beat? Was she killing the vibe? Was Kendrick's words forewarning her to shut the fuck up and ride? She glanced in the backseat, noticing that the kids had fallen asleep.

"Your kids are beautiful," she complimented. *Why the hell am I making small talk?* She thought.

His silence was so intimidating, so cold. He sat, leaning against the driver's window, as his graffiti-covered forearm extended to the steering wheel, his hand gripping the woodgrain. His brow was set in a grimace, as if he were in deep thought. One side of his face held scars and was hidden out of her sight, but she caught glimpses of it, as they passed by city lights and it reflected against the window pane. The other side of him was flawless; so smooth and dark that it looked like he was made of chocolate. He was a mystery to her.

"I'm sorry," he said. He paused to clear his throat. "About your daughter and your brother. You said you lost them," he reminded. He had to get that off his chest. His condolences came off as casual. He knew she would brush it off. How could he be sorry? He barely knew her. She would never know how sincere he was.

"Why? You didn't kill them," she said, her myriad of emotions returning. She was angry and sad and lost and resentful. She was too many things to count and she snapped off the words before she could stop herself. "I'm sorry. I didn't mean to…" she sighed. "I just wish people would stop telling me they're sorry. Sorry doesn't do anything. It won't bring them back. It's just something people say when they don't know what to say. I'd just rather they didn't say anything at all."

"Or maybe they really mean it and you're just in too much pain to receive it. Either way, I don't say anything just to say it," Ethic answered; and even though she didn't know him, she believed him.

Time passed, quickly, as the two let the music do the rest of the talking. When they pulled up to her job, Erykah Badu was crooning about the next lifetime and it felt appropriate, as if this was a man she had run into at the wrong time, under the wrong circumstance. Perhaps, if they had bumped into each other in the supermarket or the mall, hell, even a night club, he might have taken her number. The weighted way under which their paths had aligned didn't leave any room for anything but sympathy rides to work. She was hesitant to reach for the door handle. He had been nothing but kind to her, a true gentleman. She hadn't come across many of those, these days. In fact, she couldn't recall even one. Even her daughter's father had been one of the bad ones; and although a beautiful creation had come from it, the scars he left behind still affected her to this day. She cringed at the thought of her child's father and quickly dismissed it, not wanting all the negative things she felt about her past to infect her present.

"Daddy, I have to use the bathroom," Eazy's voice interrupted them.

"I'll stop in a little bit, big man. Can you hold it?" he asked.

"Noooo," Eazy replied, as he began to squirm.

"He can come inside. There is a bathroom right inside the lobby," she said. She popped open her door. "Thank you for the ride. You don't have to worry about getting me home or anything. I can call a cab or an Uber or something." Alani had no idea how she would get home. Her accounts were overdrawn, and she didn't have a pot to piss in or a window to throw it out of. Every dime she had was going into the burial of her family, but no way could she infringe further on this man's time. *He was nice enough, just bringing me all the way out here,* she thought. She climbed out of the car and Ethic exited with Eazy.

"I'll be right back, Bella. Lock the door and don't open it for anybody," he said.

"Dad, I'm not a baby," Bella protested, as she placed her earbuds into her ears.

Ethic didn't need the reminder. He saw her growing and changing every day, but to him, she would always need protecting.

Alani could see Ethic's disposition change and she smiled, slightly, as she closed her door. "Don't worry. All girls go through that phase. What is she? Twelve? Thirteen?" They crossed the parking lot and Ethic looked back at the car.

"She's 12. How did you know?" he asked.

105

"She's just at the age where you're no longer the center of her universe. All dads get hit with the pre-teen curse," she chuckled. "Don't worry. It'll pass. She's just looking for some independence."

Eazy ran ahead of them and opened the door for Alani.

"Ladies first," Eazy said, with a toothless smile, as he extended his hand for her to walk by.

"Ohh, so you're raising a little gentleman I see," she said, astonished. She couldn't help but chuckle. "Thank you. You are quite the charmer."

"He knows when to turn it on... that's all," Ethic said, with a smile that was charming all on its own. Alani drank him in. He was dark, brooding, and mysterious, as he stood before her. He was perfection on one side, handsome with the perfect jawbone and skin so black, so smooth that he looked like a work or art. Then, there was the opposite side, damaged and scarred, but filled with so much character that Alani, instantly, wondered what story accompanied the flaws. It was like God had molded him too perfectly and decided halfway through the process to even things out. There had to be balance in the world, and a man that looked as wonderful as Ethic's good side would be nothing but trouble without a little something to humble him.

He walked inside the building with his son and Alani.

"The bathroom is right down there to the left," she said, pointing.

"Go ahead, Eazy. Handle your business, big man. I'll be right here, waiting for you, and don't forget to wash your hands," Ethic stated. "He's charming until you find out he forgets to wash his hands."

She laughed aloud at that, as Eazy turned around and held up a balled fist, letting his father know he had overheard.

"I'm glad you find your tardiness funny!"

The stern voice that cut into their conversation was one that made her cringe - her boss...Mr. Taylor.

Alani turned, embarrassed that her boss was about to chew her out in front of Ethic. "I'm sorry. My car is broken down and I told you about the situation that is going on with my family. I got here as soon as I could."

"And you can walk right back out those doors," Mr. Taylor replied.

Alani's mouth fell open, as she shook her head in disbelief. "Mr. Taylor, my daughter just died. I can't even afford to bury her. I need this job," she said, lowering her voice so that Ethic didn't over hear.

"Well, you should have thought about that before you let your shift start uncovered. Mrs. Smith has been laying in a soiled diaper for over two hours. Her family came here to find her soaked through the damn bed sheets. You know the policy. If you're going to be late, you get somebody else to cover you. You didn't even call. This is the third time you've been late this month. I'm sorry, I've got to let you go. This is, exactly, why I don't like to hire girls like you."

"Mr. Taylor!" Alani shouted, in protest, as he began to walk away. She glanced back at Ethic and could tell he was, purposefully, trying to appear as if he hadn't overheard. She wanted to walk away, unbothered. She wished she was too proud to beg, but she needed her job. She was already in a financial bind. This would only make matters bleaker. "You can't do this to me. Please." Tears were stinging her eyes, as desperation filled her. "I'll do *anything*." Mr. Taylor stopped walking and turned around. Alani knew the old, white man would respond to that. He liked his girls fraught and vulnerable. He had taken advantage of plenty, young nurses, by threatening them with unemployment or worse. Alani still remembered how one of her co-workers had sold her food stamps at work only for Mr. Taylor to find out and threaten to report the girl for fraud. The young girl had thrown Mr. Taylor some pussy, just to buy his silence. Alani hadn't understood why, but she could more than relate now. She was willing to do anything just to keep her job.

Ethic was uncomfortable, witnessing the scene unfold, and knew it was best that he saved her some dignity by leaving. He didn't want to make the situation anymore humiliating for her. Truthfully, he should've already been out the door, but the word 'anything' made him take pause. Was this beautiful sister literal in her meaning, or was he reading too much into it? He felt a nagging in his gut that told him to intervene, but he wasn't trying to get too close to this woman. He had wronged her, and to be around her but not inform her of the role he played in her misery, felt like cruelty. He didn't want to disrespect her space. No mother should be subjected to the presence of their child's killer, and Ethic was just that. A child killer. No matter how handsome, how suave, how enlightened, or appealing he was...he had taken her daughter from this earth. Intent didn't matter when it came to that fact. His bullet had ended her life; and despite the many lives he had taken prior to that fateful night, he was certain it was that one deed that would be his undoing on his judgment day. He shouldn't be near Alani. Didn't even deserve to breathe the same air as her. Still, he couldn't help but think, *Fuck she mean by anything?* Eazy came running out of the bathroom and Ethic corralled him, easing out the front door, without as much as a goodbye. He led his son to his truck, all the while Alani's voice played in his head.

I'll do anything.
Anything...
Anything...

No woman, especially a black woman, should have to do *anything* to keep *anything;* but somehow, every woman had done just that at least once in their lifetime. That *anything* that made them feel cheap, that made them feel dirty, and worthless, always seemed to be just the thing that kept the lights from being turned off and kept the bellies of nappy-headed boys and girls full, while their mothers' bellies growled through the night. Children rarely knew of the sacrifices their mothers made, but the effects of them were forever burned in the minds of the women who had to make them. Black women made ways out of no way, by pulling that '*anything*' card. Even though it wasn't Ethic's place to intervene, he couldn't and wouldn't pull out of the parking lot as the white man inside held his privilege over Alani's head. As a black man, wasn't it his place to protect a queen who had forgotten how worthy she was of respect? This was the part of life that still puzzled him. How could he bask in his regality in this instance, but then take arms against his brother in another? It was in these moments that he knew that he was still victim to the conditioning of a society that made him feel justified to kill Lucas, but feel obligated to protect Alani. Was the life of a black man not as valuable as that of a black woman? Perhaps, Ethic should have spoken to Lucas, man to man, educated him, forgiven him…brother to brother… perhaps? Ethic didn't know how to change his perspective. All he knew was that he had ridden to protect "his", but this overwhelming desire to protect Alani meant she somehow was "his" as well. They belonged to the same tribe, the same, black-skinned, dark-hearted, Afro-American tribe. They were all the same. All, only a few generations removed, from the ships that brought their ancestors over here in chains. So yes, that black woman, who was inside doing "anything" for that white man, was "his." This meant, Lucas had been "his" as well. Same skin.

109

Same tribe. Yet, Ethic had done, exactly, what society had bred him to do - exterminate blacks. Hate blacks. So, did he hate himself? *Same tribe, same skin, same nigga...damn, niggers? And I say that shit like it's cool,* he thought. He had said the word so much, that he no longer valued a black man as a human being. Lucas had been just another nigga to him. It was a different spelling, and he had tried to fool himself into thinking that it meant something different, but the word, ultimately, had always been the same. That was the illusion. That was the point of it all. While niggas were busy killing niggas, white men - like the one inside - was busy taking advantage of the black queens, and Ethic had fallen for the banana in the tail pipe. Confusion plagued him. Angst tightened in his belly. He could not just do nothing. He had to do everything to stop Alani from doing "anything."

"Hop in, big man," Ethic instructed. He looked in the back seat at Bella. "Watch your brother. Lock the doors. I'll be right back."

He felt the burner inside his shoulder holster, beneath his jean jacket, and walked inside. The lobby was now deserted, but he followed the florescent lights further into the building.

He opened door after door, finding patients sleeping quietly behind each one and cursing himself for ever walking out, leaving Alani, in the first place.

Ethic was normally controlled and collected, but his own thoughts tortured him. He had put her in this position. She was in a desperate state, trying to bury her family, because he had taken them away. The guilt was heavy; and as he pushed open a door at the end of the hall, only to find it locked, he knew he had found the right one.

Ethic knocked on the door, forcefully, with a flat hand.

His temper was raging, and his nostrils flared slightly at the thought of what was happening on the other side of the door.

"I'll be out in a minute! Whatever it is, handle it!"

Ethic heard the old, white man's voice and it was all the motivation he needed to plow through the door. He rammed it with his shoulder, twice, causing the hinges to break as the door flew open. Her tear-filled eyes, as she knelt in front of the man. The sight of his belt buckled undone, as if Ethic had interrupted just in the knick-of-time.

Ethic drew on him and placed the gun, point blank, on the man's head.

"You ever put your hands on her again and I'll kill you," Ethic threatened. He didn't yell, but his eyes burned with so much conviction that he may as well had been shouting.

The man held up his hands. "I'm...I'm sorry. Just take her. Just go..."

Ethic wanted so badly to curl his finger on the trigger; but instead, he looked at Alani. "Let's go," he said.

Her reaction took him by surprise, as she pushed by him with anger. "Mind your God damned business," she snapped, through gritted teeth, not sparing him a ghetto girl neck roll as she rushed down the hall before disappearing into the bathroom. Ethic blew out a sharp breath, in frustration. He had never understood black women. When they should be appreciative, they showed anger. When they should be happy, they cried. When they should be sad, they were frustrated. Black women were anomalies to the black man. No matter what they did, it always seemed to be the wrong thing; and now, he had to go about figuring out what he had done wrong when all he had were good intentions in the first place. Putting together her puzzle would prove challenging. He swiped his face with a hand of frustration, as he was taken aback by her unexpected response.

Ethic went after her, storming into the women's restroom behind her. She was sobbing. As she stood over the sink, her head bowed in shame, she cried from her soul.

"Do you know what you just did? You took my job away. He's been coming at me for a year, trying to fuck, trying to pay me for it. I always said no, even though other girls here jump on the opportunity to make the extra money. I said no, until today; and you know why? Because I thought that my integrity meant something! I thought that if I stood for something I'd be able to teach my daughter to stand for something, but then she disappeared…right before my eyes. She's gone, almost like she never even existed, and I need to bury her. I'll do anything to make sure that happens! Even this! You just fucked things up even more for me!" She was screaming, and Ethic stood there, watching with sympathy.

A canyon-sized hole filled him, as he witnessed her undoing. She was drowning in an emotional flood that he had caused. Her turmoil, her pain, was the realest thing he had ever witnessed. It reminded him of his own, but he knew that her loss had to be greater. He had lost a woman, but she had lost a seed. Flesh of her own flesh, blood of her own blood. It was like walking around with half of you in a grave. She was the living dead, as well as every mother who had ever lost a child. It was devastating to watch and even more heartbreaking to be the root of it all.

She gripped the sides of the sink so tightly, as her shoulders quaked. She shook her head, while tears wrecked her. When she looked up in the mirror, meeting his eyes in the reflection, his heart stopped. She was beautiful. Her pain, exquisite. What she had been willing to sacrifice was somehow heroic and he was drawn to her. In the past, he had

112

been pulled toward women because of their weakness, because he felt protective, and felt obligated to save them. In this moment, he felt nothing but admiration for her strength. He wished his children had a mother whose love knew no limits; whose sacrifice had no boundaries. In her, he saw power; even though he could see her depletion on her face. He walked over to her, standing behind her and wrapped his arms around her body. His height, his sturdiness, behind her was what she needed. It was what every woman needed... a man to carry the weight when it got too heavy. Too many black queens were forced to play the role of king because of the absence of the men in their lives. Some man had put her in a position to parent alone, and now that she needed someone to hold her up, she was left on stuck. Ethic couldn't leave her. Shock shone in her eyes, as he stood behind her, holding her up, arms securely around her, as they both faced the mirror. "I'm sorry," he whispered, as he lowered his face in the groove of her neck, inhaling her scent of honey. The way his strong arms cocooned her transferred warmth to her body, defrosting the cold that had set into her bones ever since the moment she found out her daughter had died. This hug felt life-changing. Suddenly, it didn't feel like she had to stand up all on her own. He felt her legs give way, as her body melted into his. She closed her eyes and exhaled, as she wrapped her arms around his. Ethic's heart beat wildly in his chest, when she turned around to face him, throwing her arms around him. Ethic closed his eyes. Instinctively, he fisted her hair and tightened his grip, as her face rested in his chest. He wanted to absorb her, press her so close to him that two became one, so that her pain became his. He barely knew this woman, but this moment was so intimate that it felt like he had been her rock all his life. Her cries pulled at his guilt, drawing it out of him like a syringe, and his eyes burned with emotion. *Damn,* he thought, the culpability of his actions mounting as he witnessed her grief firsthand. He knew he didn't deserve to touch her, but he held her tighter anyway because he knew she needed this hug. "Let it out," he whispered. When was the last time she had been held like this? The energy she was transferring to him had been building up for a long time and he accepted it all. They didn't know each other, but her need for him was transparent as she wept. He fisted her hair tighter, and the arm that circled her waist drew her in nearer. Everything in him told him to walk away, but he couldn't. She had him at hello.

"I'm just so tired," she cried.

"I know," he replied. "Shh. I got you."

He had no idea how long it had been since she had heard those words. He held her for a good five minutes, and would have continued forever if the bathroom door hadn't opened, interrupting their moment.

She pulled away, as if a spell had been broken and cleared her throat, as she frantically wiped at her eyes as another woman walked in. "I'm so sorry." Her embarrassment was evident.

"Don't be," he said. "Come on. I'll take you home."

She nodded and followed, as he led her out of the bathroom.

They climbed into Ethic's truck and Bella was full of displeasure. "Daddy, you said it would be quick! We're going to miss our movie," she groaned.

"I'm sorry, baby girl," Ethic said. He passed her his cell phone. "Look up the next show time. After we drop Alani off, maybe we can catch the next one."

Bella was like a whiz kid when it came to electronics and she had checked the show time before Ethic even finished his sentence. "It's in 20 minutes. There is a movie theater right up the street. Can we please, please just go to that one? It's the last showing," she said. Ethic found it amusing that Bella was suddenly championing for the kid flick, when just moments before, she had called it a baby movie. She just wanted Alani out of the car. His daughter was jealous that way. She didn't like anyone to come and steal her father's eye.

When Eazy piped up and joined in the debate, Ethic knew he had no wins. "Daddy, come on!"

He looked over at Alani. "What do you say? You got time to catch a flick?" he asked, with an apologetic smile.

Alani peered over her shoulder at Bella and Eazy, as a small smile spread over her face. It was a glimmer of sunshine, cutting through the dark clouds of her life. "Sure, why not?" she replied.

"Finally!" Bella exclaimed, full of pre-teen impatience.

"Yay!" Eazy added.

Ethic laughed, as he winked at Alani, making her smile spread East to West across her face.

"Alright, Diary of a Wimpy Kid, here we come," Ethic announced. He was corny that way, when it came to his children. He tucked his gangster away, when in their presence, because they deserved more than that. They deserved the very best. Not many people got to witness him that way. For Alani, it felt like she was peeking in on a private moment; so, instead of staring at the marvel of a man in front of her, she looked out the window. Within minutes, they were pulling up to the theater and Bella hopped out of the car.

"Grab your brother's hand," Ethic instructed, as he watched them rush toward the door.

"I'm sorry about this," he offered, sincerely, as he opened Alani's car door.

"It's cool. I kind of love these movies. My daughter loves…" she paused and closed her eyes. Her heavy lids fluttered, as she opened them, fresh dew of emotion rested on her long, dark lashes. She was fragile. "My baby used to love them too," she finished in a whisper.

Ethic's hand had a mind of its own, as he brought it to her face to swipe a runaway tear from her cheek. He held out his elbow, a pure gentleman, and she held onto him as he said, "Come on, let's catch up, before they order everything at the concession stand. I'll be out of $200 messing around with these high-ass prices."

Alani shook her head and patted the big bag that hung off her shoulder. "Un-uh, never underestimate the power of a black woman and a big purse," she said, with a laugh. "I see your foreign truck and all that. I know you got it, but that don't mean you got to waste it. There's a CVS right next door. You give me $20 and I'll go grab all the snacks they want," she said.

Ethic laughed, looking down at her in intrigue, as she held her palm out and pursed her lips.

He peeled off a 20 and placed it in her palm. "You're a genius."

"I'm a mama," Alani responded. "I'll meet you guys inside."

Alani was in and out of the store in five minutes. When she walked back over to the theatre, Ethic was waiting outside. He held out his hand for her.

She hesitated, before she intertwined her fingers with his. Nothing had ever felt so comforting, as she walked with him, side by side, her bag of candy contraband tucked under her arm.

Ethic's touch was dangerous. It made her feel everything other than what she should be feeling. When he placed his hand on the small of her back to lead her in front of him, or grabbed her hand, gently, it made butterflies flutter in her stomach. Even when their fingers graced each other's inside the giant popcorn tub, she sucked in air to stop her heart from leaping. She felt guilty for feeling anything other than depression, at this time in her life, but she couldn't help but notice her attraction to him. He was strong, yet caring, and the vulnerability he showed with his children made her jealous that her child hadn't had anything close to that in her lifetime. She felt lucky to even be involved in this family outing because she had a feeling that Ethic didn't include outsiders very often. *Where is their mother?* She thought. *A woman would be half crazy to catch this man and throw him back into the pond.*

She found herself watching Ethic, more than the film; when the credits played, Alani felt disappointed. As the lights, slowly, illuminated the theater, they shined a bright light on her reality. This wasn't a date and her life was in shambles. As soon as he dropped her off, she would have to face her daunting reality. She was saddened, as she arose from her seat and followed the excited bunch out the movie theater.

She was quiet on the way home, and with his children asleep in the back seat, her silence was noticeable. The only time she spoke was when she rattled off directions, but still, she didn't even look at him. She peered out the window, watching the trees pass by in a blur, as Ethic's foreign car ate up the miles on the highway. When they pulled onto her block, she was almost embarrassed to show him where she lived. He was driving a $150,000-truck, while she was living in a $5,000-house that she had purchased with her income tax return from the Land Bank. It was far from glamorous. In fact, it was downright dilapidated, but it was home. It kept the snow and the rain out, which she had always been grateful for. This was the first time she had felt ashamed of it. Over the course of a few hours, his thoughts suddenly mattered to her. He placed the car in park and let the truck idle, as he looked over at her.

"Thank you, for today," she whispered. "For stopping me."

"I'm the last person who deserves thanks," Ethic said, as flashes of her daughter, dying in his arms, plagued his mind. "I'm not judging. We can forget about what happened today. I'm just a guy dropping a girl off after taking her to a movie. That's what I remember from the night. How about you?"

Alani gave a weak smile. "Sounds about right."

"I'll make sure your car is fixed by tomorrow, at the end of the day," Ethic assured.

She climbed out of the car, and when she was halfway to her door she heard, "Alani!"

She turned to him. "I like pie," he said, giving her a wink. She smiled wide at that, before waving goodbye and rushing inside the house, upset that they hadn't met under different circumstances. Knowing that a man was the last of her worries, she shook him from her thoughts. The smell of soul food wafted through the house, as she made her way into the kitchen. Nannie had left a plate wrapped in aluminum foil, sitting for her atop of the stove. It was small comfort in the face of everything she was facing. It reminded her that there was still someone on this earth who loved her and someone for her to love. Without that, Alani would have, surely, curled up and died. She took the food up to her room, making sure to move quietly, so that she didn't awaken Nannie. When she was behind the closed door in her bedroom, she opened the plate, sat down on her bed and cried her heart away, as she enjoyed a meal - alone.

Chapter 9

Nighttime was torture for Alani. It used to be the hours of the day that she looked forward to the most. She could come home after a long day of work and retreat to her dreams. Since the murders, she hadn't slept; each time she closed her eyes, all she saw was blood. So, instead, she wrote in her journal for hours, trying to release some of the angst that gripped her heart. There was a tenderness inside her chest, now. She had felt it at work the night her daughter and brother had been murdered. It hit her out of nowhere and had been ever present since. Beneath the excruciating loss was a dull ache that she was sure would remain with her for the rest of her life. It made her feel like every room she walked into was too small. It sucked the air from her lungs and the strength from her legs. While losing her brother hurt, losing her daughter was devastating. Her brother was a loss, her daughter was a piece of her flesh cut away from the bone... without anesthesia. It was her oxygen reduced for the rest of her life. So, instead of breathing, she was sipping air through a straw, existing minimally with what was left after grief chewed her up and spit her out. Alani had never felt so alone. The darkness of night was personified into a monster that she couldn't slay. She was terrified of the nightmares that awaited her when she slept; therefore, coffee and her journal made for great company. The hours ticked by, slowly, each minute seeming to last longer than the one before it. There was so much on her shoulders that she felt like she would collapse, and she knew that there was only more stress to come. She still had to deliver the news to her daughter's father and she dreaded it. They weren't on speaking terms. In fact, she hadn't spoken to him in six months, after she found out he had another girl visiting him in prison. Yes, she was that girl…the one who had fallen in love with Cream Richardson, a bad boy with a long reputation and even longer dick. The first time she took it for a ride, he had her hooked. That was a decade ago and she had stuck with him for years. She had poured her all into him, dropping out of college to cook up the ounces of cocaine he moved weekly, and lay under him all day. She cooked his meals, washed his clothes, sucked him dry, day in and day out. It was the type of relationship that kept young girls satisfied; but at the time, she was fresh, and he had her nose wide open. The thug in him was just enough to keep her excited and satisfied. He was five years her senior and old enough to make her young mind swoon. She became, exactly, what he wanted her to be, stifling her dreams of college to make sure they stayed close. He disguised her captivity under the notion of loyalty and she was a willing participant, but it ended the way all hood loves end. He betrayed her. When Alani found out she was pregnant, the idea of a baby complicated things. Motherhood transformed her into the nagging baby mama who demanded things, who needed things, who accepted less of his bullshit. With a newborn baby on her hip, Alani became less fun, less impulsive, less reckless. She couldn't be young and carefree because becoming a mother was like taking an aging pill and she immediately grew up. She wanted stability and a real family for their daughter. When she began to put expectations of maturation on Cream, the cheating began. She ignored it for years, but when he got locked up for carrying a concealed weapon, it became harder for him to balance his plethora of women. *Stupid-ass had me driving hours every other week to make sure I saw his face, only to find out I was one of many chicks in his rotation,* she thought. She was angry at him; not only for his disloyalty, but for his absence in its totality. How she had ended up simply wasn't how things were supposed to be. She couldn't help but think if he had never gotten arrested, their daughter may still be alive. Maybe he could have stopped Lucas from getting so heavily involved in the streets, or he could have protected their home from the masked man who entered it and changed her life forever. She knew it was unfair to blame Cream for things that were out of his control, but somehow, she had been left to handle it all. They hadn't spoken in over six months. After a random girl popped up to her home, carrying a baby she claimed Cream had fathered, Alani was done. She had stopped forcing her raggedy car up the highway to visit him, she had stopped answering his calls, she had stopped writing him letters. After years of holding onto him, of fighting off chicks around the way, of being known as his girl in their neighborhood - which wasn't a good thing anyway because the same way she was known as his girl, he was known to be a cheat. After all that, she simply let go. When he called, she gave the phone directly to Kenzie. He would be calling tomorrow and she would have no choice but to speak to him, because he would never hear Kenzie's voice again. The anxiety built in her chest, as she realized she would have to be the one to tell him. No matter how much disdain she had in her heart for him, she never wanted to put this type of pain on him. She had loved him, once upon a time; and despite his doggish ways, she was sure he loved her. She was going to break his heart when he realized that his flesh and blood was no more. When he realized that the connection they shared had been stripped and now they were just two people who knew one another - once upon a time. This news would break him. She knew this to be true because it had decimated her. It had torn down every fiber of the woman she had built over the years. Scraped away faith she had adopted on her journey to this day. The death of her daughter had changed her relationship with God, and she was sure it would bring out the devil in Cream.

She knew the sun was close to rising, when she heard her Nannie's footsteps going down the stairs. She cooked breakfast every morning. Grits, eggs, turkey ham, and toast. She had been doing it for as long as Alani could remember. The familiarity of it somehow comforted her. The smell of that breakfast was a symbol of the most consistent love she had ever had. Where her own mother had failed, Nannie had picked up the slack, mothering her, taking her in, teaching her how to survive. She had grown tired of eating the same thing every day over the years; but on a day like today, when everything else around her was changing, the same old, same old was just what she needed. She climbed down the stairs, her red eyes telling the secret of the midnight tears she had cried.

"Good morning." Her greeting was weak, lacking life, of purpose, and Nannie turned from the stove to stare at her niece.

"It might not feel so good, but the Lord is walking with you, baby. You can't feel anything right now, I know, but trust me when I tell you that the only thing pulling you out the bed right now is Jesus. He's carrying you. He'll carry you through it all."

Alani closed her eyes and took a deep breath. Preaching wouldn't remove the invisible knife lodged in her chest. God had let this happen. How could she turn to spirituality for comfort?

"I have to tell Cream today," she whispered, as Nannie set a plate of hot food in front of her.

"He can't hear it from anyone but you. Same way your soul lived inside Kenzie, his did as well. It's the one thing that boy did right in the world," Nannie said. "Maybe his family will help with the expenses."

"What family? None of them made any effort to help with Kenzie when Cream got locked up three years ago. They barely came around when he was out. I can almost guarantee that the help I need won't come from anyone on his side," Alani said. "It's on me."

"We can reach out to the pastor down at the church. We will come up with the money, baby. I promise," Nannie said. She stood, her old, rickety legs shaking under the weight of her roundness, as she hobbled over to the hall closet. She pulled out a white dress. "I made it for Kenzie to wear at her service."

Alani's eyes failed her, as tears flooded them. "It's beautiful. Thank you."

A horn blew outside, and Nannie said, "That's Mr. Larry. I'm going on down to the church for choir rehearsal. When I see Pastor, I'll talk to him about the church helping cover the funeral costs. God gon' make a way."

Alani offered a nod, as she wiped her tears with the back of her hands. She didn't move from that spot. She sat there until the coffee in her cup ran cold, just staring at the phone and wringing her fingers. At 8:05 a.m., he called... just like she knew he would... just like he had done every week for the past two years. It was the time that she would, normally, be getting Kenzie dressed for school. She let it ring twice, needing more time to figure out what she would say, before she answered.

"This is a call from the Michigan Department of Corrections..."

Alani's mind spun, as the automated voice spoke in her ear. *How do I tell him this?* She thought. *He's going to blame me. This is my fault. I should have been home with her.* Bile built up in the back of her throat.

"Hey, baby girl, Daddy misses you so much!" Alani's tears fell because she knew it was the last time he would ever say those words.

"It's me, Cream," she managed, the frog in her throat causing her words to come out deep and full of emotion.

"Hey, La," he said, his voice full of surprise, almost hopeful, and she hated herself for filling him with optimism. "It's good to hear your voice. Daddy miss you too. You know that, right? You know I'm sorry for how..."

"Something happened," she interrupted. "Kenzie's..."

"Kenzie what?" Cream asked, his voice now anxious and concerned.

"She's gone. She was shot!" The words ran out of her mouth in a crescendo of panic.

"Don't say that to me, La. This ain't funny. Don't say shit like that!" There was anger in his voice, but underneath it, she heard fear. He knew her well enough to know she wouldn't play about something like that.

"Someone ran in the house looking for Lucas," she shouted between her cries. She gripped the phone so tightly that her fingertips were numb. "She was here with him! They shot her!" she wailed. She slid her back against the wall until her butt met the floor. Pulling her knees to her body, she buried her head into them. "My baby's gone!"

Alani had never heard Cream cry in all the years she had known him, but the sound he made on the other end of the phone was nothing short of sobbing.

"Where were you?" Cream asked.

"Where was I?" she asked, her chest igniting with rage. "Where were you?" She shouted. "I was at work, trying to make sure she had food in her stomach and warm clothes on

124

her back! I couldn't be everywhere at once! I just needed a little help," Alani cried. She was melting down, her shoulders shaking, as she cried into the phone. "Lucas was supposed to watch her. This is all my fault. I should have been there!" Her admission of guilt was so heavy that Cream backed down.

"It's not your fault, La," he said, as he sniffed and cleared his throat. She could hear him trying to keep his composure. "I swear to God, I'm going to murder the niggas responsible for this shit. It's over for niggas." He was riding waves of emotion, going from rage to sadness in seconds, as he tried to process this. He had called to say, 'I love you', not to hear this. Now, he wished he could rewind time to moments before when he hadn't known...when his world hadn't been rocked by this news that his brain couldn't process. It made no sense. In what land did little girls die behind some street beef? In the land of Flint, Michigan. It happened every day, but Cream had never thought it would happen to him. "Niggas are about to bury their moms, their kids, their fucking baby moms. Whoever had anything to do with this is going to feel me."

"You have one minute left." The automated operator had placed them on a countdown.

"When is the funeral?" Cream asked.

"I...I don't know. I can't afford... I don't have insurance. She's laying on a cold slab waiting for me, Cream, and I don't have the money to bury her," Alani whispered.

"I'll see what I can do, La."

Alani sighed because she knew he wouldn't come through. He had been seeing what he could do for two and a half years; and so far, he hadn't done shit. She knew now was the one time she couldn't chastise him because she couldn't do a damn thing either. Somewhere along the way, the two of them had failed as parents.

125

"I'm so sorry. I love you. I do. Come see about me, La. I need to see you after some shit like this…"

CLICK

Their time was up and Alani closed her eyes, feeling even more hopeless than before.

Chapter 10

Ethic walked into the funeral home and he could smell the scent of death in the air. It had a distinct odor; one that reminded him that his time on this earth was borrowed. One day, he would have to pay it back. He only prayed it was no time soon. A woman greeted him, her eyes friendly as she said, "Good morning. How can I help you?"

Ethic removed a sealed envelope and placed it on the countertop in front of her. "Alani Hill is a client of yours. Her daughter and her brother are awaiting burial here," he began.

"Yes, sir, but what's this?" the woman asked.

"It's $30,000. It should cover the expenses for both funerals," he replied. "I'd like to donate it, anonymously."

"Oh, my Lord!" The woman exclaimed, as she placed a hand over her mouth in surprise. Tears came to the woman's eyes. "You have no idea what a blessing you will be to this young woman. She's been in here, crying her eyes out, thinking that she would not be able to pull this off. You're an angel, young man."

"I wish that were so," Ethic answered. "Just make sure she gets this."

"God bless you," the woman said, emotional. He turned his back and walked out of the establishment, knowing that her words couldn't be farther from the truth. He was nobody's blessing. He was Alani's curse and this money didn't erase that.

***

Morgan flipped through the pictures on her phone, frantically, as her heart filled with jealousy.

This bitch is with Messiah now? She thought, as she scoured through Nish's social media page to see the evidence of disloyalty right before her eyes. Morgan's chest burned with a scorn so great it made tears come to her eyes. Nish was her girl, her ace, the only person who had befriended her, despite her disability. Since they had been in elementary school, Nish had been by her side. *She knew I was feeling him,* Morgan thought, bitterly. It was just another loss that the poor, little, deaf girl had to take. A man like Messiah could never truly want her. He would never choose her over a regular girl like Nish, no matter how beautiful she was. Morgan felt like an abnormality and her chest swelled with angst, as she realized she would never be a man's choice. Being deaf made people pity her. She walked around in a constant state of misunderstanding, desperately wishing that she could connect to someone, anyone...

She had found that connection with Messiah. He had felt her, despite the silence that existed between them. He had found the rhythm of her heartbeat and she thought it meant something. *Nobody will ever want me like this,* she thought. She didn't know whom she was angrier with - Nish or Messiah. Seeing them together burned like betrayal. Nish was her best friend. They hadn't spoken since she had been raped at the motel. Morgan had kept her distance, feeling like Nish had left her there, vulnerable and afraid. Now, this. Morgan had wanted to give her friend the benefit of the doubt, but she was lacking benefit and full on doubt. Morgan wanted to blame Nish's actions that night on the drugs and alcohol. Perhaps, Nish had been just as afraid and had been too intimidated to stop Lucas and his friend. That's what Morgan had tried to tell herself; but in the back of her mind, she knew. Nish was a jealous bitch. Seeing her in pictures with Messiah confirmed it. Nish was shady, and Morgan was finally seeing the light. No, Messiah wasn't Morgan's man, but based on principle alone, Nish should have steered clear of him. Morgan reached for the medical paperwork on her nightstand, as she scoured over the details. They had been sitting there, collecting dust, because Morgan was afraid. Afraid to be like everyone else, afraid it would hurt, afraid to get her hopes up only to have the procedure fail. Morgan had been deaf all her life. She didn't know how the world would be once she could hear, but after losing Messiah, she no longer wanted to be who she was. Experimental or not, Morgan was ready to take the risk. She wanted to tell herself that her decision had nothing to do with Messiah. He was just a guy, and she was smarter than to make such a drastic choice based on the likes of someone else. Right? Wrong. Morgan was doing, exactly, that. She just wanted to be someone Messiah could love, someone less complicated, less unique, less handicapped. Morgan craved regularity, despite that she was anything but.

Morgan pressed the heart underneath Nish's photograph, letting it be known that she had seen it. Like clockwork, Nish's name appeared on her screen. *You couldn't be bothered to reach out after you left me at the hotel, but you're texting now,* Morgan thought. A guilty conscience would reveal itself in time.

BESTIE:
Hey, boo! I have so much to catch you up on. My bad about being M.I.A Shit's been crazy.

Morgan rolled her eyes, as her fingers went to work at a rapid response.

MORGAN:
Yeah? I see you've been busy. You and Messiah?
side eye

There was a long pause, as Morgan waited for Nish's response. The text bubbles on her iPhone screen kept appearing and disappearing, as Morgan smirked.

Dirty bitch, Morgan thought, knowing that Nish was fishing for an explanation.

BESTIE:
I know!!! I've been meaning to tell you! It's crazy. We always said we were going to snag us some legit niggas. His homeboy been asking about you too. I hope you not feeling a type of way about us. I know you used to have a little crush on him, but that's little girl shit. We're grown women now. You're my girl. I don't want no little shit coming between us.

Morgan was livid. She knew Nish was trying to downplay her treachery by belittling Morgan's affection for Messiah. *Or am I overreacting? He wasn't my man. I never even told her about spending time with him at the Falls, and I haven't seen her since the motel. She knew I liked him; but who doesn't like him? Every girl in the city had him in their radar,* she thought. Morgan was jealous and angry, but she wasn't, entirely, sure she had the right to be. So, instead of starting conflict, she conceded.

Morgan:
I'm good. Messiah ain't my issue with you. What happened to you that night? Those niggas did me dirty and you just disappeared.

BESTIE:

I'm so sorry, girl. I honestly didn't think it was that big of a deal. I was high as hell and just out of it. I wasn't thinking straight. Let's link up. Have lunch... I miss you and I want to make it up to you for leaving you by yourself that night. Meet me at the hibachi spot in half an hour.

Morgan sighed. She wanted to see Nish, face to face, to look her in the eyes to see if she could sense bullshit or sincerity. Morgan snatched up her handbag and car keys, before rushing down the stairs and out the door. A part of her wanted to declare war on her best friend, but she knew she couldn't. If Messiah had chosen Nish, who was Morgan to hate?

Sitting in the five-star hibachi spot, Morgan's leg bounced, impatiently. It had taken her a half hour to get to the restaurant, so Nish should have beaten her there. The tardiness added insult to injury. Nish was over an hour late and Morgan was beyond perturbed. Just as she reached for her handbag and arose from her seat, Nish came strolling into the restaurant with Messiah behind her. His head was down, as his fingers moved, swiftly, across his phone screen. Morgan's heart sank like the Titanic. He was here with Nish, in all his Versace-wearing, freshly-twisted-locs-having glory, and Morgan was mortified. When he lifted his eyes, she saw surprise flash in them, briefly. Her presence was unexpected, she could tell. He quickly erased the emotion from his face and took a seat. Morgan only sat because her legs were no longer strong enough to hold her up.

"So sorry we're late," Nish signed. Nish was beaming. Messiah had bossed her all the way up. Her normal H&M threads were replaced with labels of her own. Her hair and makeup were professionally done, causing Morgan to wish she had taken the time to perfect herself before leaving the house. Nish had come to stunt on her and Morgan was burning with jealousy. She had no emotion about the things Messiah bought Nish. It was the time he gave her that made Morgan sick.

Morgan's stomach was in turmoil, as she gave Nish a halfhearted smile. Her eyes stung with tears, as she avoided looking at Messiah altogether.

"I'm sorry too," Morgan signed. "I actually have to go. I thought this was going to be a quick lunch. I promised Ethic I'd pick Eazy and Bella up from school." She had no shame in lying, because if she sat there too long, the levee that contained her tears would break. The last thing she needed was to embarrass herself, yet again, in front of Messiah. She wouldn't give either of them the satisfaction of seeing her cry. "I'll text you later." She got up and snatched her purse out of the seat next to her, before storming out the restaurant.

It took everything in Messiah not to go after Morgan. This was his purpose of having Nish around in the first place. Making Morgan hate him would stop them from crossing a dangerous line with one another. He hadn't intended on throwing it in Morgan's face. He wasn't even feeling Nish to put claims on her. He upgraded her because he couldn't have a chick of her stature even speaking his name. He let her take her social media flicks and imply that they were together because he intended to turn Morgan off. Meanwhile, his page was dry of any female. Most of the time, they never saw the outside of his trap house; but today, she had claimed to be starving and convinced him to take her to lunch.

"Yo, get your ass up," Messiah said, as he stood.

"We aren't eating?" Nish asked.

"Nah, fuck that. You on some goofy shit right now," Messiah chastised, as he walked out. Seeing how his presence had affected Morgan had put him in a sour mood. He wasn't trying to embarrass her, only deter her interest so that he could respect Ethic's wishes.

***

Morgan sat outside Bella and Eazy's elementary school, watching as the kids ran across the front lawn, their voices carrying through the air, as they stretched their legs after sitting in a classroom all day. Her solemn mood was, instantly, lifted when she saw Bella, walking with her hand clasping Eazy's, as they approached the car. It reminded her of her sister, Raven. She once had a big sister to hold her hand too…a long time ago.

"Mo' Money!" Eazy shouted, when he saw her, letting Bella go, only to rush into Morgan's arms.

"Hey, Mo! I thought Lily was picking us up?" Bella signed.

"I gave her a break today," Morgan signed back.

Morgan and Bella had always been close, since the very first day they had met. Their sisterhood was phenomenal. They each craved a feminine alliance in their lives. Motherless girls, they needed someone they could trust, and they found that in one another. Morgan was sure that nobody loved her more than Bella. Bella and Eazy were the only people in the world who didn't look at her through sympathy-filled eyes.

"Can we rock out at the mall?" Bella asked. Her sign language was effortless, at this point. Eazy's too. They lived in a bilingual household; and while other people saw it as a handicap, Eazy and Bella always saw it as a superpower. It was like they spoke in a code that very few could understand.

"Not today, B. I want to ask you guys something," Morgan signed.

"What's wrong?" Bella asked.

133

Morgan eased her worries. "Nothing is wrong. I just need your opinion. What do you think about me getting a surgery to restore my hearing? Do you think it'll make me normal?"

"But you are already normal," Eazy cut in. Morgan smiled because she knew he meant it.

"Thanks, Eazy," Morgan signed. "You're the best, you know that?"

He smiled and quickly removed his iPad from his backpack. It was just that easy of a decision to him. She was Mo' Money, his aunt, but more like a sister. He loved her without alteration. She wished she could see herself through his eyes. He zoned out, as Morgan turned to Bella.

"He's right, you know?" Bella signed. "You're already normal, Mo. You don't have to fix yourself because nothing's broken. You're the coolest chick I know. I wish my dad looked at me the way he looks at you. You can do no wrong."

Morgan gave a weak smile. Validation from them wasn't enough to make her feel secure. They were only kids; and although Bella was starting to grow up, she was biased. They were her family and couldn't see the flaws that the world would magnify.

"I thought you liked the fact that you could block out the world?" Bella signed.

"Now, I just want to be a part of it," Morgan signed back. She started the car and put her hand on the gearshift. She felt Bella's hand on top of hers and she looked up at her.

"I love you. We all do," Bella said.

"I know," Morgan signed back. She placed her hand over her heart and gave Bella a wink, before pulling off. She had an important decision to make. She wanted to believe that she was motivated by the right reasons, but only one reason came to mind...Messiah. This was about a boy. This was about her best friend getting the guy - not because she was cuter or smarter or better, but because she could hear. For once in her life, she wanted someone to not only be fascinated by her, but to choose her. She headed straight to Ethic's shop. She knew she would find him there, under the hood of a car, putting in work for no reason because he didn't need the money at all. He had gone into the shop every day since her rape, and she felt like he couldn't even look her in the eyes anymore. When they arrived, she hopped out the car, taking the brochures for the procedure out her hobo bag, rushing into the shop with Eazy and Bella in tow.

"Daddy!" Eazy yelled, in excitement, as soon as he saw Ethic leaning over the engine of the old-school Buick.

Ethic's brow was bent in focus and, instantly, relaxed when he looked up and saw his baby boy. Every time he saw Eazy's face, he thought of Raven, and his heart healed, momentarily, only to break all over again at the fact that she was gone. Eazy had been the thing that kept him breathing after her death, but he was also the thing that haunted him the most. Raven Atkins lived through their son. That much, he was sure of. Eazy barreled into him, hugging him so hard that Ethic stumbled backward from the impact.

"What you doing here, big man? How was school?" Ethic asked.

"Good!" Eazy shouted, as he ran by his father and into the lobby where the arcade game was sitting vacant. Ethic chuckled and shook his head, as he saw Morgan and Bella approaching. They were too cool to run to him. Like the princesses they were, they made him wait, strolling slowly until they stood before him. Ethic kissed their foreheads.

"To what do I owe this visit?" Ethic signed. "How much is it gon' cost me?"

Morgan turned to Bella. "Can you go keep an eye on Eazy while I talk to Ethic?"

Bella nodded and did as she was told. Ethic frowned. This was serious. He could tell by the weary look on Morgan's face.

"I want the surgery," Morgan signed.

Ethic grabbed a towel and wiped the oil from his hands, as he gave her his full attention.

"You're sure? You've thought about this?" he asked.

"I have and I'm positive," she answered. She looked at her hands. "I'm tired of these being my voice. I just want to speak my mind like everybody else," Morgan signed. Ethic nodded and released a heavy sigh.

"I'll call and make the appointment tomorrow morning," he signed. He noticed the tears that gathered in her eyes and pulled her in for an embrace. Kissing the top of her head, he sighed. Morgan had insecurities that he didn't know how to eradicate. He had given her the love a father would for his daughter, and still, it didn't seem to be enough. He only hoped that this would be the thing to top off her confidence and get her to realize that she was enough. She was the last of a legendary tribe and that made her special. Hearing or deaf, she was a marvelous soul; but if this is what she wanted, he would give it to her, because he could never deny her of anything.

Chapter 11

Alani wasn't one to beg, but as she sat in the front row of the church, she knew she had no choice but to accept the donations from the congregation. She was appreciative for their generosity. They barely knew her. They saw her face on Easter and New Year's Eve. The rest of the year, she was missing in action. She doubted if anyone in the pews even remembered her name. That's how inactive she was. She watched the members rise from their seats to donate to the basket sitting next to her daughter and brother's pictures. It made her feel so loved. She had never understood the purpose of church. She believed her relationship with God was personal. That she could be spiritual without subscribing to the expectations that man put on religion, but seeing the support she was receiving made her understand the purpose of the church. *They're treating me like family. Some of them can't keep a roof over their own heads and their giving to me so freely,* she thought, wiping the tears from her face. She was so overwhelmed that all she could do was grip Nannie's hand.

"Church family, give from your heart. This young mother must bury her brother, bury her dear daughter. Let's wrap our arms around her, Mt. Pisgah. Let's lift her up. Let's renew her spirit and let her know that in this darkest time the devil will not win. Give from your hearts, church."

Alani's chest heaved, she was crying so hard. She was so sick of crying, so damn exhausted from wailing every day, all day. *Why can't I just stop?* She thought. The wails just kept coming from the pits of her, from the bottoms of her that she didn't know could carry hurt. That shit was spilling out of her.

137

Nobody but a mother who had lost a child could relate. She had ripped herself open to give birth to that baby girl, and she had been robbed of a lifetime of unconditional love. She was not only shattered, she was mad as fucking hell. She wanted justice. *What type of monster could kill a kid?* She thought.

"We have a representative from the funeral home who would like to say a few words," the pastor announced. Alani looked up to see Mr. Masters walking down the aisle. He took the mic and looked at her.

"Ms. Hill, we at Masters Funeral Home would like to extend our deepest condolences. We are so very sorry for your loss. A generous benefactor, anonymously, donated $30,000 to go toward the burials of your loved ones. We would like to present this check to you and your family."

Alani bent over, her head falling between her knees, as Nannie rubbed her back, gently. She had never understood the mystery of God. For days, she had stressed about how she would lay her family to rest, and out of nowhere things had worked out. She stood to her feet and hugged the pastor. He handed her the microphone. She was too emotional to speak. She stood up there, lip quivering, snot leaking, mascara running, as she lowered her head and just let herself cry.

"T…tha…thank you so much," was all she could manage, before the mothers of the church came and wrapped their arms around her. It was only their support that kept her standing; not because she was naturally weak, but because life had gotten so hard that it had depleted her energy.

Nannie escorted her to the pastor's office, where Mr. Masters presented her with the check. "Who would be this generous? I have to thank them," she said, as she covered her mouth with one hand and held onto the check with the other. "Thank all of you."

"I can't give away the identity of the man who donated this, out of respect for his privacy. We can help you finish arrangements whenever you're ready," Mr. Masters said.

Alani stood to leave and hugged Nannie. "I'm ready now. My baby has been waiting for me too long. Let's do it right now," she said.

"You can meet me over at the funeral home," Mr. Masters said.

Alani nodded, as she turned to Nannie. "I'll see you at home. I love you, old lady."

"I got your old lady," Nannie responded, with a smile, as Alani made her exit.

Alani checked her watch, knowing the next bus was coming soon. She still had to pick up her car. She would need it to run the errands needed to plan two funerals. Normally, shame would fill her, as she stepped onto the city bus. Flint wasn't the public transportation type of city. You had to be down on your knuckles to even consider utilizing the bus; but today, she didn't care. She looked how she felt and there was no point in fronting for anyone like she was okay. In fact, Alani wasn't sure if she would ever be okay again, and she just didn't have the energy to put up a visage. She dug the change out the bottom of her purse and paid for her ticket, and then took the first seat she saw. Her head rested against the window, as she watched the dilapidated city pass her by. She was tired of Flint. Every day it was a different story of tragedy. Niggas killing, robbing, raping, scamming. When she was coming up, Flint wasn't so bad. It was a hype, little city where everybody knew everybody. The most you would see was a good, old-fashioned fight after the city school basketball games. It was ruthless, now. So many things had changed. So many jobs had left. Too many babies deserted and too many crack pipes smoked. It was a lawless place and niggas didn't live by any type of code anymore. Women and children were being killed off every day. Young, black boys gunned down over the most trivial things every, single day. Her daughter had been a victim of circumstance, and Alani would carry that guilt for the rest of her life. *I should have gotten up out of here a long time ago,* she thought. She had been so busy chasing behind Cream that she had given up on her own dreams. Her potential to contribute something worthy to society had been immeasurable. She had been smart. She could have gone to college and made something of herself. It had been expected, but loving the wrong man had distracted her and she had become stuck. Her choices had led her here. Her thoughts plagued her all the way to her stop, and she shook them off as she hopped off. The bank was right up the block from Ethic's shop and she headed there first. After cashing the check, she hurried to try to catch him before it was closing time. She was eager to pay her debt to him, and even more zealous to see him. She could only imagine what he must think of her. She had damn near prostituted herself to a man right in front of him. She, practically, ran down half the block, as she rushed to get there. She was winded when she stepped inside the shop. The closed sign was in the window and it was empty, but Ethic's Range Rover sat in the parking lot, so she knew he was there.

"Hello?" she called out. She peeked into the back office and then out into the bays in the attached garage. "Hello?" she repeated. She stepped into the garage, her heels clicking against the concrete floor, as she tip-toed down each bay, maneuvering around cars until she spotted hers. She walked over to it and found a set of legs hanging beneath it. It was Ethic. Even though his upper body was hidden beneath her car, she could feel his presence. There was something about him that felt powerful, kingly, as if he was meant to dominate. She bent down to tap his wheat-colored Timberland boot. He lifted his head, slightly, to peek at her and she flattened her lips in a straight line as she waved. Ethic rolled from beneath the car and sat up, before pulling a pair of wireless *Beats* from his ears.

"Hi," was all she could think to say. "I've come to settle my debts." She stood to her feet and pulled out a wad of money.

"I told you, it was on the house," he responded. His tone was different, less approachable than it had been the first time she had been in his presence. He dusted himself off, wiping his hands on a towel, as he stood to his feet. He brushed by her, headed back toward the lobby. "Let me grab your keys and you can be on your way."

She frowned. He was cold. Something had happened. Something had shifted.

"Oh, okay," she said. What else could she say? She couldn't tell him that the only time in the past week that she had smiled had been in his presence. She couldn't tell him that the hug he had given her had made her feel the safest she had in years. This man in front of her was all business. He wasn't the caring guy she had gone to the movies with. *Maybe he thinks I'm a ho. He had time to think about what happened at my job.* He handed her the keys.

"Thanks. Have a good night," she said.

"You too," he replied. It was all so formal. So, sterile. Like a business exchange; and, technically, it was, but she wished he could have given her a little bit more of what he had given her the other day. He had poured into her that day. Today, he acted like he didn't even know her. His eyes were full of grey clouds, as a storm brewed behind his stare. There was something dark within him and it made him standoffish. She turned to leave, making it all the way to the door before she stalled. She was looking for an excuse to prolong her presence there. "You caught me in a desperate place the other day. I don't do that. I've never done that." She had one hand on the door and was facing it, as she spoke. She didn't want to turn around to face him because he had to be judging her. That's where this change in mood had come from. He had formed an opinion of her and it wasn't a good one - at least that's what she assumed.

"You said that before. You don't have to repeat yourself. I believe you," Ethic replied.

"Then why are you treating me like..." she didn't know how to finish her sentence. "Like...a...like..." she was at a loss for words.

"A customer?" he finished.

"Yes!" she shouted. She knew she sounded ridiculous. *This man just fixed your car. He was being nice the other day. He ain't responsible for making your life feel less fucked up than what it is,* she thought. She blew out a deep breath and tucked her hair behind her ear, as she closed her eyes. "You know what? I'm sorry. I don't know what the hell I'm doing right now. Have a good night." She was halfway to the door when she stopped, again, pulling the money out of her bag and turning around to place it on the counter top. "I'd rather pay." She stormed off, opening the door, only for Ethic to come up behind her and push it closed. She turned towards him.

"I have to treat you like a customer, Alani, because if I don't, I start to wonder what you taste like," his words were so frank and so erotic that it made her quiver. He was standing so close that she could smell the scent of his sweet breath mixed with his cologne. "My mind starts wandering to other shit that men think about when they find a woman they want to conquer. I'm all man, Alani; and since you walked in here the other day, with those sad eyes and those painted-on jeans, I've been thinking some shit I shouldn't be thinking about you. I have my reasons why I can't take it there. In a perfect world, you would have never walked into this shop. The fucking odds that you came in here on the one day I been here all month..." Ethic stopped and shook his head. His forearms stretched pass her head, as his hands rested on the door, trapping her in between him and it. It was a prison Alani welcomed. She pulled her bottom lip between her teeth, as he stared intensely at her, through her, directly into her soul. Damn, how did he do that? He made her feel something other than devastation. He saw more than the wreckage she had transformed into. This was the feeling she had wanted him to provide when she first walked in. "You and that lip," he said, noticing. He noticed everything about her. It was how he had known she needed rescuing from her boss the other night. He had noticed. He picked up on things that others didn't take the time to dissect. This mysterious, midnight-colored gangster was intuitive and a beautiful distraction from her real life. He had switched her focus from her grief with ease; but as soon as he took back his presence, the gift of diversion disappeared with him. That's why she was there, stalling, delaying the moment when she would have to walk out the door. "You want me to fuck your pain away, and under different circumstances, I would oblige you because you're lovely as fuck, but that's not possible. I would just pile more hurt on you. You're not crazy. We had a smooth time the other night. Normally, that would lead to something else, but this is a dead end. That's why I'm treating you like a customer. I'm not the man you think I am. I'm not the good guy in your story."

He opened the door and stepped aside, as he waited for her to exit, but she just stood there looking up at him. "Good night, Alani."

Alani walked out. She couldn't get inside her car quickly enough. Embarrassed, confused and rejected, she pulled off into the night. She didn't know why she was angry. She didn't know Ethic. They were merely strangers passing through each other's lives; and according to Ethic, that's how it would stay.

***

Morgan drew in a sharp breath, as she tried to calm her racing heart. She was nervous, and as she waited for the doctor to come inside the room, her mind raced. *What if it doesn't work?* she thought. Ethic sat across from her. He was so serious, as he rested his elbows against his knees, fingers in a steeple under his chin, brows dipped low. He was thinking, probably about all the what if's that were haunting Morgan as well. Despite his silence, she was glad he had come. She was grateful he had done the research to even give her the option to correct her hearing in the first place.

"You don't have to stay," Morgan signed. "I mean, there's no point in you waiting while I'm in surgery."

"I'm not going anywhere," Ethic signed back.

"What about Eazy and Bella?" she asked.

"They know how important today is for you. They're at home with Lily. They're fine. My focus is you, right now," Ethic answered. "Are you ready?"

Before she could answer, her doctor came into the room. "Hi. I'm Dr. Hamady. You must be Morgan and you are…"

"Ezra Okafor," Ethic said, as he stuck his hand out for a shake. "I'm her family."

"Nice to meet you," the doctor said, as he pulled out a stool and took a seat. "Now, I've reviewed your medical history and I think you're a good candidate for this procedure.

A cochlear implant will stimulate the dormant nerves inside your inner ear and help you sense sound. I must ask. Why haven't you considered this treatment before? You're 18. Your hearing could have been restored years ago."

"Well, my parents died when I was young, and Ethic raised me. He's always offered me different options to find out if my hearing could be restored, but I never wanted to. I was scared and young. So many of the procedures were new and required a lot of time out of school for therapy. I'm old enough now to decide this is what I want," she signed.

"Well, technology has brought us quite far in hearing restoration. The down time is three to six weeks, and you aren't really down at all, just managing pain. I will not activate the implants until after that time, so you'll still be signing to communicate for a few weeks."

"How much pain will I be in?" Morgan signed.

"Nothing a prescription of Tylenol 800 won't alleviate," the doctor assured. "I'm going to take great care of you," the doctor promised. "I'm going to get the nurses in here to prep you for surgery, measure your ears, and grab your vitals. They'll give you Xanax to take the anxiety away. It will probably make you groggy. You won't even realize you're going into surgery in the morning. It's the good stuff," the doctor signed, with a wink. "You'll spend the night here, and in the morning, we'll change your life. How does that sound?"

"Long overdue," she signed.

The doctor left the room, as two nurses came in carrying a hospital gown, a small pill, and a cup of water. She placed the pill on her tongue and swallowed it down, quickly, and took the gown into the adjoining bathroom. She changed, quickly, and made herself comfortable under the covers, before turning to Ethic.

"Thank you," she signed.

"I love you, Mo," Ethic signed back. His phone vibrated on his hip and he looked down, noticing a notification from Messiah's text message.

MESSIAH:

911.

Ethic knew Messiah wouldn't even hit his line unless it was necessary. Ethic's fingers, quickly, typed a reply.

ETHIC:

I'm at Hurley. Can't leave. Pull up. Room 714.

Ethic looked over at Morgan who had closed her eyes. He hoped he was making the right decision, regarding her. He hoped she knew that he had done the best he could to care for her, over the years. He didn't know what had motivated the sudden change in her desire to go through with the surgery, but he would support her through it all.

Within the hour, Messiah was knocking on the door. Ethic stood and opened the door to step into the hallway. Messiah caught a glimpse of Morgan, sleeping inside the room, and his stomach dropped. He froze, as worry seized him.

"Everything good?" he asked.

Ethic squeezed the bridge of his nose, as he replied, "She's having surgery in the morning to restore her hearing."

Messiah's gut twisted in concern. He wanted to ask more questions, but to show too much interest would be disrespectful.

"Damn," was all he could manage.

"What's the emergency?" Ethic asked.

"A nigga named Cream put word out that he got bread on whoever hit Lucas and the little girl. He's her father and he on lock up North. Rumor has it, he's coming home soon and the nigga ain't happy," Messiah informed.

"Cream who?" Ethic dug.

"Cream Richardson. Niggas from around the way call him Killer Cream...some corny shit about him leaving niggas circled in chalk. He's from Merrill Hood. He was getting a little money when he was out, nothing major, but I heard he solid. He got a couple bodies on him but he ain't go down for that. He caught a bullshit charge. He talking big, though. You know how I want to handle it. Give a nigga his wings, as soon as he gets his freedom," Messiah whispered, in a low tone.

Ethic, immediately, thought of Alani. She had buried enough people. He didn't want to be responsible for putting her child's father in the ground too.

"Let the nigga breathe, for now," Ethic stated.

Messiah nodded and backpedaled from the room. "You said it, that's law," Messiah replied. "Yo, is she good?" Messiah couldn't help but ask. He had resisted the urge to text her after the debacle that had happened at the restaurant. He wanted to explain. He wanted to tell her that Nish was nobody to him, but he couldn't, because then he would have to admit that Morgan was "somebody" to him. He wouldn't cross that line.

Ethic looked back, peering inside the glass rectangle on the door. "She will be," Ethic stated. "Keep your ears to the street and let me know if shit gets tense."

***

Morgan's eyes fluttered open and she tried to fight the haze the anesthesia had her captured under. Her entire body was freezing, and she shivered, as she closed her eyes once more, giving into the wonderful feeling that kept pulling her into dreamland. She opened them again, and noticed Bella first, then Eazy and Ethic. She could feel the implants beneath the skin behind her ears, and it felt odd, heavy. She wondered if they were noticeable. Morgan was floating and so out of it that she couldn't do anything but lay her head back. She felt Ethic's hand on hers and she gave him a small squeeze, before slipping back into a deep sleep.

Ethic turned to the door, as Dr. Hamady walked in. "She'll be out of it for a while, but you can take her home as soon as she wakes up fully and is aware of her surroundings. She did well. The nerves responded beautifully to the implants. In a few weeks, she can come in and we'll activate them and witness technology at work, as she hears your voices for the first time."

Ethic shook the man's hand and felt a weight lift from his chest, as tears clouded his eyes. There was only one person he could share this with. "Grab your jackets, guys. Let's roll. I'm going to drop you at home with Ms. Lily."

"But we want to stay," Bella informed.

"It'll be hours before Mo wakes up. You guys have school tomorrow," Ethic said. "Don't worry, she'll be home soon," Ethic said. He escorted his children to his truck and quickly dropped them off at home with his nanny. He had somewhere he needed to be, and he couldn't get there fast enough.

***

It was a beautiful day. The sky was like sapphires, blue and clear with beautiful, billowy white clouds floating by. The wind blew gently, kissing Alani's face and the birds chirped a jovial tune. It looked like a scene out of a fairy tale, as if someone had illustrated a page out of the happiest storybook in the world. It was much too pretty of a day for the task at hand. Alani was burying two people that she loved today. On the inside, there was a storm plaguing her. Alani stood in front

148

of two caskets, her high heels sinking into the green grass, as the pastor gave a short sermon. She had chosen to eulogize her brother and daughter outside at the gravesite because she wasn't sure if she could survive a full service in a church. She was numb, as she stood there. She couldn't even cry anymore. She couldn't release one more tear because she had cried them all out. She felt like she was standing there outside of herself, having an outer body experience, as everyone around her broke down. She couldn't tear her eyes away from Kenzie. She was so pretty, just lying there, as if she was only asleep. It felt like it was a sin to put something so pretty in the dirt. It was hard for her to tear her eyes away from her angel, but when she saw the police car pull up and a handcuffed Cream exit from the back of the vehicle, she wanted desperately to see him. He was the only person present who could understand what she was going through. Two officers escorted him over to the ceremony, and Alani stepped up to the casket, meeting him there. She gripped the edge of the metal box and he placed a shackled hand over hers.

"I'm gonna handle it," he whispered. He leaned and kissed the side of Alani's head, inhaling her scent. She let him, because she knew it brought him comfort. Who was she to deprive him of comfort on such a hard day? She wished it was as easy for her to attain.

"No touching," the officers behind them reminded. Alani leaned down over the casket and kissed her daughter's forehead. Her skin felt cold, clammy, like clay, like an object that had never breathed and lived and laughed before. The color of her cinnamon skin was faded and dingy, like a trifling mama had washed the colored clothes on hot. This little body was not her little girl. This sight of death in front of her tore her up inside. "I love you, baby. Mommy loves you so much."

"I spoke to a lawyer. I'm out of here in six months on good behavior. When I touch down, niggas gon' answer for this," he whispered. "That's my word." He sniffed away a tear and snuck one last kiss, planting this one on her cheek, before he was escorted away.

When the pastor lowered the lid to the casket, her numbness melted away, and her emotions were so crippling that she couldn't stand. She sat in the front row, sobbing, her head buried in her hands until it was over. As everyone walked away, she sat there.

"Baby, we've got to go. People will expect to see you at the repast," Nannie said.

"I can't leave her. Just go ahead of me. I need a moment alone with her. I can meet you back at the church," Alani said.

"Okay, baby," Nannie replied, sorrowfully, before walking away.

***

Ethic walked through the cemetery, carrying fresh, long-stem roses, as he searched for Raven's grave. He sat down on the grass, as he placed the bouquet on her headstone.

"I miss you, ma," he whispered, as he bent his knees, resting his elbows on top of them as he clasped his hands together. He bowed his head, as his eyes burned. He felt her loss all over again, each time he visited. He had thought wounds healed over time, but this type never stopped bleeding. The same, sharp pain dwelled within his chest every day, never letting up. "Mo is gonna hear. After all this time, she's going to be able to speak and hear and laugh. She's gonna be alright. I know you wanted that for her. Your wants are my wants, love. I've tried to do right by her, by you. I wish you could see her. She's beautiful. She looks like you, and you shine through Eazy so brightly that I forget he never got to know you. Even Bella still remembers you. She prays

150

for you every night. She likes to think you and her mother are friends and are watching out for her. We're just floating down here, Rae. It's hard without you to keep us grounded, to build a home with…a life with…I'm lost, Raven." He stood and sniffed away the tears that never fell. The sound of crying caught his attention and he looked around. All he saw were tombstones, but the cries were too real to ignore. He walked toward the sound and what he discovered tore his heart out his chest. Alani laid, curled in a fetal position, beside the hole where her daughter's casket rested. It was still uncovered. The dirt hadn't even been thrown over it yet and Alani refused to move. He felt like he had intruded in on a private moment, but he had seen her now. He couldn't leave her there, not like this. He bent down and scooped her up, effortlessly, in his arms. She had been lying there all day, unable to move, unable to go.

"I can't leave her," she whispered. "They haven't even come to cover her yet. Where are they?!" she was irrational, panicked, and distraught. "Please, don't leave her in a wide-open hole. She's my baby. She might get cold."

"Okay, okay," he whispered.

Alani had lost it, but he understood that grief rode a fine line between crazy and sane. He sat her down in one of the white, wooden, folding chairs that was left over from the service and he removed his jacket and his diamond chains. Emotion cut at him, as he grabbed the shovel that sat propped in the pile of dirt. He was, literally, about to bury the little girl he had been responsible for killing, and it tore away at his conscience, as he began to scoop dirt onto the grave. His arms burned, as he grunted, while gritting his teeth. Every muscle in his body, bulging, as he filled the grave with dirt. Alani sat, watching, silent tears melting the makeup from her face, as she dug her nails into her knees. Hours passed, and Ethic was covered in sweat and filth by the time he finished. He bent down over the now smooth dirt and placed one hand on top of it.

"God bless her soul and have mercy on mine," he whispered, so only he could hear. Alani stood, as he approached her.

"Can you hug me?" she choked out the words, her chest jerking, as her lip quivered uncontrollably. "Like you did the other day. Please," she begged. He obliged. He wrapped her in his arms so tightly that she felt his heart racing as they stood chest to chest.

"I can't say I'm sorry enough," he whispered. The sorrow of this woman was beautiful. Witnessing her immense grief was like watching a tragic opera, wrenching his heart and captivating him, simultaneously.

"I can feel it, all over me when you hold me," she whimpered. "Just don't let go."

Fuck, Ethic thought, as he rested his chin on the top of her head. Women like Alani were his weakness. Damaged, genuine, and beautiful...He didn't know why he attracted the same type. Perhaps, because he had never successfully saved any of the ones he had lost. This woman's chaos was caused by him, which meant he couldn't have her, despite her need for him.

They broke their embrace when the sprinklers came on, soaking them with water. Alani squealed, as Ethic reached for his belongings and they made the trek across the grass to his truck.

When they were out of the spray zone, Alani asked, "How did you know I was here?"

"I was here visiting. I heard you crying. I couldn't just leave you," he answered.

Alani looked at him, curiously. His type of manhood was an endangered species. She appreciated the pieces of his time he allowed her to spend with him. "Thank you, Ethic," she said. She backpedaled. "I wouldn't mind if you called me sometime. Maybe we could get coffee and you can tell me about who you were here to see. My number is on the paperwork at your shop." She paused, as she stared at him, wondering how this man she barely knew brought so much comfort to her wounded soul. "Okay, bye."

He nodded, as he watched her walk toward her car, knowing he would never call. He didn't move until she drove away. He would have to keep his distance from her because seeing her face reminded him of the monster that dwelled in the pits of him. Hustling had hardened him, had made murder just another day's work. That type of man was incapable of remorse and that type of man was one that karma couldn't wait to meet. He never wanted his children to reap what he had sown, which is why he had walked away from the streets. Reacting to Lucas had pulled him back to a place where a father didn't belong, and he hoped he didn't lose everything he had built because of it.

Chapter 12

Six Weeks Later

Morgan didn't know why she was so anxious. This was the moment she had waited for her entire life. She sat on the exam table inside Dr. Hamady's private office and her chest heaved up and down.

"You nervous?" Bella signed.

Morgan nodded.

"Everything's going to be fine. The hard part is over. This is the final step," Ethic signed to her.

"Can you hear me yet?" Eazy shouted. Morgan laughed, as she read his lips.

"Not yet, Eazy," she signed.

Dr. Hamady entered the room and Morgan's heart beat rapidly. *What if it doesn't work?* she thought. Her hopes were high, and she knew she would be devastated if this didn't end how she anticipated.

"Today's the day," Dr. Hamady said, as he signed simultaneously.

She nodded, as he examined the incisions behind her ears. Morgan had been in the mirror almost daily, monitoring the cuts, and putting different creams on them to minimize the scarring. They were practically invisible.

"You've healed beautifully," Dr. Hamady signed. "Are you ready to turn on the implants?" he asked.

Morgan smiled, her nerves visible, as she shook her foot rapidly, trying to shake out some of the energy. The doctor pulled a rolling stool in front of her, and opened a laptop in his lap, as he powered on the control that activated the tiny devices that now lived in her head.

"You may have some swelling. We may have to adjust the strength of the implant a couple times before we get it right. I'm going to run some tests to make sure all the impedances are firing correctly, so we can get some stimulation in the ear canals. I'll turn it up slowly, as we talk, and you let me know when you can hear. It may seem very loud because you've never been able to hear anything before. It will take some getting used to. You will probably feel the vibrations of sound before you hear anything. Okay?"

Morgan was reading his lips now because his hands were busy typing codes into his laptop. She nodded her confirmation. She was more ready than she would ever be. "Now, Ezra here thought it was important for the first voice you heard to be someone special. So, we aren't going to say anything. I'm going to play something for you, and when you hear it, you let me know."

Morgan sat still, waiting on pins and needles, as the doctor began turning up the frequency on the implants.

"Can she hear, yet?" Eazy asked, in excitement.

"Shh," Ethic coached. "Not yet, big man. It's coming, though. You'll know when she hears it."

Morgan frowned, as she waited. She couldn't hear anything but there was a vibrating in her ears that made them feel like they were itching. She stuck her fingers in them.

"It probably feels odd to her. This is a normal reaction," Dr. Hamady said, aloud. Morgan winced, as a high frequency ring hurt her ears.

"Does it hurt?" the doctor asked. Morgan was still focused on reading his lips, so he knew she couldn't hear yet. She nodded. "I'm going to lower the frequency and come back up again. Morgan nodded. She was already feeling defeated. Her disappointment was written all over her. The doctor handed her a pair of headphones. "Press play and try it now."

Morgan sighed, ready to give up, but she did as she was told. When the deep baritone voice began to play in her ears, tears came to her eyes.

"Let me tell you something, young blood. There is nothing like the love a man feels for his children. Raven and Morgan are the greatest gifts a man could possess. Raven knows it. She knows she's a jewel, but Morgan, my baby girl doesn't know it. She was born differently, and she doesn't realize it's the rocks with the most flaws that turn into the finest diamonds."

Morgan's heart stopped, as her hands began to tremble. She was hearing her father's voice for the first time. It was something she had never dreamed she would ever get to experience. He had died long ago, when she was just a young girl, and here she was as a grown woman hearing him whisper affirmations in her ear. A laugh escaped her, as she smiled and heavy drops of emotion fell out her eyes. She covered her mouth, in shock, as she closed her eyes.

"I will protect my girls till my dying day. I've never loved anyone like I love them, and I don't entrust them with just anyone. Just the fact that I gave you the responsibility of taking them with you to protect for the night means you are family. There are niggas I've known for 20 years that I wouldn't put in the same vicinity as my girls. They are my everything. Justine is the sun and Raven is the moon. That Morgan... baby girl is my youngest and she's the whole damn universe. I'll move heaven and earth for them. Thank you for what you did today."

"Why is she crying, Daddy? Can she hear?" Eazy asked, impatiently.

Ethic nodded. "She can hear." He had saved the voicemail from almost 10 years ago. He knew that after Benny Atkins' death, that one day his daughters would need to hear how much he loved them. It had come in handy, just when Morgan needed those words the most.

Morgan was in a state of disbelief, as she removed the headphones and rushed into Ethic's arms. She was so overwhelmed, so happy, so lucky and she couldn't stop the joy from spilling from her. She had been motivated to do this because she wanted to feel normal. She wanted a boy to like her, but this was so much bigger than that. She had gotten to know a piece of her father just by hearing his voice, and it had touched her soul.

"You'll come in for check-ups every month for the next six months or so, but this is a life time change. Do you want to try to speak?" Dr. Hamady asked.

Morgan shook her head. It was her greatest fear. Opening her mouth and revealing what her looks never did…her handicap. She had done it as a kid and had experienced a humiliation that had stuck with her all these years. She had taken years of therapy, speech and phonetics to teach her to mimic the lip and tongue movements of hearing people. She had memorized them all, but she never spoke in front of other people again. She was afraid of her own voice.

"I've spoken to your therapist, Morgan. You've mastered phonetics. They think you have the efficiency of a naturally hearing individual. You just have to trust yourself," Dr. Hamady urged. "There's no pressure. When you're ready, you will use your voice. Medically, there is no reason why you are unable to."

Morgan nodded, as the doctor stood to his feet. He shook hands with Ethic, before exiting the room.

Morgan was silent the entire ride home, as she soaked up the things around her. She never knew so many things made noise. Everything had its own sound, even the wheels rotating on the pavement was noticeable. It was amazing. It was like she had walked through her entire life half living without the soundtrack that accompanied it. She had a slight headache from the different sensations she was feeling inside her ears. It was all so loud and Eazy was on 10 in the backseat. His racket she enjoyed, however. His sound matched his vibe.

"Morgan, do you want to know what a fart sounds like?" Eazy asked. "Ooh, what about a motorcycle? Or Daddy snoring?"

Morgan smiled, as the entire car burst into laughter. He was being a typical boy - gross, silly, and mannish.

"Big man, let Mo chill, okay?" Ethic said. Ethic was used to the amount of racket Eazy made, but he didn't want it to overwhelm Morgan. She was used to processing only four senses. She would have to adjust.

"Daddy, chill. She wanted to hear. Let her hear. It doesn't have to be such a big event," Bella said, with a slight attitude.

Ethic turned and looked at her, sitting in the back seat, mouth in a pout, and arms crossed over her chest.

"Watch your tone, Bella. We operate with respect for each other. Every member of this house. It's been a long day for everybody," Ethic said, as he pulled into his estate. He was beginning to think the surprise celebration dinner he had planned wasn't such a good idea. He allowed Morgan to climb the steps first, as he and the kids trailed behind her. When she opened the door, she jumped in startle, as she heard,

"Surprise!!!"

It, literally, felt like an explosion sounded off in her ears, as Lily, Nish, Messiah, and even Dolce stood waiting for her. Her hands shot to her ears, as she winced in pain. It was too much, too soon, and Ethic rushed to her side.

"Baby girl, what hurts?" he asked, as he cupped her face as he watched her squeeze her eyes shut.

Morgan took a moment to breathe, as a silence fell over the room. Everyone stood, worried, gawking, as Morgan slowly opened her eyes.

"You good?" Ethic asked.

She nodded. "I just have to get used to it."

Ethic turned to the small group. "Let's keep the volume down. Her ears are sensitive to loud noises and she isn't comfortable speaking yet, so we're just taking this whole thing slow, a'ight?" he said.

Her eyes fell on Messiah and then over to Nish, who came rushing up to her. "Oh my God! Congrats, girl! I can't believe you didn't tell me! I know we've been distant, but when Ethic called, I had to come. You're my best friend, Mo. I had to be here for this," Nish said.

Morgan was grateful when Lily announced that the chef had set the table and it was time to eat.

As Morgan walked by Messiah, she could feel his eyes on her. She couldn't look at him. She was certain Ethic had invited him, but the sight of him with Nish made her stomach turn. He wore his locs in cornrows to the back, and he was dressed in hood rich attire: a Gucci sweat suit with fresh J's. She didn't acknowledge him. She was so angry, that if she did, she was sure she would cry. She just wanted to go to bed. She was emotionally exhausted, and she couldn't sit through an entire dinner with Nish sitting next to Messiah. She wasn't too proud to admit she was jealous and she wouldn't give herself an opportunity to show it. She walked into the dining room and stood next to the table.

"Thank you, everyone, for coming, but I'm in a little bit of pain and I really just want to get some sleep. I'm sorry. May I be excused?" she looked at Ethic, who nodded. She, instantly, fled to her room. She didn't have the energy to handle this tonight. She couldn't put on a poker face and bear through it. She had been through too much and she just wanted to retreat to the privacy of her room. Her head was spinning, and she didn't have the emotional moxie to pretend like seeing Messiah with Nish didn't bother her.

"Poor thing," Dolce said. "Thank you for inviting me. I've known Morgan since she was 11. I'm glad I could be here for this. I'm sorry how we left things," Dolce stated.

"Yeah, me too," Ethic answered. "I thought you deserved to be here. Mo likes you and you've been in her life for a while now so…"

"And what about you? Do *you* like me, Ethic?" Dolce asked.

Ethic rubbed the top of his head with both hands, feeling the waves under his fingertips. He didn't know how to answer that. Honesty was his policy; but with Dolce, she preferred the lies. The only time she blew up at him was when he was truthful about his inability to give her the affection she wanted from him.

"You like what I do for you," she said, whispering over his shoulder, as she nibbled on his earlobe.

He pushed her away, gently. "My kids are here, Dolce. Chill. You know I don't do the public displays," he said.

"Then let's do a private display," Dolce said. "I promise I won't get attached this time. I miss you and I have an itch that only you're long enough to scratch." She slipped her house key into his pocket and then walked out.

***

"You're taking me home?" Nish asked, as she noticed Messiah pull onto her street. "I thought you needed me to cook up?"

Messiah was tired of playing this game. Initially, he had planned to fuck with Nish because once he laid claim to her, he knew Morgan would be off limits, but she wasn't his type. When it came down to it, he couldn't seal the deal because he knew what it would do to Morgan. Instead, he taught Nish how to prepare his cocaine and how to turn soft into hard, stretching one kilo into two. She was cool, and they smoked weed together, mostly. He would feed her after a long night of watching her flip bricks in the kitchen of the trap house, but he couldn't take it there with her. The attraction just wasn't mutual; and while he knew she was trying to bop her thotty-ass right onto his dick, he always kept it strictly professional, despite her constant fronting on her social media pages. Messiah had checked her more than a few times about taking pictures of him without his knowledge or while in his car, or posted in front of his Kawasaki. It was all a stunt to make her feel big in a small city. He wasn't with the games and he was growing bored of her company. After seeing Morgan and watching her react to the noise that filled the room, all he wanted to do was talk to her. He couldn't while in Ethic's presence, but he hoped to get the opportunity soon.

"Nah, not tonight," Messiah said. He pulled up in front of her house and popped the locks, letting her know it was time to exit. He didn't even wait until she was inside her house before he pulled away. He found himself back at Ethic's, sitting curbside, as he burned a blunt, while contemplating calling Morgan. He was playing a dangerous game. Ethic had the power to shutdown his entire operation, and he knew firsthand what lengths Ethic was willing to go to, to protect Morgan. Messiah wasn't trying to jeopardize his relationship

with Ethic, and he meant no disrespect, but the pull Morgan
had on him was undeniable.

MESSIAH:

Come outside. I'm up the block.

MORGAN:

No.

Her response caught him off guard, but he didn't blame her.
Morgan was not only spoiled, but justified in the way she felt
about him. He had handled her poorly, and he knew she
wasn't going to make it easy to get back in her good graces.

MESSIAH:

You coming out or I'm coming in that mu'fucka. Which
one it's gon' be?

Messiah knew Morgan wouldn't want to cause a scene. He
didn't even know what he was doing there. He was far
removed from sneaking around to see a chick. It wasn't his
style. He was in his mid 20's and had left that high school shit
behind a long time ago. Anything immature turned him off,
which is how he knew he had a thing for Morgan. She was just
discovering the world, just getting her feet wet. At 18, she was
green but the way she looked at him made him feel kingly.
Her silence was mystical. She was like a beautiful bird that
you had to be careful not to frighten, because if you got too
close, it would fly away. That's why he had admired from a
distance. But when niggas around the city began to shoot their
shot, he began to feel territorial. He began to shoot his shot, as
in bullets, because he would body any nigga that stepped to
her incorrectly. His protection was no longer out of obligation
to Ethic, but out of infatuation for her. He wanted what he

couldn't have, and it bothered him to his core, because Messiah was a man who could have whatever he liked, with whomever he liked…except her. He waited for her response, but it never came. Within minutes, he saw her walking down the driveway and towards his car, her hands were tucked in a Michigan State hoodie and she wore short, cotton shorts that were barely visible. All he saw was legs, as she walked towards his car, flip flops slapping on the concrete ground and scowl on her pretty face. Her long braids were pulled up in a bun on top of her head. She opened the passenger door and climbed inside but didn't look his way. He studied her. Her body language was tense and full of mistrust. She was freshly showered and filled his car with the scent of Flowerbomb body wash.

"Shorty Doo Wop," he said, his baritone deep, as he peered through his low lids. Morgan was incensed with resentment. He could feel her animosity. She even leaned toward the door. She wanted as much space between them as she could get. She normally smiled when he greeted her in that way, but tonight she was giving out 'fuck you' vibes and he took them because he deserved them. "Mo," he tried again. "So, I've been fucking with the sign language a little bit."

She turned to look at him and stuck up her middle finger.

He chuckled. "Yeah, I know that one real good," he said. She smiled, only lifting one corner of her mouth. "She smiles. God must want a nigga to sleep good tonight, He blessed me with that visual."

"What do you want?" she signed, her hands flying fast in frustration.

"You got to slow that shit down for me, Mo. My teacher is YouTube. Do it again," he said.

She signed, again, and she was surprised when he answered, "I just wanted to see you and make sure you're okay."

She was astounded that he had taken the time to learn. She was sure he wasn't fluent, but the effort was nice.

"You can hear me. That's dope, Mo. I'm happy for you," he continued. He was rough with women. He rarely catered to their feelings, so he didn't know how to do this caring thing. All he had known them to be good for was pleasure. He didn't have a mother's love to shape the way he viewed women. All he knew was desertion, so he never let himself get close enough to care. If his mother had left him, all women eventually would too. To avoid reliving that feeling of inadequacy and the sting of abandonment, he never let a woman get close. When he felt Morgan shocking the dead battery inside his chest, trying to power on his heart, he did the most hurtful thing he could do to make her lose interest. He knew he had fucked up by allowing Nish to put out the perception that they were more than they were. He could feel the shift in his connection with Morgan. He hadn't anticipated how much he would miss it. She didn't look at him the same. Her gaze was no longer given in adoration, but in contempt. He had witnessed her disappointment in him; first, at the hibachi spot and again tonight. He couldn't have that. Like Ricky, he had some 'splaining to do. "So, why won't you speak?" he asked.

Morgan looked down at her hands and twirled the rings on her fingers around.

"You're afraid of what you might sound like?" Messiah guessed. "Well, I got to say, if you sound fucked up it's only fair. God got to give you some type of flaw. You probably got a big, manly voice. An ol' Beyoncé-bass-sounding-ass voice."

She smiled, and he wondered where this light-hearted side of himself had come from. He wasn't the wisecracking type, but he would do anything to break this ice with Morgan. *Baby girl got me on freeze,* he thought.

"There she go," Messiah admired. Morgan really was a sight to behold, and he didn't mind bigging her up, because he knew beneath the fake confidence was a girl with insecurities. "It's just me and you in this car, so let's talk. I'll start." He lifted her chin with his finger, forcing her to look him in the eyes. "I'm not fucking your homegirl, Mo," he said, frankly. He needed her to know, and despite her eye roll, he continued. "I wouldn't lie to you, Mo. I only bang with her on business. The rest of the shit she put out there is false."

Morgan's shoulders seemed to relax, as her eyes watered. "You hurt my feelings," she signed.

"I hurt your feelings," he repeated, deciphering the signs, slowly. "I apologize. I was on some asshole shit, trying to push you away."

"Why?" she signed.

"Out of loyalty to Ethic, out of respect; but when I heard you were trying to restore your hearing, it just fucked with me. It fucked me up that I couldn't be there, and I have a feeling you decided to have this surgery because you felt like you were competing with Nish," Messiah said. "Am I wrong?"

Morgan looked away. She couldn't admit that. She wasn't just competing with Nish. She was competing with girls like Nish, normal girls.

"There's no comparison, Mo. Real shit, some women just don't have to compete. Women out here with fake hair, fake nails, fake contacts, fake asses, drawing on eyebrows and shit, squeezing into them shits that make them skinny, trying to hit angles for cell phone cameras to make them look thick, just dumb shit. All for likes, all for attention. You know what you got to do for that?" he asked. "Just breathe. It's that simple for you. The way your chest rises and falls when you're nervous, like now, is the sexiest shit I've ever seen. The other girls compete, Mo, you just exist." Messiah sighed because he knew he might be coming off wrong, like he was trying to game his way back into her favor, but he was speaking all facts. "Listen, Mo, you can't be out here wilding, letting niggas push up on you, touch on you, dance on you, cuz when I see that, my mind only go to one place. Even if that bitch-ass nigga didn't violate you that night, I was murking him anyway. That's how crazy I am over you, Mo, and you not even mine. I only know one way to be and that's all the way in, or all the way out, and I've never felt this over any woman. I don't even give this much conversation to these hoes." Messiah was high, so the candidness of his words was unfiltered, raw, but Mo was listening. This was a heavy discussion for a girl who had just learned to hear mere hours ago. "I don't do the cuffing thing. I don't know how this is supposed to go, but I know how it is between us now don't work for me. I fuck with you, Mo."

"You fuck with everybody," she signed. "That big head bitch, Shayna, claiming you, Nish claiming you, 10 hoes behind them are claiming you. You for everybody, Messiah," Her hands were going, and he couldn't keep up.

"It look like you saying some bullshit," he said, with a smirk. "So, I'ma say goodnight."

Morgan shook her head, unable to contain the giddiness she felt, as she smiled. She cleared her throat and anxiously whispered, "Goodnight, Messiah." It was raspy, and her s's sounded more like z's, but she had heard her own voice, and the tears that came to her eyes were proud ones.

She looked at him for validation, her eyes full of worry, as she waited for him to say something.

"You gon' fuck me up every time with the way you say my name," he complimented, as he placed a hand over his heart. "Good night, Shorty Doo Wop." She popped open her door and walked back up to the house. For her, Messiah waited until she was safely inside, before pulling off into the night.

Chapter 13

E thic was a lonely man, haunted by ghosts, unable to shake his past enough to move forward to anything new. Dolce was a woman who thought she could change that, heal him, and that was her number one mistake. A woman couldn't change a man. He had to change himself. For the right woman, he would. Dolce wasn't that woman. To be fair, Raven was a hard act to follow. He didn't know why he was sitting outside her house, contemplating using the key she had given him. He knew he was playing with fire. Dolce had put in too much effort, too much time over the years to just walk away without expecting something in return. Ethic just didn't feel the soul-stirring pull that he had felt with Raven. Not for Dolce at least. Still, he was a man, full of frustration, and he needed to release it. Instead of going home where he belonged, Ethic opened the door to his Range and took long strides toward her front door. He used the key, letting himself in, and as soon as he opened the door, Dolce stood there, wearing a sheer, floor-length robe, six-inch heels, and nothing underneath. No one could ever deny that Dolce was beautiful. She was exotic. She was half Hispanic, half white and just remarkably pretty. Her light skin, long hair, and dangerous curves would be the only pre-requisites for another man to make her his wife, but Ethic was different. Ethic wanted his wife to be a sister; black, mixed with blacker, full of sweet juice and scented like shea butter. He wanted the woman he ended up with to be able to relate to his experience, to know what it was like to have strength and resilience, not because it was learned, but because it was inherited from generations of black people who had to be strong before her. He wanted nappy hair and intelligence. He wanted a woman that could make a feast out of a bag of beans and a neck bone, if he fell on hard times, and it was all he could afford. A woman who could raise his children, if his karma came and took him away prematurely. She didn't have to come with much. In fact, she could have nothing. If her soul was pure, and her heart linked to his own, he had enough to share with the right one. Dolce wasn't that woman. She was too pampered, too spoiled, and not cut from the same cloth as he was. They were compatible, sexually, but in all other areas they were opposites. Still, he was a man, and she had been sitting on his dick for years. As she approached him and rubbed the front of his Ferragamo slacks, he reacted to her. His dick had a mind of its own, as she aroused him, making it stand like a snake charmer.

"No strings, ma," he said, as he stared her in the eyes.

"No strings, Papi. Lo prometo," she said, promising.

Ethic needed to fuck. He was a man who prided himself on discipline, but the burdens he had on him didn't allow him to turn her down. He slid a finger down her slit and sucked in air, shocked at how ready she was. She was dripping; and although he was tempted, he wanted to make sure they understood one another. He brought his hand under her chin in a 'U', gripping her face with enough pressure to command her movements.

"Look at me," he said. She lifted her eyes to meet his. "If you're looking for love, I need to walk out right now. I don't have a heart to give you. This is just sex."

Dolce tried to kiss him and he pulled back. He didn't kiss. Not her. Ethic had only put his lips on two women in his life. Not even Bella's mom had felt his lips on her. Raven Atkins and Disaya Morgan were the ones he had tasted from head to toe. Dolce wouldn't be the third. Kissing was intimate…personal. That wasn't what this was about. He knew his stipulations were cold, but he was cold… he was frozen in a place where only hurt could exist. Hurt people, hurt people and he had warned Dolce of that. She was hardheaded. She wanted to accept what little he gave her… dick and fancy gifts with no emotions attached.

"I can't kiss your lips, so let me kiss this," she whispered, as she lowered to her knees. She unbuttoned the expensive pants and then rolled them down his waist as he stepped out of them. He removed his shirt, as she enclosed her mouth around him. He gripped her hair, tightly, as she sucked him into her mouth, using just the right pressure. Ethic's body was there in the moment, as she stood and pulled him to her bedroom, but his mind was a million miles away. He didn't know how he had gotten to this point. When he navigated through the streets, he had always lived by a code; now, he questioned if he had any type of morality at all. He was going through the motions, as he rolled a condom over his strength and watched as she climbed on top. Her rolls were slow and timid, as she tried to inch down on him, taking him in with caution. The veins in his dick teased her walls, as she found her rhythm. He had so much aggression, so much madness, built up in his veins and he felt it mounting as he matched her, trying to get her to ride him deeper. She was squealing with every pump. Her perfect, silicone D's bouncing while sweat trailed down her toned stomach. He lifted her. He was so strong that it was effortless for him to turn her around without ever taking himself out. He didn't want to see her face or look her in the eyes because she was pleading with him. Dolce's expression was begging him to give her a chance. She wanted more. He knew it and he couldn't look her in the eyes. She rode him backwards, her behind spreading. The sight of his blackness disappearing into her pretty, toned ass made a prickling current pulse in the tip of his dick. He was about to cum; and from the screams bouncing off the walls and the way her pussy smacked with wetness, told him she was there too. He filled the condom, as she climbed down off the ride, flipping her bedroom hair over her shoulder.

"God, I missed you," she said, with a smile. Dolce watched Ethic walk to her adjoining bathroom. Every muscle in his body was well maintained, from his thighs to his abs, to his strong arms. He was just the perfect mixture of strength and lean. *If I could just get him to slip up one time,* she thought, as she watched him flush the condom carrying his seeds down the toilet. He showered, and she went to gather his clothes from where they lay strewn in her living room. In all the years she had known him, he had never stayed the night, so she placed his clothes out on the bed as she shrugged into a robe. She went to the bathroom and closed the lid on her toilet, staring at him through the shower door. It was a shame how damaged this man was.

"Why can't things be different between us? More?"

Ethic closed his eyes and lowered his head under the water. This was why he had to draw a line with her. Women confused sex with love. It was like, when he entered her, his dick beelined straight to her heart. For him, it was simple to separate the physical from the emotional. He pulled back the shower curtain and stepped out, wrapping a towel around his waist.

"If I could give you what you wanted I would. I can't be that for anyone. It ain't in me," Ethic said. He saw her disappointment and he kissed her cheek, to lessen the blow. He dressed, quickly, in silence. There was nothing else he could say. Nothing she could say. He was leaving. It was what it was and love it was not.

She walked him to the door, with tears in her eyes. When Ethic turned back to say goodbye, she couldn't help but to plead her case. "Why won't you just try? You could learn to be happy with me," she said, eyes shining, sincerely.

Ethic knew that time wasn't what they needed. It had been 10 years of casual sex but he didn't want to be cruel by pointing that out. The fact that he had come to her home and transferred his energy, without intentions of staying, suddenly made him feel guilty. She wouldn't cut him off. He knew that. He had to be the one to show some restraint.

"We used to have fun, at least," Dolce reasoned. "Now, it's like I'm only good for one thing. I'm just asking you to give us a chance."

Ethic felt tension at the nape of his neck. "It's not my intention to mishandle you. There's a diner not too far from here. You hungry? We can talk about this over food."

You would have thought Ethic was offering a five-star meal, the way Dolce's face lit up. What he wanted hadn't changed, but he surmised that he didn't have to be so cold towards her. He didn't mean to take advantage of her feelings. The least he could do was consider her a friend. He would figure out how to tell her that over a meal. Maybe then, his leaving wouldn't feel so abrupt.

Dolce dressed, quickly, and then hopped into his truck, smiling ear to ear.

***

The diner was empty. It was past midnight and Alani sat on the barstool, with three, giant books in front of her, as she took notes in a journal. She had gone back to school to pursue writing and filled her days with classes, while waitressing filled her nights. She wasn't sleeping anyway, so she found it best when she didn't give herself time to think.

Staying busy was the only way for her to stay alive. If she sat still for even a moment, she was sure to slit her wrists. She was so backed up with emotion and grief that she felt like death would be better than living without her child. Exactly 46 days had passed since the funerals, and Alani just couldn't crawl out of the funk she was in. Her shift was almost over, and she couldn't wait to get home, so she could soak her tired bones in a warm bath. It would be a long night of studying for her. She had a test the next day that she couldn't miss. The bell above the door rang and she groaned and closed her book. *Somebody always wanna walk in 10 minutes before I clock out,* she thought. She knew she wouldn't be able to leave now, until the table was cleared. She went to the bin where the silverware and menus were stored, grabbed two place settings and then made her way to the table.

"Hi, my name is Lenika, I'll be your server this evening," she said. She smiled at the gorgeous woman who was facing her and handed her a menu. When she turned to the man the woman was with, Alani froze. She hesitated, and her falter caused him to look up from his phone.

"Hi," she whispered.

Ethic made her wait for a greeting, as he took her in. He noted the uniform and her sunken, sad eyes. She had dropped at least 20 pounds. "You work here?" he asked.

"You know her?" Dolce cut in.

Ethic ignored Dolce, as he stared at Alani who shifted uncomfortably.

"Yeah, for about two weeks now," she responded. "I'll give you guys a little time with the menu." She tried to rush off, only for Dolce to stop her.

"Umm… can you at least take our drink orders?" Dolce asked.

Alani turned. "Oh. Yeah! Of course. What can I get you?"

"I'll take seltzer with lemon on the side," Dolce ordered.

"We only have regular water. No seltzer," Alani said.

"What about bottled water? Does this dump have that?" Dolce asked.

"Two, regular waters are fine," Ethic said. "Thank you."

Alani rushed off to fix the drinks. Out of all the diners in the entire city, Ethic had waltzed into hers. She had thought of him so many times over the past few weeks that it was borderline obsessive. The hugs he gave out were like magic. It was the only thing that made her feel like she could breathe, after her daughter had died. She wished he could bottle them up and sell them because she would be his number one customer. She peered, discreetly, at the couple in the booth by the door and turned up her nose in contempt.

She ain't even that pretty, she thought. She knew she was hating. Dolce was beyond pretty, she was gorgeous, and exactly the type of woman she would expect Ethic to have. She didn't know why it angered her to see him with the light, bright, beauty queen. *He ain't your man. Let that nigga live,* she told herself. Still, she was green with envy. *Nigga's always want to get them a little foreign piece when they get some paper.* Her thoughts were fueling the fire in her chest. Alani rolled her eyes, as Dolce moved from her side of the table to be closer to Ethic. She filled the drinks and carried them over to the table, setting them down. She felt Ethic's eyes on her, but she avoided looking at him. Clearly, he was out of her league; and even if he was fair game, she was in no shape to be thinking about a man. "Y'all ready to order?" she asked.

"I'll just have the grilled chicken salad," Dolce said.

"I'm good," Ethic whispered.

"You're not eating?" Dolce asked, as she bent her brow and then looked between Ethic and Alani.

"How have you been?" Ethic asked; again, ignoring Dolce. "And who's Lenika?" he asked, as he rubbed his goatee and nodded toward her name tag.

"It's my middle name," she said. "Only my family and close friends call me Alani."

"And me," Ethic said.

She smirked. "You don't call me much of anything, though. I'm just a customer, remember? Lenika will suit you just fine." Alani looked at Dolce, before turning to walk away. "Your salad will be right out."

"We'll take it to go," Ethic announced.

"To go?" Dolce protested. "I thought we were eating? Talking? What happened to that?"

"It's late. I should get home. Check in on Mo and the kids," Ethic stated. It took all of 10 minutes for Alani to bring out Dolce's food and Ethic didn't miss her attitude. He paid the bill, leaving a generous tip on the table, and then walked out, guiding Dolce by the small of her back. Alani had never been so jealous of a back in her life. As soon as she saw Ethic's Range pull out of the parking lot, she hurriedly cleaned off his table, so she could clock out. Suddenly, a glass of red wine was calling her name.

Alani had one more table come in last minute, and by the time they left, she was drained. She threw her books in her tote and waved goodbye to the cooks, as she walked out into the cool, night air. She stopped, mid step, when she saw Ethic standing in front of his car, leaning against the hood. He was alone, and she found a bit of relief in that fact - even though he owed her no explanations.

"Come here."

It came out like a command... Like a king who was perched on a throne, giving orders to a peasant. He didn't mean to be bossy, but he was a boss. She could see it in the way he carried himself and the way others carried him. Alani was a stubborn girl, however, and nobody told her when to move or how to move. He had just flashed his little, fancy girlfriend in her face and yes, the 'little' description was necessary because Alani was being petty - something she was good at.

"It's late, I'm going home," she said.

She turned toward her car and unlocked the doors, before climbing inside. When she turned over the ignition, it didn't start.

"Please, not tonight. I got a point to prove and you don't want to start right now, with this fine-ass nigga watching my every move. Great," she groaned, as she attempted to restart her car. It chugged a little bit, but didn't start. She gripped the top of her steering wheel with both hands and then let her head fall onto her knuckles, as she tried to control the sobs that were threatening to spill out of her. Why life was this hard, she didn't know, but Alani was ready to throw in the towel. Before, she had a reason to be this exhausted, a reason to go so hard. She used to have a little person depending on her. But doing all this, appreciating the struggle, dealing with the exhaustion, and waiting for the glow up, wasn't so worth it when all she was doing it for was herself. She felt Ethic's presence but refused to lift her head. He opened the door and then rested his hands on top of her car, as he leaned down. He reached for the latch to pop her hood and then rolled up his sleeves, disappearing behind the lifted hood. "Your engine's done," he announced. He walked to her back door and opened it to grab the belongings he'd seen her carrying, and then reached out his hand for her. She didn't take it. Instead, she wiped her tears and stood. She took her tote from his grasp and started walking. It wasn't that far of a walk. She could make the 10 blocks to her house.

"Alani!"

Her feet stopped moving. It was like they were playing red light, green light and the nigga had suddenly switched the signal to stop. Alani froze. She didn't even want to, but she heard the impatience in his voice.

"I don't usually have to repeat myself," Ethic said.

Alani placed a hand on her hip and was across the parking lot in a flash. "Oh, little Ms. Seltzer Water must be super obedient," she snapped. "Who is she? Your little girlfriend?"

Ethic smirked. "I'm a little old for the girlfriend thing." Ethic showed teeth, this time, finding her amusing.

"You're a piece of work," she said, pointing a finger, as she turned to start her walk. When she thought of something else to say, she spun again, marching over to him. She was pissed he hadn't moved; as if he had expected her to double back. "And I told you not to call me Alani," she fussed.

"Is she the reason why you didn't call?" she asked.

"She's not the reason I do anything," Ethic responded. "She doesn't belong to me."

"You're lying," Alani said. "That big-head-ass girl was looking at me like she was ready to slap me for even speaking to you."

"Why does it bother you? Seeing me with her?" Ethic asked.

"Why did you double back here after you dropped your girl off?" Alani shot back. "You don't owe me any explanations and yet here you are."

"Here I am," Ethic confirmed, as he stepped towards her, invading her space. He wrapped his arms around her and she melted into him. He felt like home and she clung to him, as if he might disappear if she let go. "Can I take you home?" he asked.

She sniffed and wiped her face, before lifting her eyes to meet his. She nodded and then he led her to his truck.

They were silent, as they drove through the city. When he pulled up in front of her house, Alani didn't move right away.

"You probably think I'm crazy," she scoffed.

"That's the furthest thought from my mind, when I think of you," he said.

"What do you think?" she asked.

"I think the universe is cruel," he said, seriously. "I'll have one of my guys take care of your car in the morning. They'll drop it off to you when it's done."

Alani opened the door and climbed out the truck "Thanks for the ride, Ethic."

Ethic stepped out as well.

"What are you doing?" she asked, with a frown.

"Walking you to your door," he answered. "What type of men you been giving your time to, Lenika?"

"None like you," she said, as her eyes hooded in appreciation. "You can call me Alani. I like the way it sounds when you say it...like you've known me for a long time."

"I thought that was reserved for close friends and family," Ethic said, throwing her words back at her.

"Exactly," she said. "Friends call each other. Now, you don't have an excuse to not reach out." She smiled, and Ethic remained stoic because he knew he wouldn't call. He couldn't. He found her wildly intriguing, but to actively pursue her would be dirty. When she noticed how serious he remained, the corners of her mouth fell flat, as her eyes squinted in curiosity. *Is he blowing me off? He comes all the way back to the diner, but he can't call?* She thought. The moment was turning awkward, as embarrassment filled her. "Thanks, again," she mumbled, before rushing inside. She watched from the living room window, as he made his way back to his truck. When he was gone, she went directly to the kitchen where she knew Nannie had left a plate for her. She removed the aluminum foil from the plate, popped it in the microwave, and then brewed a cup of coffee. She sat down with her books, her food, her coffee, and her tears, preparing to battle another sleepless night.

***

"Alani!"

Alani lifted her head from the kitchen table, where she had fallen asleep, to hear Nannie calling her from the front door. She rushed to the front of the house.

"What? What's wrong?" she responded, in panic, as she joined her side and looked from her aunt to the white man standing on the other side of the front screen door.

"Are you Alani Lenika Hill?" the man asked.

"Yeah. Who are you?" she shot back.

"I'm Frank Williamson. I need you to sign here for the delivery of your vehicle," he said.

"Oh, Nannie, it's just my car. A friend had it towed. It died on me last night. I thought I had to pick it up from the shop, though," she said, signing the clipboard the man was holding up for her.

"No, ma'am. He paid extra for us to deliver it to this address," he said. She stepped out onto the porch.

"Where is it?" she asked.

The man pulled a Mercedes key fob from his pocket and handed it to her.

Alani looked at the man like he was crazy, and then at the key in her hand. "This is a mistake," she said.

"No mistake, ma'am, Mr. Okafor gave us very specific instructions. Have a nice day," the man said.

"First the man fixed your car for free, now he done bought you a new one," Nannie said. "It's gon' take way more than a pie to thank him for this one. Better give that boy some pussy."

"Nannie!" Alani exclaimed, before bursting into laughter.

Nannie began chuckling herself. "I'm not that old," she said. "The least you can do is cook the man a meal."

"Or… I can just give him back the entire car," Alani said. She rushed into the house and dressed, quickly, putting on jeans, an off the shoulder, button-up blouse, and strappy heels. She pulled her thick, curly hair up into a top knot, taking a tooth brush to her baby hair to lay it down. She went to the curb, admiring the E-Class Mercedes. It was beautiful but there was no way she could accept it. *Last night he acted like he didn't even want to call me. Now, this?* Ethic was impossible to read. She hopped into the car and drove to his shop. When she walked through the door, Redneck Larry's eyes widened.

"I need to see Ethic. Now," she demanded.

"Boss man isn't here," Larry replied.

"Well, get him on the phone, please, because I'm not leaving until I see him," she said. She sat down in one of the chairs and crossed her arms, impatiently, as Larry made the call. The old, white man wanted no problems with Alani. He had gotten all her black girl attitude before, and it was too much for him to handle. He would let the owner deal with her.

Alani waited, impatiently, because she had a test to take. It had already been an hour. If she waited much longer, she wouldn't make it to class on time. She stood. "Do you know how much longer he'll be?" she asked.

"He didn't say, ma'am. I can try him again," Larry offered.

"Can I just have his contact info? I have somewhere I have to be, but I really need to speak with him," she said.

"I can't give out that information, ma'am," Larry replied.

He's insane. He buying me cars and I don't even have his phone number, she thought.

Alani sighed. "Fine," she said. She placed the key to the Mercedes on the counter top. "Can you let him know that I left his car key here?" She checked her phone. She had 40 minutes to get to class and it was only about a mile and a half away. She had already missed the bus, and if she waited for the next one, she would be late. She stormed out and started her walk up the block. If she knew she would be walking, she wouldn't have worn heels. Her feet throbbed along the way, as she second-guessed returning the car. Her phone rang, and she pulled it out of her tote to see a number she didn't recognize.

"Where are you?"

She recognized the voice, instantly. She smiled, as she thought, *he called.* Never mind that he didn't sound pleased and that he hadn't even bothered to greet her with hello. She now had his number in her possession to reach out to him when she wanted.

"I'm headed Downtown. I have a class at U of M in 30 minutes. I couldn't wait all day for you. The key to the car is at the shop. I'm not for sale and I don't want to feel like I'm pressured to throw you some pussy just because you bought it for me. I'd rather just not take it," she said.

She heard Ethic's hard sigh. She was making him angry. The thought of her walking perturbed him. "Where are you, exactly?" Ethic asked, his tone cross.

"North Saginaw and Pierson," she said, calling out the intersection that she was passing.

"Stay your ass right there," Ethic stated.

He hung up on her and she looked at the phone in shock. *Who does he think he is?* She thought. Sure, his bossiness was kind of sexy, but Alani didn't take kindly to men telling her what to do, especially, a man who wasn't even *her* man. She kept walking, but it wasn't long before she saw his black truck drive up, cutting her off as he pulled, recklessly, in front of her. She folded her arms, as he rolled down the passenger window.

"Get in the car." That was an order. There was no nicety about it.

"No thanks," she said, as she walked around the front of his Range Rover and kept it pushing down the block. She hated men like him, who threw money at her problems to try to impress her. It was arrogant. Extravagant gifts were usually given by inadequate men. There was always an exchange of dignity when men used money to gain favor with women. She would one day be in a position where he expected her to return the favor, and Alani didn't want to get caught in that trick bag. She didn't want to put miles on her pussy just to pay him back for something she didn't ask for in the first place. She would rather just say no and walk away. She heard Ethic's door close, and she turned, as he stepped out the truck. Her heart raced, as she took him in. He wore casual, black slacks, perfectly-tailored, a black, button-down shirt, cognac-colored loafers with Red Bottom soles, and a camel trench coat that he left open, revealing the Burberry checkered print inside. The two, diamond chains he wore around his neck were tasteful, not gaudy, as the sun danced in each stone, while he walked towards her with conviction. His expression was stern, as if he was trying his hardest to keep his cool. Everything he had on his body was worth more than Alani had in her bank account, but she could tell he wasn't being flashy. This was his everyday lifestyle. Even when she had caught him at the trucking center and repair shop he owned, he was dressed in impeccable taste, getting designer clothes greasy and dirty like it didn't take the average person months to afford shit like that. Ethic just existed on a different level than others around him; and not because he was trying to impress, but because certain men just lived certain ways. Where was he going and why did he look so damn good? Ethic held out his hands. "You're that stubborn where you can't accept a ride?" he asked. He was filled with irritation, impatience, and a bit of intrigue, as he stood in front of her, staring down at her. He wasn't used to people defying him.

"My feet work just fine," she said.

Ethic held out his hand for her to proceed. "You want to walk, let's walk," he said.

"You're going to walk me all the way Downtown?" she asked, doubtfully.

"If that's what it takes," he said. He looked down at her feet. "Or you can rest your feet in the car and let me take you. It would be much more convenient for us both."

Alani rolled her eyes, as she shifted in her heels. Her feet *were* on fire. As stubborn as she wanted to be, she knew she would be nursing blisters if she strolled the rest of the way.

"Fine," she said, as she headed toward the truck. He walked her to the passenger side and opened the door for her.

"Stubborn-ass," he whispered, with a smirk, as she passed him.

"All this because you don't want me walking?" Alani asked.

"All this because you got a hard head. This is Flint. This same block just got lit up two days ago," Ethic replied. "Buckle up."

He got in the car and headed toward the local college. "I'll take you to class and pick you up to take you back to the shop to grab the car. You're keeping it, it's not up for discussion."

"It's a Benz, Ethic. I can't accept that. I don't know what type of woman would accept that from a man she just met. That's out of my price range. I can't pay you back for that, so even if it's a loan, I can't accept it."

"It's not a loan, it's a gift. I saw a need. I filled it."

Alani scoffed. "Listen. I have a leaky roof, blood-stained floors, a light bill that's past due, a furnace that needs replacing, and $20 worth of food in my freezer that I have to make stretch until the next time I get paid, and you want me to drive a $60,000 car? Where am I supposed to park it? In the middle of my hood? I guarantee it'll be on four bricks by tomorrow morning. Based on the type of woman I saw you with last night, I know these are the types of gifts you're used to buying, but it's not required to get to know me. I can handle my own. If I need a car, I'll buy it myself when I can afford it. Until then, the bus works just fine. I've been taking it all my life and not a hair is out of place. I'm anything but high-maintenance." They arrived at Alani's school. "You don't have to fix my life, Ethic. I just really enjoy when you're in it. It's about the only thing I enjoy these days."

"What time are you out?" he asked.

Alani smiled and shook her head. "I said all that and you're just not going to acknowledge it?"

"We're no longer discussing that. Now that I know what else you need, I'll work on that for you too. Your car is safe in your neighborhood. Word already touched down that you're protected," he said.

Protected? Who the hell is this man? She thought, as she wondered how he had the power to make that type of call.

"Now, what time you want me here to pick you up?" he asked.

"Four o' clock," she responded. She got out the truck and looked back at him. "You sure you want to do this?"

"What's that?" he asked.

"Whatever this is that you're doing? You don't do the girlfriend thing, so what is this? I just don't understand this level of generosity. We're not having sex, you barely know me, but you want to do all this nice stuff for me. What are we calling it?"

"You need a definition for it?" Ethic asked.

"It would be nice to just know," she responded, genuinely confused.

"Let's call it friendship," Ethic replied.

She smiled, and to his surprise it reached her eyes, brightening them, briefly, before they went dark again. "Okay, but just so you know... I'm the type of friend that'll slap hoes for trying to be your friend too. I'm jealous and I'm selfish, Ethic."

Ethic laughed aloud, something he rarely did; something that only his past loves, Raven and YaYa, had made him do before. "Noted."

Ethic drove away, headed to Bella's school. It was where he had been on his way to when he got the call from Redneck Larry. He hadn't meant to drop everything for Alani. She was making the car a much bigger deal than what it was. Sixty thousand was nothing for him - just a drop in a bucket of

185

money. When he had purchased it with cash, he told himself that he owed her. He had taken something from her that no amount of charity could replace. She didn't know that he was trying to ease his guilt, and he liked to think that was his only motive, but every time he was in her presence he just felt healed. Alani made him feel like a whole man, like she had the power to glue his fragmented heart back together. When he left her, the hurt reverted all over again; and as he pulled away from the college campus, he felt her energy fade from the car. The greater the distance between them, the less he felt her. This was a dangerous game he was playing, being this close to two murders he had committed. He would have to tread lightly, his freedom and his future depended on it.

Ethic arrived at the school and stepped out of the car, his determined strides filled with anxiety, as he headed directly to the front office. As soon as he stepped inside, he saw Bella, sitting slouched in the chair, her arms folded across her school uniform.

"Hey, baby girl. What's going on?" he asked.

"Mr. Okafor. Welcome." He turned toward the voice to see the principal standing behind the countertop. "I'd like to speak with you and Bella in my office."

He felt blindsided, as he looked to his daughter, searching her face for answers. She wouldn't look him in the eyes, but she hopped up from her seat and followed the principal into her office.

"Mr. Okafor, we've been having some issues with Bella, lately. Her grades have declined, drastically, this semester. She's failing almost every class. This is odd for her, because as you know, she's had straight A's until now. I've spoken to her teachers and they are all very concerned. You see, Bella is scoring in the 99th percentile on all standardized tests, so she knows the material, but she isn't turning in any assignments. She's also disrespectful in class, talking a lot while my staff is trying to teach, and today, we caught her and a group of girls skipping out of first period. They were behind the bleachers on the football field when they should have been in class. She's in the sixth grade. She'll be going to middle school next year. It's important that we iron this out before then," the principal said. "The choices you make, Bella, are starting to become more important. You're a smart, young woman and I just want to help you work out whatever is bothering you. Is there anything going on at home? Any changes that we should know about here at school?"

Ethic waited for Bella to respond. He had no idea that she was falling behind in school, so he needed answers too. Bella provided none. He saw so much anger, as she sat there, refusing to look at him, refusing to speak at all. Ethic sighed and looked at the principal.

"I'll speak to her and address the issue. It's important to me that she stays focused. You will see an immediate change in her effort and attitude." Ethic turned his attention to Bella. "Right?"

"Yes, sir," she whispered.

It was in these moments that Ethic wished there was a woman in their lives to help him navigate through parenthood. He could reign over businesses, run illegal enterprises with some of the most dangerous people in the world, and run the streets of Flint with ease, but raising children alone was his greatest challenge of all. Morgan was still giving him a run for his money and she was grown now. It seemed Bella's time for rebellion had come and he wasn't prepared for it. Eazy was the only one cutting him some slack.

Ethic turned back to the principal. "I'm going to sign her out for the rest of the day. She'll be back in class tomorrow," he informed.

The woman went into her desk and pulled out a flyer to hand to Ethic. "I don't normally do this, but I realize you're a single father. Bella is a young girl and she's in a transitioning stage of her life. There is a debutante ball at my church. It's for young ladies in the community. You don't have to be a member. I think it would be good for her to participate. It's sort of a ceremony to celebrate her growth and maturation. The first meeting is in a few weeks."

He took the flyer and nodded. "She'll be there," he said. "Thanks for your time." He stood and escorted Bella out of the school. He was angry, confused, but most of all concerned. They didn't break the silence until they were inside his truck.

"What's going on, baby girl?"

"Nothing is going on," Bella snapped.

Ethic grit his teeth, as he looked out his window. He couldn't even put his truck in drive because his heart was wrenched inside his chest.

"Bella..."

"I'll start turning in my homework, okay? It's not a big deal. It's not like you care, anyway. You're too busy worrying about Mo to even notice me," Bella mumbled.

And there it was, the true root of the problem. Bella was jealous of the time he put into Morgan. He knew he had overcompensated with Morgan over the years, but he never thought how it would affect his own children. Bella was his first born, his baby girl. He had tried hard to make Morgan feel the same love that he, organically, produced for Bella. Perhaps, he hadn't poured into them as equally as he had intended.

"Bella, just because I love Mo doesn't mean I love you less. You are my daughter - blood born. The first person who taught me what forever felt like. You and I have a bond that no one can ever break. I love you each, equally, and I know

I've given Mo a lot of attention because she was deaf and because she lost her parents and we all lost Raven. I'm sorry, baby girl, if I dropped the ball somewhere, but while I was loving her extra, it was only to make her feel like she got as much as you. You know that I love you, right?" he asked.

"Yes," she whispered. "It's just always about her; and I love Mo too, it's just sometimes I want it to be about me."

Ethic could see the hurt in her and it tugged at him the hard way. She didn't even know that everything he did was about her…for her.

"I'll do better," he promised. "But I need you to do better in school. If you have a problem, you come to me. I'm your father. You can always talk to me about how you feel. Even if you think I'll be upset, you come to me. About anything, Bella."

She nodded.

Ethic held out his hand. "Cell phone," he said. She sighed, as she reached down into her Gucci backpack and held it out for him. He slipped it inside the inner pocket of his trench coat. "You'll get it back when you make up all the homework you've been skipping."

She blew out a breath of frustration and stared out the window.

"Are you upset with me? Or are you upset with yourself for making bad decisions? I've always told you that your voice matters. If you feel a type of way, say it. Let it out, because when you hold it in, you act out in other ways and it leads to consequences like this. Now, how about we spend the rest of the day together, you and me? We'll go to Ocean Prime and then we'll hit the bookstore, so you can start playing catch up on your work, without Eazy bugging you."

"Okay," she agreed.

Ethic pulled away from the school, knowing he wouldn't make it back to pick Alani up on time. He liked to be a man of his word, but he couldn't keep two promises. If he had to choose, Bella trumped all. He pulled out his phone and sent a text to Messiah, hoping his young bull could pick up the slack.

***

"Why the fuck does she want to meet here?" Morgan whispered, as she pulled up to Berston Field House and noticed that the parking lot to the recreational center was jam packed. She didn't even know why she had agreed to meet Nish. She wasn't feeling her, lately, but after receiving a long apology text from her best friend, she had decided to at least hear Nish out. She had barely spoken to her at her surprise dinner the other night, and Morgan knew she would eventually have to clear the air between them. They had known each other for too long to let a man come between them. Right? That's what good friends promised to never do - let dick divide what had taken years to build. Morgan was feeling Messiah, but she hadn't heard from him since his pop up a few nights ago. Ethic was standing in their way, placing restrictions on who she could and couldn't see, and she knew it was unlikely that Messiah would defy that. A crush wasn't worth losing a lifelong friend, so she tucked her pride and forced herself out the car. She made sure to turn her location on her phone off, so Ethic wouldn't see that she was within the city limits. Berston was a popular spot for pick-up basketball games that got out of control. Many bullets had rung out after the crowd had gotten too rowdy. She just hoped it didn't happen today. It was her first day out the house, since getting her implants turned on, and she hoped she wasn't biting off more than she could chew.

Morgan climbed out her car and, instantly, drew attention from some of the fellas that loitered in the parking lot. Her leather leggings were skin-tight, showing off her beautiful figure and the lace, cropped camisole she wore revealed her toned middle. She toned down her sexy with a duster that read, REAL GUCCI, in graffiti writing. Black, Valentino, block-heeled, combat boots finished her look. She had taken out her braids and her real hair fell to her shoulders, in a flawless silk press. She wrestled with the wind as it blew the style all out of place on her way to the door. Nish waited inside, thumbing through her iPhone, as Morgan approached. Morgan tapped her on the shoulder. Nish looked up, smiling.

"Hey, boo!" Nish's greeting was genuine. "You look good!"

"I started not to meet your ass," Morgan said, truthfully. She could barely hear herself in the loud building, so she didn't know how she sounded. She was still getting used to her own voice. A look of shock covered Nish's face because she had never heard her speak before.

"I'm so happy for you, Mo. Seriously. This has been such a long time coming for you," Nish said. "I didn't realize how much I missed you, until I saw you the other night. I didn't even know you were having surgery. I don't want to fight with you, but I really do like Messiah, Mo. Why do I have to choose?" Nish said.

Choose? According to him, you're nothing to him, Morgan thought. Somebody was lying, and Morgan grew heated thinking of all the things Messiah had said to her the other night in his car.

"So, y'all *are* together?" Morgan asked.

"I've spent every night with him for the past month. Of course," Nish answered. "But I don't want you to be mad at me, Mo. I know you liked him, but he approached me, he pursued me, and it was just a crush to you. I didn't' think it would be such a big deal, especially, not something we'd fall out over. He is one of Ethic's workers and I knew you would never go there; but still, I should have talked to you before I started talking to him. It was fucked up and I'm sorry."

"And were you sorry when you left me at the motel that night? They raped me, Nish," Morgan whispered, sharply, her face contorted in pain from the memory. She shook her head, as if she could shake the entire episode away.

"I was high and drunk and so stupid, Mo. I passed out that night, and by the time I came to the next morning, my panties were gone, and I was bleeding down there. I don't have anyone to run and tell, so I just didn't say anything, and then I heard Lucas was killed," she whispered. "I've been dealing with my own shit from that night, Mo. We haven't talked, so I couldn't tell you," Nish said. "Messiah came along at the right time and distracted me. You not the only one going through stuff, Mo."

Morgan's mind was spinning and the emotion she saw in Nish's eyes made her more sympathetic. She didn't know whose side of the story to believe. Nish's version was backed up by months of social media posts and pictures she had taken in Messiah's house and car. The more she thought about it, the angrier she became.

"Look, can we just go in here and have a good time, like we used to?" Nish asked.

Morgan felt foolish. She nodded, giving Nish a halfhearted smile, before walking into the gym. When she saw Messiah on the court, her temperature rose even more. He was shirtless, revealing a large tattoo of praying hands that spanned across every muscle in his back and fused into the sleeve tattoo covering his entire, right shoulder and arm. Even his hands were covered in ink. Sweat made his body shine, as he worked his opponents on the court, not caring that he was scuffing the Retro Jordan's that covered his feet. His groupies were out in full effect as the packed gym reacted to the three-point jump shot he had just put up. Morgan and Nish sat on the bottom bleacher closest to the court. When Messiah and his crew were on defense, he came running past them, his eyes falling on Morgan. It was like he picked her out of the crowd, instantly, as if his sole purpose was to find her. His eyes burned into hers and she looked away, completely pissed. She avoided looking at the court the entire game.

"Yo, baby girl, you in my seat."

Morgan looked up at the handsome, six-foot, caramel-skinned man that stood in front of her. His Cartier shades, navy, Tigers baseball cap with the white 'D', and gold link chains that rested against his fitted, white V-neck, screamed Detroit. He had soft eyes with hard features, including three tear drop tattoos on the side of his face.

"I didn't know there was assigned seating," she shot back, as she raised an eyebrow in challenge. She, clearly, wasn't moving.

He licked his lips and grabbed the edges of his cap, making her notice his tattooed forearms. He was her type, if she ever had a type, but she kept her face unaffected, not revealing her intrigue. She glanced back out onto the court, letting him know she wasn't releasing the seat. Messiah was burning a hole through her, as he tried to assess the situation and keep his eye on the play. She could practically see the steam rising from him, when the guy bent down to whisper in her ear.

"Yo, beautiful, you gon' make me stand or you gon' share the seat? You're more than welcome to sit on my lap and watch the rest of the game," he said. Morgan stood.

"You can have your seat back," she said. She felt his hands on her waist, as he pulled her down on top of him.

Her eyes were on Messiah, his eyes were on her, as he cut one hand across his neck, letting the other players on the court know the game was over.

She tried to stand, but Detroit pulled her back down, "Relax, baby girl, I don't bite," he said. She didn't think he did, but she knew Messiah's bite was vicious. She watched Messiah make his way over to the sideline. He slipped a shirt over his head, never taking his eyes off her. She held his stare as well, all the while entertaining Detroit. *He want to play games, he can watch me with the next nigga then,* she thought, as she smiled in Detroit's face. Messiah passed his duffel to one of his little soldiers and then walked across the court, slapping hands with a few fellas he knew, on his way over to her. Morgan smirked at his cockiness. He didn't rush to intervene, instead he sent her warning shots in the form of intense stares. If he made it all the way across the court and she was still seated in homeboy's lap, it was going to be a problem. She knew it and yet, she didn't budge.

"I'd love to take you out sometime," the guy said.

Before she could answer, Messiah stood in front of them, glaring at her. Nish stood and went to hug him, but he snatched his arm away.

"We got a problem?" he asked. The question was intended for Detroit, but he was staring directly at her. Normally, Morgan wouldn't have caused a scene, but she was livid with him.

"It's whatever," Detroit said, as he lifted Morgan from his lap and stood, pulling his shirt up to reveal a pistol that rested on his hip. Detroit had no bitch in him, but Messiah was a fucking menace. He grabbed Detroit by his neck with one hand and snatched the pistol from Detroit's waist with the other.

"Messiah!" Nish screamed, but he was already on 10. Messiah had Detroit wedged between the bleachers and was pistol-whipping him with the man's own gun. Messiah's crew was off the court, ready to curl triggers, if any other Detroiters felt the need to intervene. Messiah stood, leaving the guy bloodied and looking for his teeth in the stands.

Morgan was horrified, but oddly turned-on, as she watched Messiah pass the burner to one of his goons.

He snatched her arm, practically dragging her out the gym. When they were in the hall, he backed her against the wall and pointed a stern finger in her face.

"I told you I only know one way to be, Mo," Messiah said. "Every nigga that you entertain, I'm using for target practice. You gon' have a lot of mamas out here pulling out black dresses."

"Why?" she asked. She was so mad that she signed and spoke the words at the same time. "Why you mad, Messiah? You fucking with Nish, anyway. You forgot to mention that you've been spending every night with her for the past few months. What you want to bag best friends? You want another notch on your belt? Got us out here fighting, while you finessing us both!"

"For one, I don't need no more notches on my belt. You big and bad, so I'ma be straight with you. I'm not starving for pussy. It's a hundred bitches in there I can play eenie, meenie, miney, mo with and fuck anytime. I told you I don't fuck with your homegirl. She work in the trap, but that bitch is canceled."

Morgan rolled her eyes. "The trap? You spending nights with her and you want me to believe it's all business? You're a liar, Messiah."

"I stay all night because I don't trust that bitch with my product, but she got a golden wrist, so I watch her like a hawk. That's the extent of my dealings with her, but you want to let her play mind games with you and get you riled up," Messiah thundered. "This the same bitch that put you on IG when them niggas ran a train on you. That ain't your friend; and today you showed me why I can't be your man. I'ma get locked up fucking around with you." He pulled in a deep breath, calming himself, because he knew he was going too far. He was starting to say things that were too harsh, things he didn't mean. He closed his eyes and pressed his forehead against hers, trying to stop himself from kissing her. He had just made it known to half the city that he was fucking with her. It was too late to backpedal now. Morgan waited for him to kiss her. She silently begged him to close the space between their lips, but she could see he was struggling. When she saw that he was about to walk away, Morgan threw caution to the wind. She kissed him, making the first move, as he wrapped one hand around her throat, gently, as he kissed her deeply. She wouldn't be surprised if there was a puddle at her feet. That's how wet he made her. She had kissed boys her age before, but this was a grown-ass man. The way he commanded her, the way she felt his anger transfer into her, the way he fisted her hair, fucking up her silk press as he fed her his tongue, it was unlike anything she had ever felt before. Isa and the rest of his crew emerged from the gym.

"Five-oh!" Isa announced, letting Messiah know the police had been called. Messiah pulled away and grabbed her hand, as she was rushed out of the field house. He spotted her car and tucked her safely inside it. "Go home," he said, closing her driver side door and patting the roof of the car, before she drove off.

Messiah rushed to his bike, threw on his helmet and rode off with Isa and his crew. When his built-in Bluetooth rang in his ear, he spoke, "Answer." The call connected.

As he hit 80 mph down the city street, Ethic's voice streamed through his helmet. "You never responded to my text, did you handle that?" he asked.

Messiah's phone had been in his gym bag all day. He had been balling all day and hadn't checked his messages yet. "Nah, big homie, I been at Berston. What's good? You need me, just say the word," he said.

"Nah, it's alright, I can handle it," Ethic replied.

"I need to pull up on you about something tomorrow," Messiah said.

"Come by the house in the morning," Ethic instructed.

"Bet," Messiah finished. He knew a conversation about Morgan was long overdue. He wasn't with the sneaking around; and if he was going to be running up on niggas in the street over her, she had to be his to defend. It was time for him to sit down with Ethic and lay out his cards like a man.

Chapter 14

Alani checked her watch. "Where are you?" she whispered, as she stood inside the lobby of the English department, her eyes constantly fretting over to the pick-up lane outside. Ethic was over an hour late and she had already missed the last bus. Her phone was dead, and she was beginning to wonder how she was supposed to make it home. He didn't seem like the type to flake, but as the two-hour mark approached and the sun began to set, she wondered if she should just start the long walk home. Anxiety filled her, as she tried to occupy her time. When she, finally, saw the head lights to his Range pull into the parking lot, she sighed in relief, but her impatience was, instantly, transformed into anger.

She marched out of the building on fire.

"You're incredible, you know that? I've been waiting here for you for two hours!" she exclaimed, as she stormed toward his car. When she saw the passenger door open and Bella hop out, she paused dead in her tracks.

"I got held up. My apologies, Alani," he said.

"No," she corrected. "You and I are back on Lenika status," she said, as she climbed inside the car. She turned toward the backseat where Bella had moved to. "Hi. Bella, right?" she asked. "It's really nice to see you again," she said, with a smile.

"Nice to see you too, Alani," Bella returned.

"Oh, so she can call you Alani?" Ethic asked.

She cut her eyes at him. "She can, you can't," she said, as she crossed her arms.

"You know, if you would have just taken the car, we wouldn't even be dealing with this right now," Ethic stated, as he rubbed his goatee, smirking at how quickly he was able to rub it in her face.

"You know what? I think you owe me dinner for making me wait," she said. "And I may be modest when it comes to gifts, but when it comes to food, I accept only the best." Her smile let him know that all was forgiven.

"No greasy diner food for you?" Ethic shot back.

"I'll take J. Alexander's, thank you very much," she replied.

"What do you think, Bella? You up for dinner?" Ethic asked.

"I didn't mean tonight," Alani said. "I have to work! I'm just saying," she paused, as she looked out the window. She felt comfortable with him, and demanding dinner was just an excuse to see him again. "Soon."

"Soon," he assured.

He pulled up to his shop and she hesitated before getting out.

"The key is in the car," he informed, nodding toward her new whip. "Good night, Lenika."

"You can stick to Alani... for now," she said, as she climbed out. "Good night, Bella."

"Good night," Bella returned.

The door closed, and Bella looked at her father. She saw a look in his eyes that she didn't recognize. "Daddy, what's wrong?" she asked.

"Nothing, baby girl," he said, as he put his car in drive. *Everything,* he thought, being honest only with himself.

***

Ethic sat at his desk, looking at the pictures of the little boy that he pulled from the envelope. He smiled, as he thought of the woman who had sent them to him. YaYa had been a woman he loved once. He had thought she was carrying his child, but come to find out, it belonged to her husband; and though disappointed, Ethic knew that was best. She still wrote him sometimes, following his instructions of old-school letters, so that he could have something to keep of her. She always concluded it with a kiss, and he fingered the red, lip stain at the end of the letter, remembering the way her lips felt against his. They were friends and always would be. He would body something, if she ever needed him, but she wasn't his. She belonged to another man. He wrote a check out to her for $5000. He would keep sending them every month, just to make sure she was straight. Ethic was just solid like that. He hadn't loved many, but those he had, he liked to take care of, even if he no longer had a place in their lives. A knock at the door caused Ethic to fold the letter and place the pictures in his desk drawer.

"Come in," he said, as he stood and walked to the window that overlooked his backyard. He had built a comfortable life for his family. As he watched Bella swing Eazy around before tossing him in a huge pile of leaves in the backyard, he scoffed. Morgan stood near them, snapping pictures on her phone, and he admired the sight of the trio. They were carefree. They knew nothing about surviving or going without. Morgan had a brief history of struggle, after her parents died, but he had done all he could to make up for whatever damage that time had caused. They were his life, his purpose, but they were growing up. Morgan was a young woman and he was sure he would be losing her to the world soon. She would want to stretch her wings and fly. The thought of Bella being not too far behind her saddened him. Eazy, he had more time with; but eventually, they all would leave, and he had no queen to share his castle with after they were gone.

"Lily let me in."

Ethic turned to Messiah and motioned for him to take a seat. "You drinking something?" Ethic asked.

"Nah, I'm good, fam," Messiah said. "It's quiet than a muthafucka around here. Where Eazy at?"

"He's outside with Mo and Bella," Ethic said, with a chuckle. "He'll be upset if you don't holla at him before you leave."

"I don't know, OG, I might not be welcomed here after I say what I got to say," Messiah said.

Ethic leaned back in his seat, staring, intently, at Messiah. "I already know what you're here to say. Word got back to me about your stunt at Berston. You broke the nigga nose and knocked out his teeth," Ethic stated. "You want to explain that? Or you want me to tell you what I think?"

Messiah knew that Ethic didn't ask questions without already having the answers, so instead, he said, "I'm not coming in here on no disrespect, fam. I've kept my distance, but the first word she said was my name, OG. That's like a man hearing his child say 'dada' for the first time. She's mine. I ain't even want her to be mine either. I was keeping my distance, out of respect, but when I saw a nigga talking fly in her ear, I just reacted."

"I get that. I've been there; but let me tell you something about Morgan Atkins. She's not yours. She's mine. I feed her, I clothe her, I stayed up all night with her when she was sick, I held her to my chest when she cried, and chased away the boogie man under her bed when she was scared. You think coming in here for permission makes it better?" Ethic asked.

"I ain't no Romeo type of nigga. I know I'm rough around the edges. I ain't no college boy. I'm in the streets heavy and I love that shit. I know I'm not who a father would want for his daughter, and I know that's what she is to

201

you…your daughter, but that girl make me feel something, OG. You know better than anybody that I don't feel shit. Not for my mama, not for my daddy, not for kids with cancer, none of that shit moves me. Mo moves me. She give me this tender feeling in the middle of my chest."

"Do you love her? If you love her, you got to be a man and tell me you love her. You doing all this dancing around. Square up with me. Tell me straight what it is. Do you love her?" Ethic stated. He was angry. Messiah was as thorough as they came, but he wasn't what Ethic wanted for Morgan.

"I think I do," Messiah stated.

"Do you know how her sister, Raven, died?" Ethic asked.

Messiah shook his head.

"I know you don't, because I can never speak truthfully about how she lost her life. It's a part of my past that I've lied about so many times that I've started to believe it. I tell people she died giving birth, because I like to think it sounds noble, like she was a mother who sacrificed her life while bringing life into the world. Other times, I just say she was sick. People don't ask about shit like cancer. I think of any lie to tell to avoid the truth. The lies paint a prettier picture. People don't pry too much when they understand why a girl died so young. The truth is, my love for Raven is what killed her. I called the play that ended her life. I killed the girl I loved." Ethic grit his teeth, as his nostrils flared. "She was with a bad nigga. I thought I had to protect her from him, help her escape from him. He used to put hands on her. I never understood how a man could destroy beauty the way he did. So, I intervened. I took her for myself. I always loved her, but she was a lot like Morgan: sheltered, naïve, spoiled," Ethic stopped to chuckle, as he stood and went back to the window to watch over the three people he cared for most. "She got pregnant with Eazy, but she was so afraid of him, she went back. She gave birth to my son, while she was living with him. She told me he wasn't mine. She lied. She named him after her father, and as an ode to me, gave him my middle name. Benjamin Ezra Atkins. I changed it to Okafor years later. I still remember the day she called me to come get her. She was terrified. I could hear it in her voice when she begged me to come. I decided right then that the nigga she was with had to die. I put word in the street that there was a ticket on his head. I couldn't have known that she would use his car to come meet me. We were supposed to leave Flint. We were so close. We were supposed to have a life together; but instead, I saw the men I hired spray the Audi she was driving. It was a miracle that Eazy survived because he was in the back seat of the car. She died because I ordered an execution and I haven't been the same man since. Men like us aren't built for the good girls. It always ends badly."

"And Morgan is a good girl," Messiah stated, somberly.

"That she is," Ethic agreed. He turned to Messiah and handed him a letter. Messiah read the heading. It was from Michigan State University. "She got in. They're willing to allow her to come mid-semester. If you love her, walk away."

***

Rehashing his truth had Ethic zoned out. He had soaked up love from his trio, sending Lily home early, so that he could spend time with them. After they were all asleep, he had the overwhelming urge to see...her. Alani Lenika Hill. The woman whose life he had changed for the worst. He needed to lay eyes on her. When he walked into the diner it was empty, just like the first time he had patronized it. Alani sat at the bar, curly hair twisted out and big around her tired face. Her bags told him she wasn't sleeping, and he knew he was the cause. He had stripped her of her peace, and it was something he had to add to his list of things to mourn. "Lenika," he called.

She looked up in surprise, defensive at first, but at first sight of him, her lips spread into a smile. "Alani to you," she said. "What are you doing here?"

"I'm starving," he said, and it was true. He was famished from lacking the nutrients a woman provided for a man and he hadn't realized the famine he had been in until he met her. It took all his will to keep his interactions with her in a friendly place.

"Well, let's feed you. Cheap, greasy, diner food," she quipped. She extended both her hands and motioned for the barstool. "Let me serve you, dear Sir."

Ethic wanted nothing more than for her to serve him. He needed a woman that would do so, lovingly, without feeling like he was oppressive to her independence, because in return he would be subservient too, when necessary. Her words stirred something inside him, but he knew there was no hidden meaning to them. She was just talking about food, so he slid onto the bar stool, accepting the menu she held out for him.

"I don't recommend the meatloaf. It's from yesterday," she whispered.

"I'll just take the pie. Peach," he said. She bit her lip, trapping it between her teeth, as she leaned onto the bar, standing directly across from him. He lifted his hand to release her lip with his thumb.

"Don't do that," he said, with a wink. She blushed.

"One slice of peach pie coming up," she announced. She cut him a slice herself and slid it in front of him, placing a fork on the plate as well.

"What are you going to school for?" he asked, as he noticed the books she had been reading before he had interrupted.

"Writing," she said. "I used to love it, a long time ago. After my daughter died, I sort of picked it back up. It helps me. I want to write a book one day, so I'm taking some creative writing classes."

"I can't wait to read it," Ethic responded.

"The car is beautiful. Thank you," she said. "I promise, I will pay you back. As soon as I publish my first book and strike it rich."

"If that makes you feel better about accepting it, that's a bet," he said, with a sly grin. He cut into the pie and lifted the fork to her lips. "You're looking kind of thin. Maybe you need this more than I do."

She accepted the fork between her lips and closed her eyes as she enjoyed the sweet bite. "I just don't have an appetite. I'm surviving off smoothies. My Nannie won't let me go too long without a warm meal, though. She cooks every night. There's always a plate with aluminum foil waiting for me on the stove when I get home. I may not always eat it, but it's there, so you don't have to worry about me," she said.

"And you don't sleep," Ethic said, out of observation.

"Sleep brings nightmares," she whispered. "Can I ask you something?"

"Anything," he said.

"I know why I'm sad; but why are you? I see a lot of hurt in you," she said, quietly.

"That's a story for another day," he insisted. "Let's just say, I know loss. I understand the hurt you feel."

"Have you ever buried your child?" she asked, defensively.

He was silent because he saw the flicker of anger in her eyes at his comparison of grief.

"I didn't think so. You don't know anything about my type of hurt," she said, passionately. "Nobody understands. It's like everybody just wants me to move on and I'm stuck." She cleared her throat and stood up straight, tucking her pain behind a fake smile. "I'm sorry. I don't mean to be rude to you. We barely know one another and I'm already doing too much with you. You probably think I'm a mess," she said.

"I think what you're going through is hard and you're handling it with grace," Ethic answered. "Now, about this dinner I owe you?" he asked, changing the heavy subject to something much lighter.

"I was thinking. How about you just come over and I cook for you," she proposed.

"You cook?" Ethic asked.

"Cook? I burn, okay?" Alani bragged. "What you want me to make? Some hot water corn bread? Black eyed peas? Fried chicken? Anything Southern, I got it covered." She beamed at him, as she continued. "You just let me know what you like, and you can have it."

"All that sounds legit," he said. "I look forward to it."

"Tomorrow then?" she asked.

"Tomorrow," he agreed.

***

KNOCK! KNOCK! KNOCK!

"The fuck?" Messiah grimaced, as he climbed out of bed and picked up his phone to check the time. It was 9 o'clock in the morning and Messiah was a night owl. He had just closed his eyes three hours ago and the disturbance at his front door wasn't welcomed. Nobody even knew where he lived. He hadn't stayed at his trap house last night, so he wondered who was knocking like the police so early. He reached in the nightstand beside his bed and pulled out a .45 caliber, chrome pistol, as he went to answer. He was about to send somebody's Jehovah's Witnesses straight to heaven for knocking on his shit so damn early. He pulled open the door, in irritation, his gun gripped tightly in his hand at his side.

"So, you just kiss me and then go M.I.A? You don't answer my texts, my calls…"

"Come in," he said, as squeezed the bridge of his nose and closed his eyes. He wasn't prepared for this conversation, but he knew it was inevitable. He stepped to the side, as she entered. She was livid, but as she took him in, standing before her wearing only boxer briefs, her anger waned. His body was incredible. The semi hard morning wood was downright distracting, and as her eyes drank him in, he smirked.

"You ain't ready for it, li'l girl, chill out," he said. He disappeared for a minute and returned wearing grey sweatpants. "Have a seat. What's on your mind?"

"You," she said, not wanting to lose her nerve. "All I can think about is you, Messiah."

Messiah swiped his hand over his nose and mouth, sighing. "Yeah, about that," he started. "I messed up by kissing you the other day. I don't really want to take it there with you like that, Mo. You're a cool girl, but I just ain't feeling it; you know?"

He could visibly see the effects of his words, as Morgan recoiled. She blinked rapidly, as her eyes watered. "You're lying," she whispered. "Why are you doing this?"

"Look, I ain't with the 21 questions, Mo. I don't explain myself. I just move the way I move and that's it. This is how I'm moving with it. What you still doing slumming it in Flint, anyway? You can hear now. Ain't nothing holding you back. Go to Michigan State. That's where you belong. In the real world, living life. This shit ain't for you. I ain't for you," he said. Messiah didn't want to push her away. If he was a selfish man, he would be between her legs right now, with her pearl in his mouth, swallowing her soul to convince her he was good enough, but he knew Ethic was right. If he loved her, he would let her go, set her free.

"Messiah, don't do this," she whispered, desperately, as a single tear slid down her cheek.

His gut hollowed at her sadness, but as he thought about Ethic's warning, he couldn't cave to spare her feelings. Gangsters and good girls didn't mix. He didn't want to have his actions jeopardize her and he wasn't ready to leave the game alone. He was young and thugging it, getting money hand over fist, and Morgan wasn't built for that. He would rather hurt her feelings than to give in to his own, and one day be the cause of her tragedy. It had already happened to her sister. Messiah wouldn't be the one to allow history to repeat itself.

"Messiah," she pleaded. He leaned over in his chair, resting his elbows on his knees, as his head hung in turmoil. His hands were clasped against his forehead. *Fuck, Mo,* he thought. His name on her lips was his weakness. It was the way she said it, as if she had practiced in her head a thousand times before she ever had the courage to try it aloud. These tears she cried and her pleading his name... Messiah wanted her. "Messiah!" This time, it was angry, but still she was calling him. His dick swelled, his heart thundered. God he wanted to fuck her...to love her...to keep her. He did the one thing he knew would make her go and dead all possibilities of them ever having anything together.

"I fucked Nish, Mo," Messiah said, as he lifted his head to look at her. He may as well have slapped her, the way the false confession landed like a blow to her chin. The way

her eyes fell in disappointment... It broke his heart. Every
piece of his cold heart thawed. He loved her, and if there was
any doubt before, it was gone now. Her hurt was his, but he
wouldn't take it back. It was for her own good. "Go to school,
Morgan, there's nothing left for you here." He envied a blind
man at that moment. Watching her leave was the worst feeling
of all, because this time, he knew she wouldn't return.

Chapter 15

Morgan could barely function. She was overly emotional, as she packed her things in the cardboard boxes that covered her room. She was leaving home, venturing out. Instead of the excitement she should have felt, she was forlorn. She had gone through so much to get Messiah to want her, to get him to see her, only to be rejected. He wasn't who she thought he was and her miscalculation in judgment stung.

"Mo?" She turned to see Bella standing in her doorway. "You need some help?"

"I'm about done now," Morgan replied. Bella walked over to the bed and sat down.

"It feels weird seeing you pack up," Bella said, the normal gleam in her eye missing.

Morgan could see Bella was sad. They had been together since the day they met. "Hey," Morgan said. Bella looked at her. "Sisters forever," Morgan signed. It was their thing. It was what they did when they needed each other.

Bella returned the sign. "Sisters forever."

"Now, help me get some of these boxes in the car," Morgan said.

"Why? Daddy got Messiah and Isa downstairs already to move all your stuff," Bella said.

"What?" Morgan exclaimed.

"Yep. So, we don't have to do any work," Bella stated.

Morgan gave a half smile. "I'll have plenty of work you can help me do when we get to my new place," she teased. "What you can do now is make sure Messiah and Isa don't break any of my stuff. You're in charge."

"Where are you going?" Bella asked.

"I'm going to drive ahead of everyone. I still need to sign my new lease and get my key," Morgan explained. The truth was, she was running. She didn't want to face Messiah or even be in his vicinity. She grabbed her handbag and rushed down the stairs.

"I'm headed up to sign my lease. I'll see you there!" she shouted to Ethic, as she rushed out the house.

She didn't even wait for his response. She was already out the door.

It only took Morgan an hour to get to the college town. Since she was joining so late in the year, she couldn't stay on campus, so Ethic was financing her an apartment close by. If she kept her GPA strong, he would do so until she graduated. As soon as she got her key and opened the door to her new place, all the heaviness she felt, all the sadness, all the drama dissipated. This was her chance to do something with her life and to put the ghosts that followed her in Flint to rest. She was no longer afraid to face the world by herself because she was just like everyone else. She had been through hell and back, but this felt like a chance to make a new life; one where she wasn't the poor, little, deaf orphan.

Ethic showed up first with Bella and Eazy in tow. He was nothing less than the proud father. He had raised her, and she could see he was trying his hardest to keep his emotions in check.

"This is so dope! I'm coming to visit you every weekend," Bella said, as she looked around in amazement.

"I'm going to hold you to that. I don't have any friends here, so I'm going to need your company," Morgan said, laughing.

"Where is all your furniture?" Eazy asked, as he did cartwheels in her bare living room.

"It'll be delivered sometime today," Morgan answered. "Are you going to come visit me too?"

"Mmm, hmm," he answered, as he bounced and jumped and ran around her. Morgan laughed. He never sat still, like ever, and his energy always cheered her up...at least when it wasn't working her nerves.

"Yo!" Messiah's voice made her heart drop, and she watched him enter her place without knocking, as if he, himself, were the financier. "Shorty Doo Wop, where do you want us to put your boxes?" he asked.

"You can just set them anywhere," she said, without looking at him.

"I've got to go. I've got to be back in Flint by this evening. I just wanted to come down, look around, make sure you're comfortable. If you need anything, Morgan, you call me. You understand? We're family." Ethic asked.

He was always so cautious. So serious. He worried about the well-being of everyone else constantly, but neglected himself.

"I'll be okay," she said.

He stood in front of her and looked off into the distance, as emotion caused his eyes to water. He squeezed the bridge of his nose and pulled her in to kiss the top of her head. "A'ight, Mo. Messiah and his mans will get your boxes in and get you settled. I'm going to head back."

She didn't realize how fatherly he was until he was walking out. Ethic was the man that would walk her down the aisle, who her future children would call Grandpa, and who she could always run to with her problems. He was the man she would measure every man against; and as she looked out her window, she teared up watching him and the kids walk to the car. She stepped out onto her balcony. "Ethic!" she yelled.

He looked up at her.

"I love you!"

"I love you too, baby girl!" he said, as he shot his hands up in salute.

Morgan barricaded herself in her room, while Messiah and Isa unloaded her boxes from the truck. She didn't even say thank you when they were done. She simply told Messiah to let himself out, without even looking his way.

***

Messiah made it all the way back to Flint, before he decided to turn around. He dropped his man off and then jumped right back on the highway headed back to Morgan. She had ignored him all day, and although he understood her attitude was created by him, it still affected him. He had pushed her away, and now that she was gone, he felt the impact from her resentment. She didn't bang with him at all. Whatever affection she had for him had turned to hate. He could see it. He could feel it when in her presence. He cut the hour drive in half, as he sped down the expressway. When he arrived, he didn't bother to call. He stormed straight to her door and gripped the side of the frame as he knocked hard.

She snatched it open, face bent like she was ready to cuss somebody out for the interruption, but when she saw him, she rolled her eyes as she crossed her arms across her chest.

"What you doing here? I thought you were the pizza guy," she snapped, with an attitude, as she shifted her weight on her back foot, causing her voluptuous behind to stick out of the bottom of her tiny boy shorts as her back curved in an arch.

"You answer the door like this for the pizza guy?" he asked, territorial, as he looked her up and down. Her cut-off, green sweater barely covered the bottom of her breasts, her toned stomach was on display, and half her behind was hanging out. He could see it from the front and he was steaming. Even the sight of her pretty, white, painted toes pissed him off.

"What I do is not your concern," she said. He walked into her place, without invitation, and she closed the door. "You made it crystal clear. So, if I want to order up dick with a side of special sauce and have it delivered to me, it's my business."

Messiah advanced on her, backing her up against the wall until she had nowhere to go. "Don't make me fuck none of these college boys up out here," he threatened. "I moved all these fucking boxes up here. I could have hired strangers to do that shit for you. I don't even be getting my shit dirty like that," he said, holding out his palms as he spoke. "I did it because it was you and I want to see where you rest your head, and you couldn't give a nigga a thank you."

"Excuse me?" she snapped. "I didn't ask you to move anything. I would think you were too busy putting dick in my best friend to be bothered with me," Morgan snapped.

"Man, fuck that girl! I never touched her. I said that shit, so you would come here. So you would get the fuck away from Flint and live your life, chase your dreams, shorty." Messiah said, as his eyes appreciated her entire body, roaming her from her pretty toes to her flawless, bone straight hair and lingering on all the goodies in between. His dick jumped. "Man, go put on some clothes. A nigga come to the door with a pizza and see all that, he gon' try and get it," Messiah fussed, bothered by the idea of a random man seeing her body.

"You ain't want it. Now, you don't want nobody else to have it," she snapped, her eyes ablaze in anger. She didn't even know how they had started arguing over the pizza man.

214

Messiah was crazy and jealous, but not even her man to be any of those things at all.

"I want it," Messiah conceded. He kissed her lips, soliciting a moan that she didn't mean to let escape. "Damn, I want it," he repeated, as he kissed her neck, making her head fall to the side and her eyes close.

"You said you didn't want it," she groaned.

"You know I want that shit," he whispered, as his hands roamed underneath her sweatshirt and found her nipples. They pebbled at his touch, as Morgan pulled the entire shirt over her head. His lips and tongue circled her areolas, as he went from one breast to the other. Morgan quivered.

"You don't act like you want it." Her protests were just foreplay now, because if he wanted it or not, she was giving it to him. His dick pressed into her and she whimpered, as he slid her panties to the side and lowered onto his knees.

"Let me show you," was the last thing he said before he tasted her. Morgan's back arched, as her hands wrapped around his head and he put her legs over his shoulders. Messiah's tongue was so warm that it melted her center, as he rotated his entire head in circles. He assaulted her clitoris, sucking and pulling and licking and flicking.

"Agh!" she screamed, as she rolled her hips, increasing the pressure on his tongue. She was glazing his entire face, as she frantically pushed her sex into him. It was the best thing she had ever felt. He put two, thick fingers inside her, as he hummed while eating her. Some people hummed while they ate great food. Messiah hummed when he ate good pussy. Morgan was serving him the best meal he had ever had. It was like she was feeding a starving man. He devoured her. Messiah laid her down on the floor and then pulled back her fat lips to give himself better access to her pearl. He paused, briefly, to admire it as it swelled, and her juices dripped from it.

"Damn, I want it, shorty," he growled, as he dove back in. "You taste good as fuck. I could eat this pussy all day."

A rush came over Morgan and she clenched her thighs around his head. "Wait, Messiah, wait!" she cried. She had never felt anything so intense. Her whole pussy was tender to the touch. Every time he pulled at her clit, she felt like it was a piñata, taking as many licks as it could before she would explode. He lifted her ass off the floor, his hands kneading her backside, as she rolled upward, grinding his face. When he stuck a finger in her backside, Morgan erupted. He didn't stop licking until she went limp in his arms and he lowered her back to the floor. He wiped his face with his hand and came up from between her legs. She reached for him and he kissed her. Softly. Slowly.

"That's my shit," he said, as he gripped her chin and stopped their kiss to look her in the eyes. "You hear me?"

She nodded.

"No more answering the door for the pizza man in your panties and shit," he said, as he kissed her, biting her bottom lip, gently. She laughed, as he pulled her on top of him and stared up at her.

"You know we can't tell Ethic, right?" she said, her expression fretful.

"I'll figure that part out," Messiah promised. "It just might take me some time, but not having you is no longer an option."

She reached beneath her and grabbed his dick, lifting slightly to guide herself down onto it. Her mouth fell open at his girth. Morgan was inexperienced and still so tight that it hurt a little. He flipped her on her back. "You're not ready for that," he said. He slid into her, slowly, rocking, giving her the dick inch by inch, until all 10 of him was nestled inside her. "Let me know if I'm hurting you." He stared at her, his hands on the sides of her head. "I don't want to hurt you, Mo."

She could see the worry in his eyes. His words had a deeper meaning, but she trusted him. "You could never hurt someone you love," she whispered.

He began to grind into her, the muscles in his entire body tensing, as she touched his face. She lifted her head to kiss him and he kissed her back. The flavor of her womanhood lingered on his lips. "I love you, Messiah," she whispered.

He grunted, as he fucked her slow; each stroke deeper than the one before, as if he was trying to dig his way to her soul. He didn't believe anyone could love him. Nobody had certainly ever told him, and the melody of her voice…that rasp, the sincerity. Fuck, if he didn't love her too. "Tell me again, baby," he said, as she threw her body back at him. Like waves in the ocean, crashing against one another, they rocked the boat. "Oooh," she moaned, her face twisted in an ugly pleasure, as she bit into her lip as he took control of her body. He was straddling the line between being delicate and going beast inside her. He had flirted with the idea of this night many times in his mind, but nothing was like the real thing. "I love you, Messiah," she groaned. "Fuckkkk," she screamed, as the sound of their skin meeting, slapped throughout the apartment. Her pussy sucked him in and spit him out, massaging his manhood again and again. When she had been raped, they had robbed her of her virginity, but Messiah was the first man to enter her by choice. She wished they hadn't stolen her gift before she could give it to him, because the way he was working her body over, made her never want to know what it was like to have someone else inside her ever again. "I'm cumming," she whined, as she pulled him into her, gripping his ass and locking her thighs to keep him there in her depths. He knew he should pull out. He wasn't strapped up. He was never this reckless, and he was about to press eject until her heard her say it again. "Messiah," she moaned. *This fucking girl gon' be the death of me,* he thought, realizing he had found his weakness, and in the same thought, deciding that he had to keep her hidden because there were niggas who had been searching for his soft spot for years. If it was ever discovered that she was it, she would be a target. Messiah groaned, as he planted his seeds inside of her, and then moved her hair out of her face to see that she was crying.

"I love you," he finally answered. "I've never done this before, so if I start loving you wrong, you got to let me know." She nodded. He kissed her tears away and then rolled onto his back, pulling her on top so that he could hold her. He had never wanted to be this close to a woman, never trusted them enough to stay after sex, but this was different. It scared him. That's how he knew it was real.

KNOCK! KNOCK!

"That's the pizza," Morgan said, standing up and heading to her door, naked.

Messiah stood and chased her to the door, catching her by her waist from behind, and sending her into fits of laughter. Messiah pushed her behind the door, as he smiled and opened the door, naked, dick swanging, hitting mid-thigh even when it wasn't fully erect. He was sculpted like an African king. He grabbed the pizza, roughly, from the college, pretty boy standing in front of him. "How much I owe you, homeboy?"

The light-skinned boy stammered, as he looked up instead of straight at Messiah. "T…twenty bucks," he said.

Morgan snickered behind the door, as Messiah handed her the pizza and walked over to his pants, pulling a wad of money from the pocket. He peeled off a hundred and walked back to the door to hand it to the pizza man. "Keep the change.

And ayo, if you ever come here and my girl answer the door wearing some skimpy shit, and you start thinking about trying her, remember me, my nigga. It's good, but it ain't worth dying over. Have a good night."

Morgan's laughter bellowed, as Messiah closed the door. They shared a laugh, as Morgan put the pizza on the counter. They ended the night in her kitchen, naked, as she sat on the countertop beside the box and he stood between her legs feeding her pizza. Messiah had never been so relaxed with a woman and Morgan had never been without an insecurity. She always worried about the way people saw her or how she sounded. In this room, with just the two of them, they realized that discomfort didn't exist and neither wanted the sun to rise and burst the bubble they had created.

Chapter 16

"Pastor asked me to see if you would mentor in the debutante pageant this year," Nannie asked, as she moved around the kitchen, preparing a meal fit for a king, as Alani sat at the table, writing in her journal.

Alani's pen paused, as she looked back at her aunt. "That doesn't sound like my idea of a good time. Being around all those mothers with their daughters…"

Nannie removed her silver pans from the oven and placed them on top of the stove. "Well, I already told him yes. All that money the church donated when you were in need, you better have your butt down there tomorrow morning for the rehearsal. There are a lot of girls who need mentors. Everybody don't have a mother to participate with. I'm sure whoever you get will appreciate you. And, girl, get your narrow tail up and come help me with something. You invite a man over your house for dinner and got me fixing it," she fussed. A horn honked outside, and Nannie went to grab her purse. "Now, I'm going down to the bingo hall with Mr. Larry. I'll see you later."

Alani kissed her aunt's cheek and walked her to the door. "And don't you let them biscuits burn."

"I won't," Alani called. Alani checked her watch. It was almost time for Ethic to arrive. She had cleaned her house from top to bottom, but it was only so much shining she could do to an old shoe. Her house was worn and old, but it was clean, and she hoped Ethic didn't judge her. It was clear he was used to living a certain lifestyle. He had blown $60,000 on her, without batting an eye. She didn't come from that. Spending the $60 it had taken to put together tonight's meal had been a big decision for her, and she would have to eat the leftovers for days to make up for the splurge. He was worth it, however. His friendship made her pain dull a bit; and for that, she wanted to show appreciation. When he knocked at the door, Alani checked herself in the mirror, fluffing her day-old twist out, trying to tame it a bit. She frowned because her fluffing just made it worse. She hurriedly pulled the hair tie off her arm and pineapple'd all the curls on top of her head. She hadn't had time to get super cute. She had just left class a few hours before. The long sleeve, black, maxi dress hugged her nicely, but it wasn't date material. "Good thing this isn't a date. Thank God for just friends," she whispered. This was as good as it was going to get. When she heard the bell a second time, she hurried to the door.

Ethic stood there, dapper as ever, without even trying. The cowl neck, Ferragamo sweater, dark wash, denim jeans, and Prada shoes told her this was as casual as he was going to get. He emanated grown man, even down to the scent of his cologne.

"Hi," she greeted.

"I didn't know what you drank, so I just brought wine. It's a 1999 Bordeaux," Ethic said, as he handed her the bottle.

"Considering that I drink 10-dollar Moscato, I'm sure I'll enjoy it. I'm not very hard to please," she said, smiling. "Thank you." She looked at the box he held as well.

"Can I take that for you?" she asked, unsure of what he was holding.

Ethic was distracted. He had forgotten about the box he held in his hands. It was eerie being back inside Alani's house, and his mind kept drifting back to the sight of her daughter dying in his arms. "I'm sorry. Yeah, they're for you. I don't know the rules to this new-school dating thing, so I brought these just in case it's still the thing to do." He said. He handed her the box that had the words *La Fleur* written on it in fancy script. She opened it to find the most beautiful bouquet of roses she had ever seen.

"Wow," she said. "They're so pretty. I don't think a gesture like this ever goes out of style. Thank you." She now felt guilty for not putting more effort into her look. *He said the word 'date',* she thought, suddenly anxious, as she led him to the table.

"Food smells good," Ethic said, as he took a seat. "You made all this?" He eyed the food on the stove. It had been years since he had a good, old-fashioned meal. Lily was under strict instructions to keep him and his children on a lean diet. He didn't want the generational curses of high blood pressure and diabetes to affect his family; so instead, he was very strict on what he put in his body. He would cheat tonight, however. This type of food was made with love. Alani had put in a lot of effort, from the looks of things, and a woman took pride in feeding a man.

He sat at the table, as she went to the stove to fix his plate. His eyes bounced around the room, taking in her home. It was where she was most vulnerable, where she hid the ugly parts of her from the world. How she lived would tell him things that her words would never say. Like, the fact that the carpet was spotless, told him that she was particular about people taking off their shoes. She had been polite by allowing him to wear his inside. The flourishing plants in the window told him that she had good energy because plants didn't grow around negative forces. Only light made them grow, and despite her circumstance, Alani illuminated without trying to. The way she kept her bathroom would tell him of her cleanliness, but he wouldn't snoop that far. He had discovered Dolce was trifling by just pulling back her shower curtain. Ethic didn't have those worries with Alani. He could tell from the way she kept her nails groomed, the back of her feet impeccably smooth, and the scent of almonds in her hair that she was meticulous. She sat a plate of food in front of him and then took her seat across from him. She placed a cloth napkin onto her lap.

"You're nervous," Ethic said, aloud.

Alani lifted her eyes to his. "I just don't invite people here," she said, as she looked around the kitchen, slightly embarrassed.

"Because you value your privacy or because you're ashamed?" he asked, frankly.

"I guess both," she said.

"You own this house, right?" he asked.

"Yeah," she answered. "It's nothing to write home about, though. I bought it from the land bank with a tax return when my daughter was born. I moved around a lot when I was little. My mama showed me, exactly, what not to do when I became a mother. She was a prostitute, still is probably, if she's still alive out there somewhere. We were always running out on a landlord, couch surfing with her friends, or staying with strange men. I hopped from school to school. I was always afraid because I didn't have a safe place to retreat to. I was always sleeping in somebody else's bed, eating someone else's food. I didn't want that for my daughter, so I bought this place to make sure she always had a consistent roof over her head. As you can see, my budget wasn't very big, but at least she knew that she would sleep in the same place every night."

"A small win is still a win," Ethic replied. "You own this house, this land. It's yours. There's no shame in that. If you did it with this house, you can do it with the one next door and the one next to that. Before you know it, you're a black woman with a whole block - with assets. This is the first step

223

to building wealth. That's something to be proud of. I'm sorry about your mother, by the way. That had to be tough."

"It was," she said, her eyes on her plate. "…but it made me stronger."

She focused on her plate, scooping up a bite of homemade mac and cheese because she didn't know what else to say. The conversation had gone to a heavy place, bringing up memories that she didn't dwell on often.

"How is it that you're not taken, Ethic?" she asked, as she cocked her head to the side, looking curiously at him, as she lightened the mood.

He chuckled. "It takes a lot to keep my interest. I've loved a great woman before. Not many women measure up," he said, honestly.

"Do I?" she asked.

"Do you what?" he asked.

"Measure up to this great woman?" she asked.

Ethic set his fork down. "I don't know if anybody will ever compare," he said, honestly.

"Well, you seem to really love her," Alani whispered. "She's an idiot for letting you go."

"She's dead," he admitted.

Alani dropped her fork, causing it to clang against the table, as she covered her mouth. She had been so busy fishing for compliments, trying to gauge how he felt about her, that she had neglected to see the mourning in his eyes. "I'm so sorry," she whispered. "I didn't know."

"It's fine," he assured. "She's my past. You're the present."

She smiled at that.

"Tell me about your daughter's father," he said. Ethic knew that Cream wanted smoke; and sure, he wanted to know more about the potential threat that loomed over his head, but it wasn't a great concern of his. Ethic wanted to know the history of her heart... Who had broken it and what had yet to be prepared. "Where is he?"

Alani grew uncomfortable, shifting in her seat. "He's not in the picture. He's locked up; but even before that happened, we had our problems. I loved him, and he just walked all over me. When you love someone, you give them your heart to hold, hoping they won't fumble it. You trust them to keep it safe. He didn't keep me safe. He fumbled me every opportunity he got. He cheated and lied, and like an idiot, I forgave him over and over again. The crazy part is, I'm not even that type of girl. The one to stay after I feel disrespected, but he turned me into someone I didn't recognize. I was a crazy person with him; checking phones, emails, switching cars to follow him around the city just to catch him in a lie. All to reinforce what I already knew. I began to question myself. What was I doing wrong? What were other women doing that I wasn't? It just became too much. He wasn't for me."

"And if he gets out?" Ethic pressed.

"He's getting out soon, actually," she said, confirming the information Messiah had already told him. "But he and I will never be together again. It's not happening. I'm not weak enough to go back."

Their conversation flowed from the complexities of their past to the simplicities of their preferences. Alani wasn't shy about asking 21 questions. She wanted to know everything about Ethic, even down to the most trivial things like his favorite color. She hadn't ever met a man so gentle, yet with an err of unspoken authority that told her he was masking great power. Why he would hide his gangster, she didn't know, but she was glad he didn't flaunt it. The subtly of his dominance made her like him more. He was generous, yet somehow, she knew he didn't lavish just anyone with the gift of his time or his money. How she had gotten him to come to her ghetto, little house, and break bread over what she was sure was a ghetto meal to him? She didn't know...but she was grateful for his company. By the time they finished talking, she had fed him two helpings and dessert. She stood and grabbed his plate, and he felt his dick jump, as he watched her walk away.

Behave, he thought to himself. *This ain't that.* He knew he shouldn't even be in her proximity. There was too much at stake for him to risk being this close to her, this close to the dirt he had done, but Alani was like a flame and Ethic was her moth. It wasn't the obvious things that attracted him to her. Her body was average. It was beautiful, but far from perfect, and evidence of her motherhood was present on her hips and thighs. He would bet his last that stretch marks covered her ample behind. It was exquisite, but her small waist let him know that her thickness had been a side effect of child birth. The modest, maxi dress she wore looked like lingerie wrapped around an ass like that. It sat on top of thighs that were made for wrapping around a man's back. Her waist was thin, and her face was pretty. Ethic was a man in position, so he had attracted prettier, but prettier had never attracted him. Her vibe was refreshing, it was authentic, and he was swimming in troubled waters. It was the little things about her that he appreciated. Her domesticity was refreshing to a man that lacked it. She didn't want to be on the scene, eating 100-dollar dinners. She had invited him to her home, prepared the meal herself - or so he thought - and was now putting leftovers in old, *Country Crock* bowls and using aluminum foil to cover them. She was a black woman, making shit work, and the sight of her made Ethic's dick hard. He wanted to lift her dress, take her from behind, and put babies in her because she was the type of woman that raised children well. Then, he remembered he had robbed her of that opportunity. His eyes shot to the living room floor - to the blood stains - and his guilt burdened him. He was disrespectful for even coming back. He stood.

"It's getting late," he said, as he walked up behind her, as she placed all the dirty dishes into the sink.

"Yeah, my aunt will be back soon. I guess we should call it a night," she replied. She cut off the water and turned to face him, instantly noticing his disposition had changed. He had opened up to her over the past few hours, but she could see that he had restored his guard. "I'll walk you out." She saw Ethic to the door and he went into his pocket to pull out his wallet. He opened it and removed ten $100 bills. He placed it on the hutch that sat near the door.

"To replace the money you spent on the groceries to prepare this meal. Thank you," he said.

"Ethic, that's not necessary," she declined.

"A man that have you cooking food he doesn't provide is not a man," he said. "Lock up," he instructed, bossing her around in her own home. Alani felt cheated, when he walked out without touching her. She needed his transference of energy. She was offended that he hadn't offered it; and being the big mouth that she was, she had to let him know.

"Ethic!" she shouted, as she stepped out onto her porch with bare feet.

He turned back.

"Every time you see me, I need you to touch me. It just makes everything better," she said, as she approached him.

"I can't," Ethic declined. "I won't be able to control my hands, Alani, and I can't offer you more than what I'm giving. Even this, tonight, was too much." Ethic saw no point in lying. He was running out of restraint with her.

"That's not fair. Why is this too much?" she asked. "I walk through every hour of every day feeling like I'm bleeding on the inside. It feels like I'm dying, and the only time it doesn't is when I'm with you. I'm fine with friends. I know you don't do the girlfriend thing, but I just need to feel your arms around me."

This was getting too deep. He had taken things with her too far. He could see she wanted more from him and he could handle that. What bothered him was that he wanted it too…that she soothed his ails as well…she was the anecdote that he had been searching for and he couldn't have her.

She was crying, as she walked up to him, lifting her hands to his face. She tried to touch his scars and he pulled his head away, slightly, but her gentle fingertips coaxed him to allow her free rein. She cupped his face in her hands and then closed the space between them, sliding her hands around his shoulders, as he wrapped her in his embrace. She rested her forehead against his chest, as she lowered her head, closing her eyes. *God, this man is energy,* she prayed. *Please, help him let me in.*

"I've got to go," he whispered.

She stepped back and nodded, before rushing into her house, because the last thing she wanted to do was watch him leave.

***

"Do I have to go?" Bella complained. "I made up all the work I missed. I haven't skipped any classes. I swear it won't happen again, Daddy. Please, don't make me go to this."

"You're going, Bella. End of discussion," Ethic stated. Ethic knew that his daughter needed female mentorship, and participating in the church's debutante pageant would give her that opportunity. He was a man. There were certain things he couldn't help her with; and with Mo out the house, he didn't want Bella to have to figure it out on her own. He had to provide connections to women he could trust. If that meant going to church, then so be it.

"We don't even go to church," she moaned.

"It won't be that bad, Bella. Just give it a chance," he said.

She didn't speak with him the entire ride, but it didn't change his mind. As a single father, his worst fear was to have Bella be lead astray due to his lack of guidance, so he felt this was necessary. He climbed out the car and then walked around to open the door for her, before leading her inside.

"I'm not even going to know anyone here. All the girls probably go to this church and already know one another," she mumbled.

They followed the sounds of voices into the sanctuary and Ethic grabbed Bella's hand to lead her over to a woman that looked like she was in charge.

"Good morning. How can I help you?" the woman asked, as she smiled. "I'm Alicia White."

"Ezra Okafor, and this is my daughter, Bella," he introduced. Bella gave a tight-lipped smile.

"Nice to meet you both. We're happy to have you participating this year, Bella," the woman said. She grabbed a piece of paper off the front pew and handed it to Ethic. "This is the list of rehearsal dates. There are only two. You'll be required to wear an all-black suit for the father and daughter dance. Bella is required to wear a white, floor-length gown. Bella's mother will need to also wear white for the mother-daughter portion of the ceremony."

"I don't want to be in this pageant!" Bella said, as tears filled her eyes. "Can we just go, already?" Bella was emotional and turned to storm off, but Ethic grabbed her by the wrist and pulled her into his chest.

"Did I say something wrong?" the woman asked.

"We lost her mother when Bella was younger," Ethic stated, in a low tone, as he kissed the top of Bella's head.

"Oh, baby, I'm so sorry," the older woman said. "But, baby, you have to participate. You are in God's house and his angels are watching. I'm sure your mother would love to see you dressed up and taking this passage into womanhood. We have mentors who volunteer to participate with the girls who don't have their mother's in the picture."

Bella was sobbing, and he felt her shaking, as he held her. The chatter from the other girls and mothers across the room ceased, as they all focused their attention on Bella. It was then he realized he was the only man in the room. Every other girl had a woman present, supporting them. Ethic could provide and had provided a lot for Bella over the years, but nothing could make up for being a motherless child. She bolted from the sanctuary and Ethic turned to the woman. "I'm sorry," he said, before going after his daughter.

As soon as he made it to the hallway, he was shocked at the sight before him. Alani stood there, holding Bella, as she cried hysterically on her shoulder. Confusion, empathy, and hurt resonated in Alani's eyes, as she looked up at him.

"Shh," she whispered, as she caressed Bella's head, gently. Ethic stepped toward them, but Alani put up one hand, stopping him, as if that one hand possessed some type of magic that cursed his feet from moving. Her other hand was wrapped tightly around Bella. It was a motherly embrace, a comforting hold, one that Ethic knew his daughter needed. "I've got it," she said. "Come on, baby girl," she said, as she whisked Bella into the women's bathroom. Ethic didn't know where Alani had come from, but he was grateful for her presence because his daughter was hurting, and he had no idea what to do.

Alani grabbed Kleenex from the sink and cupped Bella's chin in her hand, as she wiped her tears. "It's okay to cry, Bella, let it out," she whispered, as her own eyes misted. There was so much pain in this little girl. Bella's entire body quaked.

"I told him I didn't want to come here," Bella said, hyperventilating between words, trying hard to catch her breath. "Everybody in there is with their moms. Mine is dead and it's just not fair."

Alani's heart throbbed in recognition, as she said, "Oh, sweetheart. I know it hurts really bad being without your mother. I'm so sorry you have to go through that. There will be a lot of times when you just need her and wish she was there; but let me share a secret with you about mothers and their babies. We never leave. There is nothing that will make a mother leave her child. Even after every bit of air has left our lungs, we are still with our children. You can feel her, can't you?" Alani asked, as she pointed to Bella's chest. "Have you ever had a decision to make that you were unsure about and a voice inside your head told you what to do?" Bella's cries had dulled but tears flowed still, as she nodded. "That's your mother, Bella. That's the part of her that she planted inside you the day you were born. You want to know how I know?" Bella looked up at her. "Because I'm heartbroken too. My daughter died, and I still feel her. I still talk to her every night when I pray, and she visits me every night when I dream." Alani was the one crying, now. They were crying together. They related to one another.

"It's just not fair," Bella said.

"It isn't, and you have a right to be mad, Bella. I'm mad too and it isn't something that anyone understands, if they haven't been through it; but I understand, and if you ever need to talk, you know your dad is a great listener," Alani said.

"He doesn't get it," Bella cried.

"Well, I know we just met, but I'm a pretty good listener too and I'd like to be friends; if that's cool with you? One thing about me…" Alani paused to wet a paper towel as she wiped Bella's face. "I'm a really good friend and I'm always there for my friends when they need me."

"I'd like that," Bella whispered.

"Now, listen. I never got to be in a debutante pageant before, and I'd love to be in it with you, if you'll have me. We can make both my daughter and your mother happy, because I know that they will both be there with us. I know I'm not your mom, but I'd really like to experience this with you. What do you think?"

Bella rolled her eyes to the sky and then closed them, as she tried to compose herself. "I can't believe I just embarrassed myself like that."

"Nobody's judging you here," Alani said. "How about we go back in there together?"

"Okay," Bella said.

Alani held up her finger. "One second," she said. She pulled out her concealer and nude-colored lip gloss and applied a little bit to Bella's face.

"Nothing like a little makeup to erase all evidence of tears," Alani said. Bella looked in the mirror and smiled, and then allowed Alani to escort her out.

"We're ready," Alani said, with a smile, as she emerged with a hand around Bella's shoulders. The look of worry on Ethic's face as he hugged Bella moved Alani. There was nothing more attractive than a man that loved his children.

"Thank you," he mouthed.

She nodded. "Bella, we better get in there. We can't let these other duos show us up," Alani said, with a wink.

"Alani said she'll be my mentor, Daddy," Bella said.

"If that's okay?" Alani said, her brows dipping in concern, as suddenly she felt like she may have overstepped.

Ethic nodded, as he watched them walk back into the sanctuary. He entered moments later and took a seat in the back pew, while he watched Alani interact with his daughter. She was so nurturing, so calming. At that moment, she was God-sent and Ethic hated that he would have to give her back because the greatest sin he had ever committed had been against her.

When the rehearsal was complete, both Bella and Alani were all smiles, as they approached him. She didn't have to ask for his touch, this time, because right after he hugged his daughter, he pulled Alani close. "Thank you," he whispered in her ear.

The doors behind him swung open and Alani's smile grew brighter. "Oh, Nannie! Perfect timing. I'd like for you to meet my friend, Ezra, and his daughter, Bella."

Ethic turned to greet the woman, but as soon as she looked him in the eyes the woman's face contorted on the left side as she mumbled, "The man that he God kill my..." The woman was speaking mumbo jumbo, as she staggered forward, her weight falling into Ethic.

"Nannie?" Alani screamed, in panic. Nannie had her mouth open in an O of fear, as she laid paralyzed in Ethic's arms. "Nannie! Someone call 911!"

***

"If she dies, I don't know what I'll do," Alani whispered, as she sat in the waiting room at the hospital, clasping her hands together, as she rocked back and forth in the chair. "Thank you so much for staying here with me. I know you have kids and..."

"I'm not going anywhere. My nanny, Lily, can take care of my kids for the night. I'm right here," Ethic assured. He knew in his bones that Alani's aunt had recognized him. There was something about the look in her eyes that told him so, and he knew if she died, he would be responsible.

"I've got to tell you something, Alani," Ethic said. She looked at him, eyes wide and full of worry; but before he could speak, a doctor walked into the waiting room.

"Lenika Hill?" he called out. Alani jumped up. "That's me. How is my aunt?"

"Please, sit," the doctor said. It felt like the ground was pulled from underneath her, as she fell into the chair, preparing herself for the worst. "Your aunt has suffered a massive stroke. She's alive, but there was significant damage. She's in a coma and her scans show very limited brain activity."

Alani reached out and gripped Ethic's forearm. "What does that mean?"

"It means you have a decision to make. Since you are her power of attorney, you need to decide how we proceed from here. Right now, there is a machine breathing for her. You can remove her from life support and let nature take its course, or you can keep the machine's breathing for her."

"I can't just unplug her. What if there's a chance that she can wake up?" Alani's voice was childlike. She felt three feet tall and defenseless against a world that wanted to leave her alone.

"The chances are very minimal, Ms. Hill. If there was some motion of the lines of her CT, I'd be more hopeful. I don't believe she can recover from a stroke of this size. I'm sorry," the doctor said.

"Can I see her?" Alani asked.

"Of course," the doctor replied. She turned to Ethic. "Will you come?"

Ethic leaned into her, as he whispered, "I don't think I should."

"Please, Ethic," she cried. "I can't do this alone."

She was distraught. Another hurt caused by him. Another life destroyed because of him. "Okay," he said. She sniffed, as she stood, and they followed the doctor to Nannie's room.

"I'm going to be right here in the hall," Ethic said, feeling fucked up about being a part of this moment at all.

Alani went inside the room, and when she saw all the tubes coming out of Nannie's body, she turned right back around. She ran into Ethic's arms. "Get me out of here," she cried. Ethic picked her up and carried her out of the hospital. He couldn't take her home and expect her to be alone, so he broke one of his rules and took a woman to his house.

By the time they arrived, it was past midnight and even Lily had fallen asleep on the couch. Ethic went to wake her, and then sent her home, before escorting Alani to one of his guest rooms. She sat on the bed and Ethic kneeled on the floor between her legs, as she placed her hands on his head, tracing the pattern of his waves as he bent his head in despair.

"I'm sorry, Alani," he said. "You'll never know how sorry I am. I need to be honest with you. There is no easy way for me to tell you this…"

"Stop, Ethic," she whispered, as she lifted his face and stared him in the eyes. "I can't take any more bad news. I can't. It will be the thing that breaks me. So, whatever you are about to say, just please, I'm begging you; if you know it's going to hurt me, just don't say it."

"Alani, it's important…"

"Just get out!" she shouted, louder than she intended.

Ethic stood and backpedaled from the room, knowing he couldn't tell her now. It wasn't the right time. He would let her have some peace to mourn all she had lost. He checked in on his children, feeling guilty that they were tucked safely in their beds while everyone Alani loved was in peril. His mind was chaotic, his humanity challenged, and his spirit was destroyed. He wasn't a bad man, but then again, maybe he was. His actions were speaking loudly, drowning out his intentions. No matter what he did, destruction followed him. He had to discharge some of this negativity that was choking him. He retreated to his room and changed clothes, before heading to the one place in his house where he could find peace.

Chapter 17

I shouldn't have snapped at him, she thought, as she gripped the sink in the guest bathroom in Ethic's palace. She cleared the steam from the mirror in front of her, looking at herself. She was wrapped in a plush towel, her hair was soaking wet, shrinking her long curls up to her shoulders. Alani could see the exhaustion in her face. She had so much on her shoulders, so much sorrow, so much weight that it was almost intolerable. She walked back into the guest room and pulled open the drawers, hoping to find a clean shirt she could sleep in. She pulled one of the neatly-folded, Oxford shirts from the drawer and put it on. She couldn't help but grow jealous of whoever had laundered it. They had taken the time to spray his signature scent onto it and she wondered if it was the woman she had seen him with at the diner. The scent of his cologne surrounded her, as she pulled the collar to her nose and inhaled it. She hoped he wouldn't mind. She doubted he would. Ethic had been the most accommodating person she had ever met, and it surprised her because she knew he was anything but friendly. In fact, he was downright guarded. *I'm the asshole,* she thought. Alani had asked him to leave. Had put him out of a room in the house he owned, even though distance from him was the last thing she wanted. Alani didn't know how she was supposed to manage this new relationship she had with Ethic. He had come to her in the most confusing and torrential time of her life. *I should have heard him out,* she thought. She crept out of the room, as quietly as she could, not wanting to wake his children. She had to see his face, she had to feel the rise and fall of his chest against hers as he hugged her. She needed to feel that pulse he sent through her like shock pads to her heart. He revived her when she was circling the drain. She went from room to room, in search of him, wanting to apologize, hoping he would give in to her need for him. Death surrounded her. It suffocated her and drowned her in suffering. A bullet to the head would have been more civilized than this. Besides suicide, Ethic was her only relief. She needed more than a hug, she needed his tongue against hers, his body connected to hers, inside of hers, so she could feel all the healing he had to give. Alani was sick with loss and Ethic was the only remedy that worked. She noticed a door on the first floor was slightly ajar, and she slowly descended the steps into the basement. It was like she could sense that he was down there. Her entire body reacted, as she drew near. When she saw him, she stopped, and her breath caught in her throat, as she witnessed God's art at work.

Alani felt as if she were a voyeur, watching an intimate moment, one that wasn't meant for anyone's eyes, but still she enjoyed it. Ethic's body was like a statue, sculpted by years of discipline. His strength present but not overwhelming. Had she seen any other man practicing yoga, she would have judged him. She probably would have surmised he had a bit of sugar in his tank; but the way Ethic moved fluidly from one position to the next, his muscles bulging from the intensity of it all…hmm, nothing had ever looked so masculine. He was all man. All chocolate and Alani wanted a taste of him. The Nike, football, training tights he wore proved that his manhood was not to be denied. The outline of him teased her, as she bit down into her lip. He was strong, full of stock from

African kings, royal blood coursing through his veins, thick authority swinging between his legs. Alani quivered, as nature caused her southern lips to produce a sweet nectar. She was lusting, in heat, as her biological affinity for man caused her body to respond. Her nipples hardened and rubbed against the fabric of his shirt, and the scent of his cologne only heightened her desire. He was a beautiful man. Yes, beautiful, because handsome just would not suffice. She had never met a man like this. Ethic made everyone before him seem boyish, as if all other men were still swimming in the kiddie pool, and he alone was on some grown man shit. He noticed her out of the corner of his eye.

"Come. Here." It was a command and it startled her that he knew she was in the room. She flushed in embarrassment, as she rocked on her heels, suddenly feeling like she needed to run the other way. Had he seen her gawking? Was he watching her, watch him the entire time? He didn't look her way or stop his routine. He simply waited for her response. "You gon' stand there and watch or you gon' join me? It helps when your mind is at war to bring peace to your body," he said.

"I'm nowhere near flexible," she replied.

"I find that hard to believe," he countered. "Come." There was something about the way he called her. When he beckoned, she obliged. It was an order she looked forward to following. She submitted, without protest, fighting against her apprehension. He stood behind her, his sweaty chest sticking to the back of the t-shirt. Her bare feet against the cold, wooden floor caused her nipples to tighten even more, as she felt him behind her. His warm breath was sweet, like honey, as he spoke into her ear. His full lips touched her earlobe and she drew in a sharp breath. If they felt this good on her ear, she could only imagine how they felt on her... *Oh my God,* she shuddered at the thought. She wondered if he knew what he did to her. Did he purposefully arouse her? Did he want her to soak through her panties? Did he know that he was close to making her orgasm, without even touching her? *What type of super negro is he?* She thought, almost bursting out in amusement, as a smirk crossed her lips. The way she felt when in his presence was unreal. It was like all her life she had been dulled to just coast through life, and now, her every fiber was alive. She felt everything when she was with him. She noticed her heart beat when he was around. He simply made her feel.

"Relax," he coached. "You're too tense."

He was standing so close to her that nothing separated them, and she took a deep breath, as he placed one hand in front of her and the other on the small of her back, pushing her forward, folding her in half.

"Touch the ground in front of you and close your eyes," he instructed. She added an extra measure and took it upon herself to bite her lip. She had to stop herself from moaning, as her behind pushed into his pelvis. She felt all of him, amazed at his size because he wasn't even erect. His manhood was nice and thick and long, and God she wished it would go hard. The sensation of him against her made her pussy clench in yearning. She could feel the familiar pulse begin to drum in her clitoris, and she squeezed her thighs together to try to douse the fire threatening to spread within her.

"Let me know if it's uncomfortable," he said. "You good?"

"Yes," she breathed out. It took everything in her not to shake her ass a little. She hadn't realized how long it had been since she had felt a man against her. Ever since her baby daddy had gone away and taken his fuck boy promises with him, she had gone untouched. Ethic had fallen into her lap by way of fate, at least from her perspective, and he was so different from any man she had ever experienced before. She was sure he could get her to try anything once.

He took her through a series of poses, challenging her, his hands roaming her body to guide her form. Every place he touched felt like soft kisses, and soon, she was not only sticky with sweat, but wet from the tension building in her panties. The places he planted his hands made her body tingle, and as he moved effortlessly with her, she realized this was the clearest her mind had been since losing her daughter.

She felt herself being affected by Ethic, her lust blossomed, as her nectar wet her inner thigh. She could smell the sweet scent of her flower in the air. Her pheromones were all over the place. She was in heat. Her heart was racing, and she could feel her pulse everywhere.

God, if this man don't stop pressing into me like that, she thought. He was in control of her body, and as he laid her on the mat on the ground, he positioned himself between her legs. Stretching one out toward the floor, and the other toward the sky, he began to lean forward into her, as if he were about to throw one leg over his shoulder. The tension pulling at her hamstrings mixed with him pressing against her body was something other worldly. She felt him, growing, but not fully hard, and she arched her back, causing more friction between them.

Her leg was near her ear now, as he pushed her to her limits and his dick hardened, pushing directly on her clit, causing her to gasp. They were straddling a line between using this as an excuse to feel one another, without asking, without trying. This was turning sexual and she was so close to her peak, as she rolled her hips beneath him. He had her there and he hadn't even removed her clothes. Just when she thought he would take her all the way, he pulled back. It was like

241

somebody's mama had entered the room and killed the vibe, as he abruptly stood to his feet. Her chest heaved, as she lowered her leg and looked toward the ceiling, putting both hands over her eyes.

"It's getting late," he said. "You should get some sleep, so I can take you back to the hospital in the morning." He snatched up a towel from the leather couch and wrapped it around his neck.

She stood, shifting from foot to foot, as an insatiable throb filled her clit. "I don't want to think about anything but what's happening right now," she said.

She approached him, and he stepped back, confusing her as she frowned. There was alarm in his expression.

"I thought," she paused, as she ran a hand through her hair. "Wait, what's happening right now?" she asked, suddenly confused. They had been in a vibe, she had felt it, she knew he had felt it.

So, what's with the disappearing acts? She thought. Rejection was worse than loneliness, and suddenly, she felt humiliated. *Maybe I'm misreading the signs,* she thought.

"This isn't right," Ethic said. "I shouldn't have let it get this far." He ran his hands down his head and then his face, as if he were kicking himself, regretting every moment he had spent with her.

"What's not right about it, Ethic?" Alani asked. "I know what I want. Right now, I want you to fuck me." He knew she was angry because sweet Alani had turned into kick ass Lenika, and all her frustrations were aimed at him. "Are you not attracted to me? Have I been imagining our chemistry? Cuz I'm going crazy right about now. So, if I'm misreading this shit, let me know."

"It's not about my attraction or the chemistry, Alani. It's more to it than that," Ethic stated.

"And more is bad?" Alani was lost. "I'm a grown woman, Ethic. I can handle it. I can handle you. What are you running from?"

She was chasing him now, desperately, and she felt pathetic for it. This sounded a lot like begging, and Alani had never begged a nigga for anything a day in her life. He had reduced her to the type of woman who didn't allow a man to walk away. She couldn't let him leave it like this, not without understanding, not without an explanation. They had enjoyed each other's company for weeks. She had thought they shared a connection, that they were building something. Their chemistry was undeniable, but still, he was spinning her. As he walked away, he wouldn't even bless her with an answer.

Her confusion turned to aggression, and she pushed his back, as he headed for the stairs. Alani was angry that he had lifted her out of her sadness, that he had distracted her from the hurt, only to freeze up when it mattered most. She wasn't asking him to love her. She was just asking him to stay, asking for one night, asking not to sleep alone because when she did she cried herself to sleep. He ignored her assault, as he kept marching toward the stairs.

"Ethic!"

He spun around, abruptly causing her to bump right into him. He gripped her shoulders. "Stop. Stop asking for something that will destroy you. I'm not the man you think I am. I'm the one you should run from, not toward. Just leave it alone," he said, as he shook her slightly.

His words stunned her to silence and she could see behind his intense stare that he believed what he was saying. He was warning her. She could read between the lines, but she had always been a stubborn girl. She would have to learn the lesson the hard way.

She stood on her tip-toes and placed her hand on the side of his face, the imperfect side, touching him so tenderly that it felt like she was touching his soul.

"I've lost a lot this year Ethic, but out of nowhere you came along and made things easier. I don't know what this is, but when I'm with you I feel like I can fly. I want to fly, Ethic," she whispered, as she inched closer and closer to his lips. His body was rigid, and she felt him tensing, as she kissed his lips without permission. She became the third woman he ever put his lips on in that moment. He resisted at first, but she was so hungry for him that she bit his bottom lip, aggressively, forcing him to let her in. Their kiss was like the first fireworks on the 4th of July, it ignited her body and she wrapped her arms around his neck and he pulled her into his growing lust. It was like he was fighting with himself, as he pushed her away, only for the need of her to cause him to pull her back again and again.

He tasted like honey and she wanted to overindulge. He was so hard that she could feel him bulging against the seam of the grey sweatpants. *God, thank you for grey sweatpants,* she thought. It felt like the temperature had been turned up to 100 degrees, as he scooped her up under her bottom and she wrapped her legs around his waist. He lifted all 160 pounds of her, as if she was light as a feather. Holding her up by her ass, he kissed her, as the feel of his sex on her sex drove her wild. She just wanted the fabric that separated them to disappear. "Fuck me. Not slow, not nice, not gentle. Fuck me hard, Ethic. I want to feel every inch of you. I've been empty for so long. Fill me up," she whispered, looking him directly in the eyes, as she reached down and grabbed his length.

"Oh shit," he groaned. Whatever will he had left went out the window, as she rubbed him.

He pinned her against the wall, as she reached inside his sweats to free him. Her eyes widened in shock at the blessing she uncovered. Those sweatpants did him no justice. What she had suspected was big was more like magnificent. Ethic placed her on her feet and his head fell back, as she stroked his length with her smooth hands.

"This ain't right," he growled.

"Don't say that. Don't tell me no," she whispered. He picked her up, again, this time sliding her onto him, causing her to gasp. He was more than she had anticipated, and she dug her nails into his back, as he rocked in and out of her.

"Shit," she moaned, as he explored her depths. He was hard, and her softness massaged him as he sank into her, barely wanting to pull out before diving in again.

"Damn," he moaned.

She grabbed his chin with one hand and pulled his mouth to hers as she kissed him. Her tongue danced inside his mouth, as if she were trying to inhale him. "It's so good," she whispered. Ethic had her trapped, her back against a wall, as he touched the center of her with every stroke. She wanted to run from him, to dull the ache he caused each time he thrust inside her, but there was nowhere to go. She knew he would be good, but to be this damn good was a motherfucking sin. She would have to try hard not to feel entitled to this man. He was the type of lover who made bitches go crazy.

"Turn around." There was another one of his orders, and she followed it, as she braced herself, hands to the wall as if he were about to arrest this pussy. She felt him against her ass, knocking the top of it with his heavy manhood, as if he were waiting for her to say come in. He left her wondering for a brief second about what he was about to do. The lack of control as he took charge was a new element for her. Alani had always been the pretty, prissy girl in the hood. Few men had experienced her treasure, and those who did, usually had to follow her lead. She was old fashioned and had never dared to venture outside of anything missionary. She was a pretty bitch, so she could be boring. A man had never made her want to try too hard, but for this type of dick, she would pop her pussy on a handstand if it meant she could have it forever. She was a control freak and didn't like anyone else manipulating her body. She liked to say when, where, and how; but with Ethic, she felt safe. With Ethic, she felt lucky, and she was in it to please, instead of to receive. Her body tensed, as she anticipated pain.

"Relax. I'm just admiring the view. You're brilliant," he whispered. "I want to do things to you that you're not ready for."

"I'm ready," she moaned. "Please."

He smirked. Ethic lifted her right leg, resting it in the crease of his arm as he entered her from behind. She cried out.

He fucked her up the wall, lifting that leg so high that he had access to depths unknown to even her. She needed his yoga lessons, because with him, she would have to be flexible. He was stretching her to her limit - both inside and out. There were no idle hands and he paid attention to every part of her body, as he teased her clit in the process.

He reached around her body, palming her V, as she fell into a frantic grind against his hand while his thickness beat up her insides. "This is too good, Ethic, please. Wait...stop!"

"If I stop, I won't hear what you sound like when you cum," he said, as he kissed the back of her neck. "I want to hear you." He paused, suddenly halting the intense pleasure he was causing, driving her crazy as she anxiously feigned for his next stroke. "Or you want me to stop?"

"No, don't. Keep going. I need it." Alani didn't even recognize this voice of desperation. It was sultry and deep…pleading. *Am I begging for this dick?* She thought, as her face contorted in pleasure. Had this man read the manual to her body? How did he know which buttons to push, how to get her to gush, how to elevate her arch? Alani was on one tiptoe, he was fucking her so good. She just knew she would die if this ended too soon. This raw, passionate, animalistic sex, was unlike anything she had ever experienced, and she felt Ethic pouring all his doubt into her, as they did what men and women were meant to do. Her breasts bounced, and she clawed at the wall, as sweat covered every inch of her body. She had never gotten this nasty for a man, and suddenly, she just wanted to taste him. "Agh!" she cried, as she rained down over him.

"That's good," he coached her, as she went limp against his body. Alani had never experienced anything so pleasurable, so uninhibited, so natural. It was like he was the first man and she was the first woman. Together, they were figuring out their symmetry. This was that Adam and Eve shit; the stuff God got a refund on after the bitch ate that apple. This was the bliss that only God himself could have created; the pleasure that manifested when Eros was at play. Something other worldly had just happened within her, stimulated by him, and Alani wanted more of it. She faced him and then looked up into his eyes, coyly.

"I don't know what this is…" She paused, as she placed her hands on his chest, gently tracing the outline of his tattoos. She took a second to gather her thoughts. Her head was spinning, and her heart was pumping pure emotion. She didn't want to come off clingy or scare him with confessions of love. She knew that to him this could very well be just sex, but she felt something…different…rare…with this man. She had felt it the very first time he wrapped his arms around her and not telling him would torture her.

"I just want you to stay, okay?" she finished, afraid to say much more. It was at that moment that he knew he could never tell her. He had finally found her. He didn't want to jeopardize what they could be together. He didn't care if he was building his foundation with her on secrecy and lies. Before he knew what she felt like on the inside, he could have done it. He could have let the truth push her out of his life, but not now…not after she had let him discover the secret that heaven was between her legs. Ethic knew it was selfish, but he hadn't felt a love like this before, not even with Raven. Their love had been young and passionate, something he never thought he would find again. But this thing with Alani Lenika Hill, was more potent than anything he had ever felt.

"I'm right here," he replied.

"I know," she whispered. "But men leave. They always do, eventually, right down to my daddy. They just are here one day and decide I'm too much work the next. I don't want you to leave me." She saw his eyes widen, slightly, and she knew that her words were coming on too strong. "I'm not saying you have a responsibility to stay, but I like this between us. I mean…" She felt herself talking too much. *I probably sound crazy right now,* she thought. She knew she was rambling, but she couldn't quite express to him how good he made life feel without sounding like she was expecting too much. "I just want to explore whatever this is. I've never met anyone that I was willing to change for, but you make me feel differently. I want to be what you like. I want you to want to stay, so if I'm ever doing anything to make you feel like you don't want to explore this with me, just tell me and I'll change it. I just really don't want you to leave; and if it's not like that, just tell me now. We can leave it right here, right now, as is…just one night."

248

Ethic's eyes burned into hers and she anxiously awaited his response. She knew she came off needy, but shit, she did need him. What woman didn't need a man like him?

"I don't leave. I don't fold. I don't run," he responded. She believed him. "Promise me that you won't run when you discover the worst parts of me, Alani."

"I promise," she said, without hesitation.

Alani began to rub him, encouraging him to go hard once more, as she dropped to her knees right in front of him. After years of fearing intimacy, of not being touched, of not trusting anyone to explore her body, she suddenly desired affection. She craved connection; and as his strength grew in her hands, her mouth watered. It was like she wanted to please him, to prove to him, that he didn't have to go anywhere because she could be all that he needed. When she put her mouth on him, she felt him tense and then relax as she bobbed her head. Sliding along his length, barely able to handle all of him, she wet him, massaged him, as her tongue and lips put in overtime. Alani had never done this for anyone. No man had ever made her want to; but with Ethic, it felt natural, as if it was her sole purpose to pump his seeds from his magnificent flesh. His grunts of satisfaction and the way he bowed his head, as he placed both hands on the wall in front of him, made her confident that she was doing it right. She placed her hand on his solid thighs, bracing herself, as she felt him throb against the back of her throat. She wanted to go harder, wanted to swallow him deeper, wanted him to be the one calling *her* name. Alani wanted him to stay, not only for tonight, but for as long as he made her heart leap with delight just from his presence. She was showing him...right there on her knees...without any reservation. He was wet with her saliva and she moaned when she tasted the hint of sweetness on the tip of him. Normally, the idea of going further would have repulsed her, but she anticipated his release like a child anticipated an ice cream cone on a scorching summer day. He was her treat. To lick him was her delight. He provided healing to things that had been damaged long before the death of her child. When she was with him, she forgot that she was in mourning. She forgot the heartbreak that came before him. There had to be a reward for that. Maybe swallowing him would allow some of the happiness to plant itself inside her and grow within her. That way, she wouldn't need him around all the time to feel joy. He was pulsing now, as one hand fisted her hair, his knees weakened. He had reached that point and Alani enjoyed every second, as she massaged him until the end. He pulled her to her feet, rubbing her arms up and down, as he rested his forehead against hers. His eyes were closed, as if he were in deep contemplation.

"I've taken this somewhere it shouldn't go," he whispered.

The statement stabbed her...injured her, and she placed her hands on his cheeks. "Look at me, Ethic."

He did, and she saw so much pain in him that it brought tears to her eyes.

"Wherever it goes, good or bad, I'll follow you there," she said.

She kissed his lips and he picked her up, carrying her up the stairs to his bedroom. As he laid her down on the sheets, she wondered about the layers that dwelled beneath the surface of this man. She wanted to peel him back, piece by piece. She had no idea that at the pit of him was a secret that would destroy her, but he was aware, and it was only a matter of time before her adoration turned to hate.

Chapter 18

Alani awoke first, and as she rolled onto her side, she admired Ethic. She hated to be naive and to place unrealistic notions of fairytales on what was happening between them, but she had fallen for this man. In his bed was the first night in months that she had slept through the night. She trailed her nude-painted fingertip down his strong abs, awakening him.

"It's six in the morning," she whispered. "Go back to sleep. I'm going to catch an Uber home, before your kids wake up and catch me in your bed."

She moved to get out the bed and he wrapped a strong arm around her waist, pulling her back down.

"Ethic, I should go," she whispered. "I don't want you to have to explain my presence to them. We don't even know what this is."

"*I* know," Ethic said, as he pulled her chin to him.

"I know too," she admitted, as she kissed his lips. "But this isn't the type of thing that you spring on your kids."

Ethic knew she was right, he wasn't ready to let go, however. Waking up to her was a sight. She filled every void every woman had left him with before her. A man without a woman was half of a man, emotionally stunted, and overcompensating in every area of his life to make up for what he lacked in companionship. A king could not reign without a queen to keep him strong. If man was the walls of a house, holding everything up, bearing the weight of all that inhabited it, his woman was the foundation. You could tear down walls, but a foundation was rock solid. Even Raven had been too young when he had loved her for her to give him that. Alani

251

made him feel like he was standing on solid ground. He knew she depended on him for   strength, but she didn't deplete him, because she somehow replenished whatever she took from him. It was the rare gift of reciprocity.

"I know, you're right," he said. "But I'll be damned if you're taking an Uber. Take my truck."

"Then what will you drive?" she asked.

"I'll manage," he said, not wanting to sound pompous by mentioning the Tesla he had sitting in the garage. "I'll come by later, after Lily arrives."

"Okay." She smiled, as he placed a strong hand on the side of her face, his fingers wrapping around her neck, as his thumb caressed her cheek.

"There will be a day when you question if this was real," he said. "It is. It always has been, and it always will be. No matter how flawed it becomes, or how wrong it is, or how much it ends up hurting."

He pulled her face to his and kissed her so intensely that she shivered. She pulled away and walked out. She made sure she was silent, as she hurried to the guest room and slipped back into her clothes from the day before. When she stepped back into the hallway, Bella was standing in her doorway, rubbing her eyes, sleepily.

"Alani?" she called out.

Alani froze like a deer in headlights, as her mouth fell open.

"I'm sorry. Did I wake you?" Alani asked. "I was just...um..."

"How's your aunt?" Bella asked.

"She's not so good, baby girl."

It was Ethic who answered, and Alani turned around, so grateful that he had intervened. "Alani was upset after seeing her aunt in the hospital," Ethic continued. "So, I let her stay the night, so she wouldn't have to go home alone."

"Good," Bella said. She walked up to Alani and hugged her, taking Alani by surprise. She looked up at Ethic in shock, as she hugged his daughter back.

"You give the best hugs, Bella. Thank you," she said. "Must be something that runs in the family."

Alani winked at Ethic and then released Bella.

"Are you staying for breakfast?" Bella asked.

"Oh, um…no, I can't," Alani said. "I'm sorry, I have to get going. I want to check on my aunt. Next time; okay?"

Bella nodded, as Ethic said, "Come on, B. We can get breakfast started before Eazy wakes up." He turned to Alani. "The keys to the truck are in the study inside my desk."

Alani was so glad her encounter with Bella hadn't been awkward, but she didn't want to try it again with Eazy. She hurried into the study she had passed the night before, when she was looking for Ethic, and walked over to his desk. She opened the drawer and picked up his keys. Her hands froze when she saw the funeral program with Kenzie's face on it. Her breath caught in her throat, as she picked it up and, instantly, her legs gave out. She sank into the plush, leather chair behind her. She opened the program with shaky hands and a handwritten note fell out.

Thank you for your generous donation. God bless you.

Alani gasped, as her heart seized in her chest. *He donated the money for me to bury them,* she thought. *He didn't even know me that well then. Why would he…*

She found strength in her legs and walked toward the sound of laughter coming from the kitchen. The sight of Ethic and Bella cooking together would have normally warmed her heart, but she was too full of confusion to appreciate his fatherhood.

"W…what is this?" she asked, as she held up the funeral program and the note.

Ethic turned to Bella. "Bella, can you go upstairs and get dressed? I think we'll go out to eat this morning."

It took all Alani's will to wait until she heard Bella's footsteps go up all the stairs. "Why do you have this? You're the one who paid for the funerals?" she asked. "Is this what you were trying to tell me last night?"

Ethic wanted to receive her appreciation. He wanted to be the good guy who did good things, for good reasons; but the truth was, his guilt had urged him to cover the burials. He had always been taught to clean up his mess, and the death of her loved ones was his mess. He didn't want to hurt her, but he couldn't look her in the eyes and lie. He couldn't let her praise her daughter's murderer.

He sat in one of the chairs at the table and pulled one out for her. "Alani, please sit," he said.

She was shaking. Finding her daughter's picture had unnerved her.

"Ethic, you have to say something," she whispered. "Please, just tell me what's going on."

He grit his teeth, his temple throbbing, as he placed his elbows on his knees. His palms met each other in prayer, as his eyes burned. Ethic could count the times on one hand that he had cried in his life. He pinched the tip of his nose, his face contorting, as he lost control. He was a man who was about to destroy the woman it had taken him 34 years to find.

"What do you feel for me, Lenika? Could you see yourself loving me?" he asked.

"Ethic…I…"

"Please, just answer because I'm about to hurt you, Alani. I'm about to erase any chance that we have. I just want to know what it would have been like," Ethic stated, as he took a deep breath, taking his mind to a place of selflessness and strength. He wanted to be selfish and tell her falsehoods. He wanted to make up something that would explain the things she found and still allow him to keep her, but he couldn't. He respected her too much to not answer her truthfully. Light always uncovered darkness, and one day she would find out about what he had done. He wanted her to hear it from him.

"I don't have to imagine what it would be like to love you one day, Ethic. I love you now. I am in love with you, Ezra."

His head fell between his knees, his strong arms flexed, as he swiped his hands over the top of his head, in despair. Her words gutted him. He was bleeding out.

"I love you so fucking much, Lenika. I waited so long to love you…so long for God to reveal why I experienced so much loss. It was because when I met you, I needed to appreciate the gift of you. I'm so sorry, Lenika."

"Why are you calling me Lenika?" she asked, her eyes misting, as a weight settled onto her chest. This was not how she had expected his confession of love to be. This didn't feel good. It felt like goodbye.

"Because you won't recognize me after I tell you this. We'll go back to being strangers, because you don't know the man that did what I did," he whispered.

"What did you do?" Her voice was barely audible, as she sucked in a breath, holding it as she anticipated his reply. She placed a hand on his knee, as a tear slipped down her face.

"It was me," he whispered. "I'm responsible for killing your daughter and your brother."

She pulled her hand back so quickly, it was like she had touched fire. Suddenly, his touch felt harmful, as if she was suddenly staring into the eyes of evil. Nannie always told her that the devil didn't come in the form of the boogie man. He comes in the form of everything you ever wanted. Alani was looking at the devil in human form. This man that she had fallen in love with, this beautiful soul that had come into her life and planted love when sadness had ruined her soil, was the one behind her pain to begin with. He was the hand behind the trigger that killed her family. The hair raised on the back of her neck and she took a step backward, as her shoulders tensed.

"Get the fuck away from me," she whispered, as her eyes widened in shock, and she stumbled as she stood, trying to backpedal away from him.

Ethic stepped toward her.

"I SAID GET THE FUCK AWAY FROM ME!" she screamed, at the top of her lungs.

Ethic couldn't tear himself away from her, if he wanted to. He should have, months ago, before it ever went this far, but he hadn't and now the truth had revealed his deception. He had wanted to tell her so many times. He had tried to tell her, but he knew as soon as he spoke the words that what they shared would die. Selfishly, he had wanted to hold onto her a little bit longer. He knew she would be hurt, but the fear that he saw in her eyes broke him.

"Let me explain," Ethic said.

Alani was like a pot of boiling water. As the revelation settled into her soul, violent bubbles of anger ballooned inside of her.

"Explain? You want to explain yourself? You want to tell me how you took my daughter's life? How you shot my brother? Or do you want to tell me why you came into my life, watched me self-destruct right in front of you..." she couldn't even finish her sentence. The pain in her stomach was crippling. The sickness in the back of her throat was building. "I was torn apart! My heart was in fucking pieces and I stitched my shit up for you! I salvaged whatever I could and handed it to you on a platter. For you, Ethic! You made me love the person who murdered my daughter!" she wailed. "My brother! Taking them wasn't enough for you? You had to take my dignity too?" She had to grip something to keep from falling. It was instinct for Ethic to go to her, to touch her. It was what she always needed when she was weak. His touch. To feel. Him. Now, it burned.

Before Alani knew it, she was swinging. She had boiled over and her attack was relentless. "I fucking hate you!" she shouted, like a madwoman, as she beat his chest. "I hate you!" He stood there, with misted eyes, telling her he was sorry. He was staring at her, as if she was about to disappear before his eyes… as if she were a good dream that he was about to wake up from. The kind of dream that made you feel good but that you couldn't remember once you opened your eyes. He didn't want to wake up, but as she hit him, slowly reality became clear. "Don't look at me! Don't you dare look at me!" She was so enraged that she spit in his face, then slapped him with so much force that his head turned on impact.

Bella ran down the stairs. "Daddy!"

"Go upstairs, Bella, everything's fine," Ethic said, sternly.

"But, Daddy?"

"Go!" He didn't look at Bella. He was too busy looking at Alani, but he heard his daughter's footsteps as they traveled up the stairs.

Ethic was visibly injured - not physically, but her reaction harmed him. He opened his arms, inviting her to assault him.

"Get it out," he said.

Alani pushed him. She punched him. If she had a gun, she would have shot him where he stood, but it wouldn't have taken this feeling away. She crumpled to the ground, sobbing.

"Goddd," Alani moaned, so stricken that she felt like she would be sick.

He swiped his hand over his mouth, wondering how he could remedy this. If God was real, he needed him in this moment. He needed God to fill her with some type of forgiveness.

He sat on the ground and pulled her into his arms. She was limp, void of all fight, as if she had exhausted all the strength she had left. Or perhaps, he had exhausted it. Maybe loving the representative and meeting his truth had depleted her. He didn't know, but he was grateful that she was no longer on the attack.

She melted into him, crying into his chest so hard that he was sure she couldn't breathe.

"I'm so sorry," he whispered. She gripped his shirt, as her chest rocked with grief. She was ashamed. Ashamed of the fact that she was still there, in his arms, and that these strong arms comforted her strangely. Ethic was the only one who could ease the hurt because he was the man whom had caused it. She knew it was backwards, she knew it wasn't right, but melting into his embrace as she felt his racing heart, anxiously awaiting the next words she would speak, feeling his tension, his desperation, his angst, as he held her. They had always connected through touch, and this moment was no different. It was the most confusing thing she had ever felt, and she was ashamed. As a mother, she should want revenge, but all she wanted was to feel him, to have him take some of this aching away that he had put on her. He sat with her between his legs, stroking her hair, as he tried to commit as much of her to memory as he possibly could. The feel of her against his body, the scent of coconut Shea Moisture in her hair, the sound of her cries, he wanted it all retained in his mind, like a secret that he would never share. Ethic knew, once they climbed up from that floor, that he would never get close to her again. She would never allow it and he had no one to blame but himself. He kissed the top of her head, breathing her essence in. He knew every second that lingered on was her gift to him because she should have left the moment the words fell from his mouth.

"I can't be here," she said, as she tried to squirm away from him. She made it all the way to the door before his words froze her in place.

"Don't leave me," he said. He sounded like that little boy who had begged his mother to stay all those years ago.

She didn't turn to him, but it was like he was Spider-Man and had spit webs at her feet to hold her in place. She breathed, rapidly, her chest heaving up and down as he continued. "I swear to God I will spend the rest of my life loving this pain away. This is as bad as it will ever get." She tensed, because his voice was drawing closer, as he closed the distance between them. "Don't leave me, Alani." His lips were on the back of her neck now and she closed her eyes, shuddering, as he wrapped one arm around her body. It was a moment in time that stood still, as Alani let herself love him one last time because she knew this was over. Alani knew the moment her eyes fluttered open this thing between them was a wrap. She paused, and they stood there for a few seconds, acknowledging the end of a love they didn't even get to explore.

She snatched out of his grip and headed for his front door. She felt him following her. She didn't even look back at him as she said, "Stay the hell away from me." She pulled open the door, leaving it wide open, as she walked away.

Alani didn't look back, because she knew if she did, she might turn around. She didn't know if she would go back to kill him or to kiss him, but distance was the only thing that gave her clarity. The more steps she took, the clearer her mind became. She cringed, thinking of the ways she had opened up to him. She had let him into her head, let him between her legs, let him tie his soul to hers, only to find out he was the Grim Reaper in human form. She felt like a fool. His level of deception was so great that she saw him now as the ultimate liar. His cruelty knew no bounds. He was the master of betrayal and the man to make her never want to love anyone - ever again. She sat in the driveway to Ethic's home, gripping the steering wheel to his truck, as tears slid down her face. Images of him touching her, infiltrating her body, seducing her mental, haunted her. She hit the wheel in frustration, as she saw him emerge from the house. She hurriedly shifted the truck in gear, not wanting to see him, unable to breathe the same air as him, and peeled out of his estate at top speed. Distance minimized him in the rearview mirror, until finally, he disappeared. She cried an ugly cry. The kind of cry you allow yourself to have after your mama beat your ass with the switch she made you pick yourself. Alani had let the enemy in, and now she didn't know how to get him out her system. Crying him out wasn't working. With every sob came a gulp of air. She was only drinking him back in. Alani was so wounded that she was shaking. She gripped the steering wheel with her thumbs and held out the rest of her fingers, as they quivered. She knew she shouldn't be driving. Her mind just wasn't right. She kept sweeping her thoughts, trying to remember if Ethic had ever given her any indication that he meant her harm. She didn't know who to trust and there was no one to turn to.

Chapter 19

Alani found herself at the hospital, sitting at Nannie's bedside. "I'm so sorry," she whispered. "You recognized him, didn't you?" she asked, as she sat in the chair beside the bed and held her aunt's stiff hand while crying. "He's the reason you're lying in this bed. You knew he was the one who did it. When you saw his face, you went right into the stroke."

Alani had gone through her entire life guarding her trust, and the one time she let someone in, she opened the door for chaos. It felt like there was a hole in the center of her chest. She sat in the same spot all night, sobbing, as she replayed every interaction with Ethic over and over in her mind.

"I'm not a good man," he had told her.

She hadn't believed him then, but he had been right. *I should have listened,* she thought. Alani had thought she had a keen sense of who people were. She was normally such a good judge of character. She had always avoided the fakes and pointed out the real in people. *How was I so far off with him? The man I thought he was could never hurt a child... my child. Oh, God, my baby,* she thought, in despair.

Her thoughts tortured her through the night, and when the sun light crept through the hospital windows, she stood to her feet. She hadn't slept a wink and knew that she wouldn't for many nights to come. "I really wish you would wake up, Nannie," she whispered, as she bent down to plant a kiss on her forehead. "I need you."

She didn't know how she made it home. She didn't even remember driving there, but as she pulled up to her house, she saw Ethic's Tesla sitting in her driveway. It hurt her that fear was mixed with her pain. He had gone from a man she had thought would never hurt her, to one that was unpredictably dangerous. She knew he had committed murder. Was he there to console her or to finish the job and make sure he was never connected to her at all? Alani's heart beat furiously inside her chest. She thought of driving off, but she had nowhere to go. This was home, and no one was about to scare her away from her home. She looked out the window and noticed the group of kids playing basketball on the rollaway hoop in front of her house. She would, normally, run them away from her house with all their noise, but today, she was grateful for their presence. They made potential witnesses. Ethic wouldn't dare hurt her with so many eyes watching. She saw him, slowly, climb out his truck and the pit in her stomach deepened. She held her breath momentarily to calm the falling feeling within her. She didn't know how she hadn't noticed how intimidating, how looming, how terrifying Ethic was until now. She exhaled and placed both hands on the steering wheel, as she lowered her head. She couldn't look at him. She was afraid of the devil that would reflect in his eyes. He opened the door and she could smell his Armani cologne. The scent repulsed her.

"I'm not going to the police. I'm not going to say," her voice cracked in emotion. "...anything. I just want you to leave me alone. Please..."

She felt wetness on her thighs and she opened her eyes to see her tears raining on them. Memories of her daughter and brother slid down her face and shattered against her skin... skin that she had let their murderer touch.

"That's why you think I'm here?" he asked. "To stop you from going to the cops?" Ethic shook his head. "Alani, look at me," Ethic's voice was pleading. He was always so stern and sure. It was the weakest she had ever heard him.

She shook her head. He leaned on top of the car, looking down at her.

"Do I need to worry about someone coming here to hurt me, now that I know?"

Finally, she looked up at him, her concern etched in the creases of her stressed forehead.

"I would body anybody that touched a hair on your head. I do that. I learned to move that way over the people I love a long time ago. It's not right, and there will be a reckoning for that one day, but it's necessary. Your brother raped Morgan that night. I didn't know your daughter was in the house. She was sleeping on the other side of him on the couch, when I pulled the trigger. By the time I realized she was there, it was too late…"

"Stop it!" Alani whispered. "Just stop! I don't care if you didn't mean to, if you didn't see her! If it was a mistake! I don't care if you're sorry! None of that brings my daughter back to me." She stood to her feet, a snotty, sobbing mess. Alani could see the remorse in his eyes. The pride-filled, strong, honorable man she had come to know, stood before her half of himself. He was sorry. After all the lies, that much was true, but Alani wasn't a forgiving woman. She felt no sympathy for his guilt. She hoped it tortured him. She stood, and he blocked her, pushing her against his car. "Am I not free to go? After everything you've taken from me, are you taking that too? My choice to walk away?" It seemed her tears were filling the air with thick humidity. Ethic couldn't breathe. It felt like she was twisting his heart with a pair of pliers. He had felt a lot of loss in his lifetime. He had lost people to death, he had lost a woman to another man, but this loss felt uniquely significant. To lose Alani because of his own wrongdoing was tormenting. It felt inhumane to love her; and then to not be able to have her when she was standing so close, right in arm's reach. "I need you to leave me alone," Alani cried. "Please, Ethic. I swear to God, if you don't, I'm going to do something crazy. I want to hurt you. I want you to pay, and the only way to make you pay is to feel the loss of me. You have to stay away from me, because if you can't, I will take myself away - permanently...from everything. You can either mourn losing me or mourn my death, because at this point, I'm willing to die to make this pain go away." Ethic knew she was serious. The last thing he wanted was for her to hurt herself. He didn't want to pour alcohol in her wound. If his presence was unbearable to her, he would have to be absent.

He made it halfway back to his car when he heard her muffle her cries. He turned to her and her hands were covering her mouth, as she sobbed while watching him leave. He felt a lurching in his stomach because he knew he would never find another love like hers. Raven had been an introduction to the idea of a woman's love. YaYa, his second, had been a reminder of how good it could feel. Alani had been affirmation that God had molded a specific help mate for him. Alani was life and he would never be able to pull the roots she had put down in his garden. The hatred in her eyes was non-negotiable and he realized he needed to give her time to deal with the emotions the truth had unveiled. He refused to give up on her, on them. She would have to kill him to stop him from wanting her. There wasn't a woman in the world that could heal him the way Alani had. He only hated that he had wounded her in the process. He didn't know how he could fix this, but he had already grown accustomed to her being his oxygen and he knew he couldn't live if he was deprived of her. With a heavy heart and bleeding soul, he walked back to his car; but before he pulled away, he prayed, *God, please fill her with forgiveness. Even if I have to live through the hell of her resentment, just bring her back to me.*

Alani was so distraught, she barely made it to her doorstep. She took a deep breath, placing the key in the door, preparing herself to walk into the empty house. She stepped inside and froze when she saw who was waiting for her.

"I'm home."

Cream sat, arms stretched across the back of the couch, legs wide, face handsome, expression grim. He was back like he had never left. He greeted her like he had woken up to her that morning, and she was returning from a grocery store run…like he was, exactly, where he was supposed to be…like he paid bills there. Cream, with all his bad boy finesse, good dick, and empty promises, was sitting in her home and Alani had no energy, no shock, no reaction to give. Ethic had already taken it all from her. Cream had done her wrong, but there was no comparison to the amount of pain that had been caused by Ethic. She hated Cream, but it didn't stop her from falling into his arms as he stood. He was the only, other person who could understand how badly she hurt; but even still, her journey was worse because she had fallen in love with the enemy. She just needed to be held, but his arms didn't have the same effect. Still, her sobs were endless.

"It's alright, La. I'm home now and I know who's responsible for all this shit. A nigga can't touch mine and live to speak about it. That's my word. It's already being taken care of. The nigga will be dead by the time the sun go down. The wheels are in motion as we speak…"

TO BE CONTINUED IN ETHIC II

Discussion Questions

Was Ethic wrong for allowing Alani to fall in love with him?

Is Messiah disloyal for disobeying Ethic's order to stay away from Morgan?

Can Alani ever forgive Ethic for her daughter's death?

Does love conquer all or are Alani and Ethic doomed?

Is Ethic a good or bad man?

Why does Ethic choose damaged women?

Is Morgan doomed to repeat the mistakes of her sister, Raven?

Was Ethic right or wrong for avenging Morgan's rape?

Follow Ashley Antoinette on social media.
Instagram @ashleyantoinette Facebook @ashleyantoinette
Twitter @novelista

Be on the lookout for my new novels

The Fairest of Them All
(Coming 2019)

Ethic II
(Coming 2019)

9 780692 089705